the sun at dawn

KIMBERLY MARIE

leaf
publishing
house

It's a funny thing, when dreams come true. Thank you Mom,
for everything.

xx,
Kimberly

For each copy sold $1 will be donated to the A21 Campign

CONTENTS

CHAPTER 1

The morning dew settled onto a new home atop the blades of grass. Warmth and light from the sun shewn through the clouds as it crept above the horizon, calling the birds awake and the stars to slumber. The moon was cast away for another day.

Sweet songs awoke her and as she began to rise she became a witness to England's first light, piercing through the warped glass of the window. Walking to the window, she gently ran her hand along the iron, embracing the warmth on her skin and the hope of a new day, or more so, the passing of the previous.

She settled at her vanity, breathing a heavy sigh as life's memories lingered in her mind. A brush ran through her silver hair as she gently embraced an antique jewel draped around her neck. The wrinkles that graced her hands were not a sign of age, but rather, a sign of survival. A sign that she had taken on life and won. She held her head high and stared at her reflection; proud of who she had become.

Gracefully ambling down the staircase in her best garments for the day, she glanced upon her lonely estate. The hollow rooms and empty halls no longer rang with laughter or cheer, footsteps and conversation, but rather, withered away with the changing seasons and the increasingly long years. Paintings collected dust and the piano no longer sang. Weeds had overtaken her vast gardens as vines crept up the stone exterior of the manor. The very thought of her aging home, slowly withering with her forced a gentle tear from her eye. The droplet coursed its way down her age-creased skin, settling in the dips and curves of each wrinkle until it reached her chin. It lingered here until the shock and delight of a voice caused her to freeze in her tracks. The tear then fell from her skin like an anchor descending into the ocean and crashed against the floor. Pulling her from her sadness and constraints of her own mind, she let a smile form on her lips as her granddaughter crept through the halls accompanied by one of her staff.

"Hello Grandmother," the spritely young girl said in a sweet and soft tone as she curtsied. Her blonde curls fell upon her face as she bowed her head. A smile on her face as she moved towards her grandmother, wrapping her arms around her for a simple, yet lovely, hug.

"Hello, my dear," the woman said as she held her granddaughter tightly, placing one tired arm around her waist as the other wrapped around her head, pulling her close. Her withered cheek laid atop the girl's curls as her loneliness dissipated.

"Grandmother," the girl began with a quizzical tone. "Can you finally tell me the story?"

"Why yes, my dear," she stated with a heavy and heartful voice. "If that is how you wish to spend the day," she continued, motioning her hand to the study.

"Will it really take all day for a story?" The girl asked as they both, arms linked, strolled into the study.

She took a seat in a large chair, made of leather and visibly worn many times over. It was clearly sentimental. Each rip had been repaired and each hole patched. It had scars, as did she. She turned her head to the leather and took in a deep breath, absorbing the scent of the weathered skin, taking in every aroma and memory that accompanied it. The young girl threw herself onto the couch in front of the fire place as her lace dress, covered in pink ribbons, flew up upon impact before slowly falling back into the girl's lap.

"Grace!" she snapped. "Young girls do not jump on the furniture. They also keep their dresses down. It is not ladylike to allow your hem to fly above your knees."

The girl apologized as she straightened her posture and folded her glove hidden hands in her lap just as she had been taught. Then, the girl rose her head and looked toward her grandmother with a soft smile as she pulled the hem of her dress down past her knees, where it belonged.

The elderly woman took in a deep breath and let out a heavy sigh as she began the story.

"She was a young girl, and daringly beautiful," she began. "With blonde hair, a shade or two darker than yours, and she was fierce."

The girl glanced down at her own curls before lifting her eyes again, this time with a wild spark in them and a bright smile on her face. She had already decided that this story was to be one of her favorites.

It was about young Annabelle Faraday, nineteen years old. A woman of medium height and a small frame, she had a pleasant face with simple beauty. Her glow made her stand out from the rest of the girls at the Auburn Academy for she had not grown up like them. For much of her childhood, she resided in happiness, but alas, she found herself waiting to be summoned as a governess in a household far richer than her. Disliked by many older ladies for her looks and pleasant demeanor, she spent her days alone, held together by memories. Her grey eyes, like crystals, were growing tired with the days, and she often wondered if this would be her future. She was almost certain of it.

Auburn, nestled along rolling hills in England's countryside, held a lovely exterior that hid the harsh interior and aggressive authority that resided beyond the walls. Almost fifty girls attended the academy, all being trained for a governess position, all competing for a way out. Each time a wealthy estate needed someone, the girls flocked to the opportunities, for staying at the academy any longer would be akin to signing your ticket to hell. Annabelle, however, did not fight the other girls, for she would rather see one of them given even the slightest chance at happiness, than to think she could ever obtain it for herself. She spent her days teaching those younger than her, hoping she could give them a brighter outlook on the future, even though she knew there was not one. But the hope, if she could only give them hope to continue to move forward, then maybe they would survive.

As one of the best educators the Academy had to offer, Annabelle found most of her days accounted for, teaching and caring for the young girls who found themselves, through the trials of life, at this school. They were training for a life of service, that is, if they didn't get married first.

She would spend most of her days tucked away at Auburn, this she knew. Her noticeable beauty would be perceived as a threat by any noble wife. Governesses were desired to be plain, hiding their beauty from the world indefinitely. Annabelle, one of natural beauty, was unable to do so. Her pleasant demeanor and awestriking smile made her the least likely candidate to be chosen to live in an aristocratic family's household.

"Too pretty," a phrase she was not unfamiliar with. "I need a governess who is simple and plain."

She was a staple at Auburn Academy, and at only nineteen, she could see her future here clearly. Not only one of the best teachers the Academy had to offer, Annabelle was also a favorite among the younger ladies.

"Annie, Annie!" Cried Emily, one of the young girls who called Auburn home. "Annie, tell me the story once more."

With Christmas almost arrived, the girls loved watching Annabelle re-enact *The Nutcracker and the Mouse King* by E. T. A. Hoffmann. She would twist and twirl and alter her voice for the different characters, recounting it from her memory, a story her mother would tell her when she was young. In this moment, all the girls, Annabelle included, forgot where they were and what their futures held. The only thing they knew was that imagination was beautiful and miracles were real.

This ecstasy quickly came to an end with one swift burst through the door. The girls gasped and shuttered as Annabelle stood in front of them, protecting them from Miss Haskill and her fury.

"I thought I told you to go to bed hours ago!" She hissed.

"I'm sorry ma'am, but we…"

Annabelle's sentence was interrupted with a swift strike to her cheek. Tumbling to the floor, she found herself looking at a group of defeated faces, blanketed in fear, watching their maternal figure struck down like a bird and a musket ball. She turned over and saw Miss Haskill standing over her, grimacing with hatred.

"I did not ask you to account for your actions, Miss Faraday," she spoke down to her. Standing up straight, in fine form, she ordered, "to bed, all of you!"

As footsteps shuffled across the floor and blankets were thrown over fearful heads, Annabelle rose from the ground, wounded and broken, and crawled into bed. No care would be found here. It did not matter if you were the best or the worst teacher, you would always be below those above you. There was no way to escape your vocation.

She spent the night shivering. She shivered and prayed and cried and felt more alone than she had ever felt in her life. With the next dawn, no new hope came. A bruise, however, found a home on her jawline to cause Annabelle pain with every movement of her skull. Back to her schedule, the only thing that kept her going were the little faces she saw in classrooms and Sunday school. The girls who needed her, the girls she needed. She searched for hope and optimism, and always found it in the face of one younger than her. One who had known less pain and understood less of the evils of the world. The freckle crossed faces and bright eyes that rose every morning pulled her out of her own bed. Her mornings were spent braiding hair and tying bonnets while listening and humming along to birds on the window sill. She often wondered why creatures so wonderful would choose to reside in a place so vile.

With days and nights spent caring for others, Annabelle never had much time to think about her own life, but occasionally, every now and again, she found herself with an afternoon. A few moments of time all to herself. She spent these in the church.

Making her way down the center aisle of the little country church, she would find a home in the pew, fold her hands, and pray. She could get lost in a prayer, in the peace of the colors dancing across the floor as the sun passed through stained glass. This, along with the tall grass waving upon the hills that bordered the road to the church, was the most color she saw in her week, and she cherished every moment of it. To escape the grey, cold, stone walls of stone in Auburn, and the dying grass that occupied the yard. To see more than just the black of her uniform and the foul air that filled the main school hall. The fresh air and the blue skies, these novelties kept her alive.

"Anna!" Fear paced through her body as a hand upon her shoulder began to whip her back and forth. "Annabelle!"

Spinning around and slipping out of the pew, onto the stone floor, Annabelle recognized the hand, and the girl that was attached to it.

"Goodness, Emma!" She berated, losing her perpetual calm demeanor. "You pulled the breath straight out of my lungs."

"Anna, please grant me your forgiveness, but you are late," Emma, Anna's single most important friend at the academy informed her. Panic struck across her face as the words left her lips. She has clearly run to the church. Her red curls were loose of their ribbon, cascading to her face that was sprinkled with sweat and her breaths were quick and shallow. Annabelle was not the only one regaining breath.

Annabelle did not utter a word. Instead, she rose from her place on the floor and shuffled out the back door of the church with

Emma at her side walking as quickly as possible without being disrespectful to their surroundings.

"Why did you not come for me sooner?" Annabelle inquired.

"I am sorry, Anna," Emma responded. "Time is lost upon me today."

Even with their quickest sprints once they were out the door of the church, Annabelle and Emma found themselves late for class, and were henceforth punished. That night, dinner had been denied them, and they were sent straight to their beds.

The cold, pale rooms faced south, and gained very little light throughout the day. The cold stone that formed the walls grew colder with the night air. With too few blankets, the girls huddled together on winter nights to keep warm. They were in this together, and they would survive together.

Daybreak brought the girls' wakeup call as another day beckoned. Annabelle was sure that her life would be spent here, teaching and pouring out hope into those younger than she, but this too, was short-lived for one day, Mr. Worthington called upon Auburn, searching for a governess for his niece and nephew.

Tall in stature and fit in frame, Sheridan Worthington of Arrington Estate walked with strength, but also with an elegance only a man in the aristocracy could attain. Riding up to the school on a great horse that was fierce as could be and as dark as coal, flying with ferocity, Mr. Worthington came to an abrupt halt in front of the school. Dismounting the beast, Mr. Worthington, a handsome, but not particularly striking man walked to the school's door and proceeded to knock loudly, making his presence known. Removing his top hat as the door opened, he introduced himself with a subtle annoyance at the very idea of having to be in this place at all.

"I am Mr. Worthington of Arrington," he began. "I sent word that my estate was in need of a governess."

"Oh, Mr. Worthington!" Miss Haskill pawed. "We are so delighted to have you. Won't you come in?"

"Not today Madam. I haven't the time nor the energy to pretend I have a considerable opinion on the matter. I am only here to check on the status of my inquiry, as the children are becoming ever more restless and I am in need of some relief. When do you suppose my need will be filled?"

He spoke with fiery intelligence, but the underlying emotion was one of agitation. He did not want his sister in his home, nor did he wish her two small children as residents, but since this became his situation, he would minimalize his responsibility of the children by acquiring a governess to be responsible for their care. Behind his green eyes was a shade of loneliness, and a harsh view of life cloaked in negativity. He was not a pleasant man, but not cruel either. Preferring to be left alone, the only place he seemed content was on his rides to and from town atop Atlas, his stallion.

The girls, at the sound of a man's voice, rushed into the main hall, around the corner from the foyer. Huddled together, they stood as close to the doorway as their bodies would allow them without being seen, listening to every word of the discussion, praying they would be the one picked.

"Mr. Worthington, if I may," Miss Haskill began. "Usually it is the misses that handles the acquisition of the governess. Can I ask you why this duty has fallen to your lot?" Her inquiries were nothing more than ammunition for the gossip mill. Like most women of her age, she found delight speaking to her acquaintances about the latest news of the town, and she was determined to gain as much information from Mr. Worthington, disguising it as necessary for the placement of his governess.

"Miss Haskill, is it?" Mr. Worthington began, a twinge of irritation in his voice. "Please understand that my affairs are not any matter that should concern you, but since I know the cows that you will feed this story to in the evening would like so very much to know, I am not wed and the governess is for the children of my sister who have come to reside with me for a season. You would already know this if you had read the letter I sent, but I can clearly see efficiency is lost upon you."

In one swift motion, he lifted his hat to his head and began to turn around. Walking back to Atlas, he shouted, "I expect a governess at my home tomorrow, the best you have!"

Miss Haskill stood in disbelief at the manner at which she had been treated. Her face flushed, and her eyes hollowed as embarrassment and shame crept upon her. He had seen right through her; something no one had been able to do in years.

Around the corner the girls muffled their giggles of amusement, wishing it had been them who had put the witch in her place. Annabelle and Emma laughed a little under their breaths, but then shuffled the girls back to their classrooms before Miss Haskill had a chance to notice they were there. Peering out the window, through the warped glass, Annabelle gazed at Mr. Worthington as he mounted his horse. Put off by his demeanor, but inspired by his bravery, she watched as he rode away, then ascended the staircase, joining her peers.

As the next sun rose, the time to assign a governess to Arrington came about. The girls were sure that Annabelle would be chosen since Mr. Worthington had inquired for the best. This did not help Annabelle's standing with the older girls, for while she had a few friends in the Academy and was popular with the younger girls, her allies in the ladies of her own age were few and far between, she did not yet know that one of them was about to leave as well. Little did they know she had sent up a hundred prayers over the night asking for it not to be her. She did not deserve happiness, at least so she thought, and she was sure she would prevent it from coming upon her. Escaping this prison would give her hope, more than she deserved, so she prayed to stay.

"Line up ladies!" Haskill screeched. "Only those of age."

All the ladies who were of age lined up in from of Miss Haskill awaiting their fate. So many young girls with so many prayers on their lips, patiently waiting for the verdict that would send one of them away and give them a chance at life that had sooner been denied.

"Catherine," Miss Haskill whipped. "You will travel to Arrington today and begin your tenure as governess. You leave at noon, so I suggest you start packing, not that anything you ladies have is really worth holding onto." Little insults were her way of staying her jealousy towards the ladies that left, while she was forced to reside at Auburn, watching her face grow older in the mirror every morn.

"That will be all."

Running upstairs, the ladies crowded Catherine as she put her few possessions into a carpetbag and readied for her journey. Between the whispers of encouragement and the tears of joy, Catherine took a moment to give each of her fellow ladies a lovely and meaningful embrace.

"I love you all," the youngest of age of the group, Catherine, spoke. "And I will miss you dearly. Please remember me in your prayers, for my time for life has come."

As she an Annabelle embraced, Annabelle looked upon her with a sweet smile.

"My beautiful Catherine, do write to me and tell me of all the wondrous things you are seeing and doing at Arrington. I will miss you so, but a letter will ease my distress and quiet my soul, just knowing you have found happiness."

None of them knew the typical life which awaited a governess. Normally one of cruelty and solitude, not of joy and hope.

Catherine gathered her belongings and went downstairs. Her embrace with Annabelle was the last time these girls would see each other, as Catherine was off to what she thought would be a better life.

That night, after the darkness began to creep into the town and the halls of Auburn, the girls pondered what Catherine's new life would look like.

"I wonder if she will find love with a stable hand, or maybe a landscaper!" One girl cheerfully mused.

"I just hope she is happy," another contemplated.

"There is no way she cannot be happy, having escaped this place," Jennifer, one of the eldest and a close friend of Annabelle's, chimed. "The only shame is that the rest of us are still here, destined to wither away like the witch."

"Now ladies," began Annabelle. "Do not bring woe-some thoughts into this pleasant discussion. I am certain that Catherine will find happiness, if not on her own, through the help of our prayers. For now, though, it is time for sleep."

As the ladies laid down to rest their heads for the night each one of them said a silent prayer for their friend.

The next day, life continued per usual and the girls were back to schooling and back to work. Annabelle was busy as ever, filling in the space that Catherine had left empty. This was good for her, though, for the loss of her friend had brought on a greater sadness than she had expected, and a busy schedule seemed like the only cure.

Nightfall came, and Annabelle laid her head to rest. She said a prayer for her friend, desperately hoping she had made it to Arrington in good condition and was about to slip into slumber when a familiar hand came upon her shoulder and began to shake her. She quickly rolled over, having to calm herself from the anxiety that ensued from the surprise. Deep breaths entered her lungs as she shut out the stress her body had begun to feel. Startles were her enemy.

"What is the matter with you," she grunted toward Emma, who had Jennifer at her side.

"Forgive me Anna, but you need to wake up," Emma whispered.

"Whatever for?" Annabelle inquired.

"We are going into town, and we would like you to join us!" Jennifer answered with a burst of excitement. "The girls are down for sleep and Haskill is locked away in her quarters for the night."

"What makes you wish to enter town at such an hour?" Annabelle inquired, not realizing the time was only eight o'clock.

"Gracious, Anna, it is only eight at night and there is a ball tonight," Emma answered. "Get up and put on your best dress! Join us, won't you?"

"Please Annabelle!" begged Jennifer. "Will you not come with us?"

"And what, pray tell, happens when Haskill awakens to find us missing?" Annabelle questioned.

"She will not," Emma replied. "And if she does, what is the worst she can do to us? We have survived all her previous torments, I think we can weather a few more storms."

It was an argument Annabelle knew she would lose, for she was too tired to argue with her friends, and they were far too awake to go to sleep now. She rose from her tired iron bed slowly to prevent as much squealing from escaping the springs as possible, and tip-toed to her case with her dresses in it. Only five to choose from, Annabelle chose her favorite. A navy dress, as simple as her tastes, with long sleeves and white lace trim around her neck, wrists and the hem of the skirt. There was no piece of clothing she owned that made her feel more beautiful. She stepped out of her nightgown and into the blue dress. It wrapped around her, fitting perfectly as if it was made just for her. She altered the garment herself when she first purchased the item. Months of savings afforded her this dress. She saved it for special occasions only, but as she hadn't had a reason to wear it since her purchase, she chose this night as special enough to require a special dress. She quickly twisted her hair into a braided bun on the back of her head and fit on her boots. The winter air held a definitive chill, and so she also brought her coat. Pneumonia would not take her tonight.

Just outside the door to the ladies' sleeping quarters, Annabelle joined Emma and Jennifer as they readied their escape. Each having lived here for at least 7 years, they knew just which piece of wood creaked the floor and which whined on the staircase. They knew which doors would alert Miss Haskill of their escape, and which would pull open without hesitation. Slowly they travelled down the staircase, taking extra care at the bottom of the steps, where Miss Haskill's room resided. Once they were certain they hadn't been caught, they hurried out the door on the side of the building, leaving a rock by the entry, propping the door open so they could return undetected.

The ball was set to begin at 9 o'clock. It was a country ball in a poor neighborhood. This called for men and women of the area wearing their best and looking to have fun. Emma and Jennifer were clearly searching for husbands, more so, a way out of their destiny. Annabelle, however, was just looking to forget. She wanted to laugh and dance and forget who she was or what she would be returning to when the night ceased. Her desire for entertainment and her pleasant features would make her a popular lady at the ball.

"Do you suppose we will meet anyone?" Mused Jennifer as the ladies walked the narrow pathway that led to the ball. Dark brunette hair and a plain face, she had such high hopes for her life, but her emotion could turn on a dime should something sour amount. She would easily fall into sadness. Annabelle took extra care with her to keep her happiness.

"Maybe I will meet a dashing gentleman who will sweep me off my feet!" Pondered Emma while she twirled long the pathway, throwing her hands into the air with a giggle. Annabelle let a smile twist onto her face at her friend's actions.

"Maybe we all will meet happiness!" Jennifer squeaked back excitedly. "Anything will do if it will take me away from Auburn."

"Oh, surely you have higher standards for yourself," Emma responded.

"A woman beautiful as you, deserves only the best of men, my sweet friend," Annabelle lectured.

"And what about you, my dear," Emma began. "Annabelle, will you meet your prince tonight?" She finished her sentiment with a smile and a childish giggle as Jennifer heartedly joined in.

"Oh stop, you two." Annabelle said with a smile as a blush wormed its way to her cheeks. She was not looking for love, nor would she encourage it, but the mere thought made her nerves rise just a little. "Can we not just enjoy our time together in the splendor, beauty and gaiety of the ball?"

"Very well," said Jennifer with a smile as the three continued to twist and skip down the road towards the ball.

Held in what seemed to be a refurbished barn, the ball was filled to the brim with townsfolk, all looking to escape for a few hours of merriment. With stone coating the floor, and candlelight brightening the atmosphere, music filled the air as deep red wine filled the glasses. A team of orchestral instruments played lurid music as men and women alike spun and leapt across the dance floor together.

These events were not new to Annabelle and she knew every dance that graced these floors by heart, but to Jennifer and Emma, this was a new and exciting world, with every possibility imaginable.

It was not long before Emma and Jennifer were swept up in the amusement of the activity. Annabelle sat back, simply enjoying the sight of her friends' cheer as they were whisked into dancing with young men.

"God, please let them find love," She whispered. "If not here, somewhere."

It would not be long before this prayer would be answered, for Peter, who courted Emma after the ball, and Samuel, who courted Jennifer would soon wed them each. For now, they were dance partners, but in a matter of weeks, Annabelle's closest friends would be swept away into marriage, finally escaping their personal hell they call Auburn.

Annabelle danced with a couple of men, all lovely in their own right, but none would cause a stir in her heart, not that she was looking for that either. She danced like an expert, spinning with grace and holding her partners hand with gentleness. She was elegant as she moved through the crowds of people, all twirling and hopping across the stones. Genuine laughs slipped through her lips as her mouth cured into breathtaking smiles. Annabelle had not felt so free in a long time and would embrace this moment for as long as possible.

Spinning around the dance floor, Annabelle caught the eyes of her friends while they twirled with their partners. Life was breathed back into them this night, as hope filled their eyes and fire resided in their smiles. Annabelle could not help but breathe a sigh of relief as she filed this moment into her memories. She would forever remember the look of pure happiness on her friends' faces.

The candles melted down and began to dim as the orchestra slowed, signaling that the jauntiness of the evening would soon be coming to an end. Annabelle bid her current partner adieu and strode to her friends, who were high from the night and were filled to the brim with love and hope.

After a night of dancing and wine, and pleasant company for Jennifer and Emma, the ladies made their way back to Auburn Academy.

"I cannot believe it!" Declared Jennifer, skipping and twirling down the dirt road laughing between breaths. "Did you see how he danced with me? Did you see how he looked at me on the floor tonight! I could not have even dreamed of such a sweet night."

"Well did you see how Peter spoke to me?" Shrieked Emma like a young schoolgirl with an innocent crush. "He looked at me as if I were a precious gem! I believe I know what love feels like. My future seems so much less bleak, and more hopeful than I could have ever imagined it would be. And oh, how he is handsome. Do you not agree, dear Annabelle?"

"Did you dance with anyone tonight, Annabelle?" Asked Jennifer.

"A few, my dears. But I was far too enraptured witnessing your happiness to even notice any men who made offers of dance to me. I kept my eyes on you both through all of my dances."

In fact, she had turned down numerous offers during the course of the evening. She was far too pleased watching her friends enjoy themselves. It was in the happiness of others that she found a glimmer of her own.

"I'm sure your partners loved that," Jennifer said with sarcasm and a smirk. "Annabelle, you should have allowed yourself to feel free and truly dance with a man tonight." She grabbed Annabelle's hands and

started spinning rapidly in circles. She was clearly high on wine and tumbled to the ground after losing her grip on Annabelle's hands after a fit of giggles hit her.

"Are you okay?" Annabelle worried. "Jennifer!"

"I am fine my dears," she sleepily replied. "I just wish you would have allowed yourself to feel joy tonight." Emma nodded feverishly in approval of Jennifer's statement.

"Silly girls," Annabelle began her reply while kneeling down beside her friend on the dark road, the only sober one of the bunch. "Your happiness brings me more joy than even an illusion of my own could bring to me." A soft smile swept across her lips and both of her friends let out giggles, the only thing they could think to do at such a precious moment.

The girls arrived back at Auburn arm and arm, shushing each other as their home was finally in view. Removing the stone and muffling their giggles of love while they shuffled through the house, the girls made their way back to bed, with a new wonderful memory to share together. Attempting to avoid the creeks and whines of the worn wood in the hallways and stairs, the girls slowly crept to the comfort of their rooms while sleep descended upon them quickly and swiftly.

Stripping out of her dress and back into her nightgown, Annabelle began a simple prayer as she readied herself for rest.

"Thank you, Lord," Annabelle whispered as she crawled back into bed. "Thank you for their joy. I could not be more content in life than to see all my lovely friends find happiness."

CHAPTER 2

Within a matter of three weeks, Christmas had come and gone as did the New Year. No celebrations were had and no visit from Saint Nicholas arrived at the Auburn Academy, although Annabelle did use her minor wages from teaching her classes to buy each of the ladies a small piece of candy. She wanted to make sure the girls felt loved, even the ones that did not love her.

The holidays were always difficult for Annabelle for she knew another life. One where Christmas would bring joy and new treasures to carry her through the year while New Year celebrations brought hugs from her parents and a kiss on the crown of her head from her father. Her mother would teach her to make cookies and her favorite apple pie while her father would dance with her next to the fire. Extended family would come and go as the days drew on, candles would burn, laughs would be had, and love would be shared. Her holidays were immaculate. Her favorite time of year as a child, but now they only reminded her of what she used to have. Of what is here no longer.

Sitting in the window of the dreary boarding room watching the snow slowly collect on the window sill, Annabelle would recount these memories. Each day she would cherish a different one to help her get through the season and each night she would dream that life had not turned cruel and she could once again experience this bliss. She would get so lost in the depths of her mind that she could almost smell her mother's holiday perfume and the cedar wood burning on the fire. She could almost feel her father's hand in her hand walking to church, and she could vividly see her father holding her mother in a close embrace on

Christmas morn drinking his coffee as Annabelle sat on the floor unwrapping the riches her parents had gifted her.

She traced the warps in the glass as she took a breath. Pulling the blanket draped around her shoulders a hair closer she sent up another prayer.

"Take care of them, Father," she whispered. "Do what I could not until I see them again. Tell them I love them and that I wish them the happiest of Christmas'. They need not worry about me, for I will be alright."

With that, Annabelle took in one more calming breath before returning to her work downstairs.

After the holidays, Annabelle's time at the Auburn Academy grew wearier as her last two friends celebrated their weddings, overjoyed with happiness during the events, Annabelle had never felt such a fierce solitude as she did after their departure. The weddings were small, but Annabelle could not think they were more perfect after seeing the love that filled the barn where her friends met their loves only a few weeks earlier.

First went Jennifer, married off to Samuel. Married in the lovely country church that Annabelle called home on her free afternoons, it was a poor man's wedding, but blissfully perfect nonetheless. They married on a sunny day in early March with few present, but enough love to last a lifetime. Jennifer had never been so joyful, and Annabelle could only hope the bliss would continue.

Simple and sweet, yet utterly perfect, Annabelle shed many a tear for her beloved friend while watching her sign her fate. Annabelle only hoped such an opportunity could only lead to happiness for her dear friend. Life is never easy, but happiness will come should you work for it.

The couple departed for London as Samuel no longer wished to work on a farm and thought more steady employment could be found in the new railroads and factories of the city. They left to stay with Samuel's family in town until he could sort out a form of employment.

Annabelle, Emma, and Jennifer cried and laughed as they packed her bags. Only two were needed to hold her life. They shared memories, giggles, and the sweetest hugs as they bid each other goodbye with a kiss on the cheek and a promise to write.

"I promise I will write!" Shouted Jennifer as she rode away in a carriage to her future. This would be the last time Annabelle would see her friend. She never did find out where life lead her, but in the first and only letter she received, she was assured of her friend's happiness and her grief over the loss of a friend was dulled with the gladness of knowing that life led her to a sweeter place than this.

"My sweet Annabelle,

I am so sorry it has taken me this long a time to write you, but my dear Samuel and I have been so very busy since moving to the city. Life here is nothing like that of Auburn, but it is all a good thing. I have never felt so loved in my life as I do with my sweet husband and can only pray you find happiness like this one day. He cares for me like no one I have ever known. We have a home in London as well, small but perfect for our little family, so we no

*longer must stay with his aunt and uncle. They had a very small
dwelling that was not fit for more than two people.*

*My sadness was left at Auburn. I can only hope you leave that
horrid place to a life of happiness as well. These past weeks have
not been easy, but I dare say that life can only be lifted from this
moment forward.*

*I promise to write more in my next letter. I only wanted to
make you aware that we are settled into our new lives quite nicely.
Please send my love to Emma and my wishes for her wedding and
marriage. I say a prayer for you each and every night.*

With all my love,

Jennifer"

Three weeks later came Emma's wedding. This separation
would prove the most difficult for Annabelle for Emma was the
first friend she made when she arrived at Auburn now 9 years
earlier, and she was her closest and dearest friend.

Annabelle's first night at Auburn was one of heartache and
uncertainty, but it was this night that she met Emma. Ten years
of age at the time, Emma and Annabelle were bunk mates and
instantly had a connection.

"Hello there," said doe-eyed Emma to Annabelle. "I hear we
are bunkmates. What is your name?"

"Annabelle," she responded in a quiet and shy tone. Tears
strewn from her eyes and pain printed across her face, she was
clearly out of place at Auburn.

"I am Emma," she said with a bright smile and caring eyes. She lifted her thumb to Annabelle's face and wiped away her tears. "No more tears. Crying is not allowed in my bunk." She smiled after seeing Annabelle's look of confusion. "Have a good cry, because tears heal, but then no more crying. I dislike sleeping on a wet pillow." Emma's face turned into a scowl as she thought of sleeping on a moist pillow.

A giggle slipped through Annabelle's lips and her eyes brightened, only for a moment. Over the next few years, Emma's funny faces and silly jokes helped Annabelle's eyes brighten so much that she was now the brightest and most hopeful girl at Auburn. Hopeful for the young girls and for their futures. She could handle her future at Auburn as long as she kept the light in her eyes. The light she had before she arrived at Auburn, and the light she regained through her friendship with Emma.

****

"Grandmother?" the little girl softly asked.

"Yes, darling?" She replied.

"Why did Emma leave Annabelle if she knew how much she would miss her?"

"She did not realize the pain she would inflict her friend by leaving," she replied. "She would never do that to her friend. If Emma knew what her absence would do to Annabelle, she may not have chased her own love and happiness." She said, moving forward towards her granddaughter's side to grasp her hand.

"Annabelle had to let her friend go and be free. She was happy, and Annabelle would have never forgiven herself for even causing her friend to think twice about love. Do you understand, dear?"

"I guess so, grandmother," She quickly replied with a tender smile and hints of confusion in her eyes. "Can you please continue the story?"

"Of course."

****

"My sweet Anna," Emma said through tears on the morn of her wedding. "How can I think to say goodbye to you?"

Annabelle, also drying tears from her eyes, replied, "My dear Emma, you are not going far. This is not goodbye."

Indeed, she was not going far. She was marrying a stable hand named Peter, who worked on at the Trowsdale Estate. She would not be out of reach, but no longer being at Auburn was already too far for this pair.

"I love you, you know that, right?"

"Of course, I do, Emma. You are a sister to me, the only one I have ever had, and I could not be more excited for your happiness. You are getting married today, no more sad tears," Annabelle said as she wiped away the tears of her friend. "Only happy ones are welcome here. We would not want you to sleep on a wet pillow on the night of your wedding."

Emma let out a small giggle and hugged her friend tightly as a few more tears caressed her cheek. Turning up to look at her friend, all Emma could think to do was smile. She smiled the most beautiful smile Annabelle had ever seen, and in this moment, she knew she would live a happy life, far away from the haunted halls of Auburn Academy.

A small and simple service, but beautiful and filled with love. Emma cried more tears of joy and Annabelle felt bliss as a melting smile swept across the groom's face as he gazed upon his bride. Annabelle could not understand how her two closest friends could be so blessed to have each found futures of love, but then she remembered to never doubt God, for he had answered her prayers.

"Thank you," she said through tears as she lifted her eyes to the sky. "This is where you have shown your love to me, through the blessings you have poured upon those I love."

And so, Emma was married on a Thursday morning in early April as the flowers began to wake up from the winter's cold and the birds resumed singing happy tunes of warm breezes and bright skies. Emma then moved five miles down the road.

Annabelle was not allowed to visit her on the grounds of the estate, so they would meet in town every Wednesday, when Annabelle had her free afternoon and would stroll through the markets together. She had to sacrifice the little time she normally spent in church, but she knew God would forgive her if the absence was in service to a friend.

"How is everything at Auburn?" Emma asked on one of their first meetings. "Have the girls treated you well?"

"Well enough," answered Annabelle. She knew lying was a sin but hurting the spirits of her friend would hurt her heart much more. She had weathered much of the ridicule from the elder girls at Auburn since Emma left, but being alone had begun to weigh on her soul. While the older girls were reading together and sharing stories, or studying together, Annabelle found herself alone. She would hum while she kept busy by doing tasks like cleaning or washing her clothes and sing with the birds in the window at days first light. She did not have many issues, just scores of loneliness. She did not especially lash out until one of the elder girls, Amelia, went through her belongings and found a pendant to which she decided she would keep.

"Give it back!" hissed Annabelle. Her sweet smile and calm voice no longer gracing her face. Her eyes were dark and lacking the light that normally dwelled in them.

"It is mine now," antagonized Amelia. She wore the pendant around her neck as she sauntered through the dining hall showing off her new prize to all the other girls. And then, with what felt like no control over her body, Annabelle lunged toward Amelia and tackled her to the ground, prying the pendant from her neck. The girls quickly gathered around this scene, drawing the attention of Miss Haskill who, favoring Amelia, punished Annabelle solely for the incident. After a lashing in front of all the other girls for her physical assault of Amelia, she went almost a week without food and was forced to do additional chores in accompaniment with her other responsibilities. This almost killed her, but she was not given leave to be ill either. In the end, though, Annabelle had no regrets, for her treasure and one of the few remaining objects from her former life was back in her possession, not to be taken again.

"Well, I am pleased to hear they are obliging and treat you well," Emma declared, snapping Annabelle away from her troublesome memories. To this, Annabelle formed her best fake smile with the hopes of deceiving her friend into thinking she was alright.

Two months similar to this passed as Annabelle continued to make do with her circumstances. As June came and the flowers bloomed, Auburn ceased to change. Brown grass and gray walls persisted through the grounds, feeding Annabelle's depression daily. Every Wednesday, however, Annabelle forced light back into her eyes and smiled her best smile as a few moments of ecstasy with her closest friend proved enough to get her through the next week. Walking back to Auburn though, she began to wish she had prayed a few prayers for her own happiness, back when it seemed almost feasible.

Annabelle decided she would continue her teaching and studying while putting on her bravest face for the young girls. She also avoided all older girls at all costs as she could not afford to be in trouble again and face an even worst punishment. She smiled when appropriate, laughed when a younger girl told her a story she should be proud of, and continued acting out stories she remembered from childhood. She could not let her sadness affect those she oversaw. While her hope dwindled, she did everything possible to ensure theirs would continue to burn brighter than ever.

This pattern continued for almost nine weeks until Annabelle's heart shattered once again with the news that Catherine, her sweet and lovely friend who had departed from Auburn just over eight months prior, had perished. She contracted yellow fever and became a victim to it.

"I am sorry to inform you of this event so swiftly and without remorse, but we must continue our work," Miss Haskill said in a solemn tone. She liked few girls in the home, but she did not especially dislike Catherine. She was more jealous of the fact that she got away.

"Annabelle," Miss Haskill began. "Mr. Worthington is in need of a new governess and I have assigned you to take the job. You leave today at midday."

"But ma'am," Annabelle interrupted, hoping to plead her case.

"I will not be interrupted," Miss Haskill demanded, raising her hand as if to strike Annabelle, causing the girl to flinch and let out a quick weep, preparing herself for the pain. "This decision is final. I am getting rid of you while I still have the leave to do so. Now go pack!"

Annabelle was surprised at Miss Haskill's decision. Typically, getting a job was viewed as a good thing. Amelia could not remove the scowl from her face while she turned to stomp up the staircase like a child. She clearly wished for Miss Haskill to choose her to be the new governess, having made it clear that she found Mr. Worthington attractive. Annabelle had no opinion on the matter, as she had only seen him riding away on a horse.

Many thoughts crossed her mind this day, mostly of confusion and anxiety of leaving Auburn, a place that had been so familiar for so many years. She did not know how to feel and did not know what to pray. It was as if God had disregarded her wishes to stay where she was safe. Unhappy, but safe. Her emotions were a mess and she did not know what to think about this new journey she would embark on. More than anything, though, she was happy it was a Wednesday.

She was not especially fond of her circumstances, but the possibility of change terrified her even more.

Change had never benefited her life, and she was sure that now would be no different.

Many tears flowed from her eyes this day as she hugged each one of her young ladies goodbye. She looked at the big eyes and bouncing curls of these young girls and her heart broke more and more as her eyes flickered to every face.

"Do you have to go?" One asked.

"I will miss you! Who will read us stories?" questioned another.

"What if my dress rips? Who then, will patch it?" A third inquired softly with tears welling in her perfect blue eyes.

She felt her heart shatter as she looked upon her sole reason for surviving. What would she do at this new home without her ladies?

"My dears, each and every one of you hold a piece of my heart." Annabelle assured the little eyes fixated on her. "My prayers are yours. Know that I am never far from you, my sweet ones."

After giving each a long and sorrowful embrace, Annabelle left the room she had laid her head in for so many years with nothing but uncertainty in her heart.

"This cannot possibly be God's plan for me," she thought.

She departed Auburn at noon, with nothing but her suitcase. Miss Haskill stood in the doorway as Annabelle walked through the halls for the last time. Determined to never let someone hurt and belittle her the way Miss Haskill had done for years, she let go of her pleasant demeanor once more for a final word with her tormentor.

"Good riddance, child," Miss Haskill whispered to Annabelle as she crossed Auburn's threshold. She quickly turned, and with a scowl on her face, and anger in her eyes, she spoke "I will never let someone treat me as you have for the past eleven years. You only know cruelty and while I keep you in my

prayers, that you will find peace, miss you, I most certainly will not. You are vile and vicious to those in your care, and if I could stay, if only to protect these young ladies from your hatred, I would, because I know what love looks like, and you Miss Haskill are most certainly not it."

Stern in her words, Annabelle turned and walked away after she finished her beratement of the witch. With orders to go straight to Arrington, Annabelle could not help but disobey them to see Emma and make her aware of the news. Meeting her in the town market, walking through the streets with her friend, Annabelle told Emma the news of her new employment, to which Emma jumped for joy, clearly pleased with the turn of events.

"That is wonderful!" Emma beamed. "Is it not?"

"I am unsure," Annabelle replied with worry across her face.

"Anna, this is exactly what you need. This has been my prayer for you for months! You have escaped and are free."

"Free to live in a home being ordered around by another person who may just be worse than Haskill herself," Annabelle begrudgingly answered.

"Where is my sensible Anna," questioned Emma as she took Annabelle's face into her hands and rubbed her thumbs along her cheeks as her eyes narrowed at her friend. "The one who looks on the brighter side of life and sees beauty in everything."

"She is on holiday," Annabelle quipped, to which they both let out a chuckle or two. "Oh, Emma, but I wish I could be optimistic. What am I to think of this new job? The very place where Catherine perished, and I am supposed to find happiness there?"

"Yes, Catherine perished, but I am sure she would take these last eight months of freedom over a lifetime of servitude to the witch," Emma responded quickly and sternly. "She would want happiness for you, and if life does not gift it to you, you must create it for yourself. Now go! We will write, I promise."

With a fond embrace the friends bid adieu for the time being whilst Annabelle walked toward her future. Moving 13 miles down the road, 18 from her dear friend Emma, Annabelle began her walk after one o'clock and hoped to make it to the estate by nightfall.

As she walked down the road, many carriages passed with none taking a moment to even notice her existence. This was not a surprise, as her faded dress and worn suitcase told passersby that she was not of much importance. It was not until a man on a dark black steed, thundering down the road, slowed as they came up beside her. Annabelle jumped off the roadway as he neared, fearing he would trample her. The only way this day could get worst was for her to get run over by a horse.

A statuesque figure dressed in the best riding attire with a pure leather halter and saddle for his horse, she could tell he was of aristocracy. "Where are you headed this day?" he inquired as Annabelle sighed with a tinge of anger, climbing back up to the road.

Seeing no escape from the conversation, she answered with her head facing the ground "Sir, I am going North to my new position as a governess."

Amused by her ignorance, he asked, "My lady, what is your name?"

She answered swift and bitter, "Annabelle Faraday, sir." She was hoping to make it clear she preferred to be left alone. Her emotions for the day were almost too much to bear and she was ready to lash out should this man stick around much longer. She normally wore her sweet demeanor, but today a bitter mask came upon her with all the changes she faced, and she let it overtake her for another moment. She was sure she would surely feel awful for her behavior later, certain her mother certainly would not have approved. At the moment, however she could not see past her thick cloud of heartache.

"Could I possibly give you a lift?" He inquired. "I must say though, a dress in that worn of shape and a suitcase practically falling apart may not be able to handle the ride on my horse." He said with intent to sting and a glare on his face, clearly being a gentleman because he had to, not because he wished to truly help her.

It was here that Annabelle once again shed her kindness and whipped around to face this man. Her grey eyes grew cold and fierce as she glared at him from below. He towered over her like castle, but she would not be intimidated.

"I am sorry, sir, if you believe that my dress is worn, and my suitcase is falling apart, but I will have you know that I am quite content with them."

"I am sorry, ma'am," he interrupted. "I never meant to offend. In fact, I am headed South to the train station. I thought to be kind and offer, but as you are so easily offended, I see I have made a mistake..."

She cut him off just as he had done to her and replied, "Yes you did. Since you rode up here you have done nothing but attempt to make me inferior to you, but I will simply not have it. I am not uneducated, sir, and I can guarantee you my birth was not inferior to yours either. I do not need the best clothes or leather halters to prove my worth to the world, as you so clearly feel you need to prove yours. Now if you would kindly leave me be, I have quite a bit of walking to do and the less noisy distractions I encounter, the better. Please, ride South to the station and leave me be." She said motioning her arm to point down the road. "I can make my own way in the world. I need no help of a man."

She bowed to him, as was the custom and continued on her way. He, however, was enticed but perturbed and rode off viciously into the distance without a word but did turn to look back just once.

"She clearly does not know who she is speaking to," he thought.

Nightfall was descending upon her as she walked up to the main house at Arrington and knocked on the large wooden door. The home was large, very large, and secluded. There was nothing for miles, but the grounds seemed to have everything anyone could need. Farmland bordered the property, while a lake and a barn resided next to the main house. Large gardens also wrapped around the back of the house and ivy climbed the exterior walls. It was peaceful and tranquil. Annabelle hoped she could find some kind of contentment here, even if just a portion.

The splendor of the estate made Annabelle forget her pain for a moment, not only emotional, but now physical as her legs began to tire and grow sore from the walking of the day.

The door was answered by a pleasant woman named Lily. The head housekeeper of the house, the aging woman was to oversee Annabelle.

"So good to see you, Annabelle," she introduced. "I am Lily Bowden, welcome to Arrington. May I show you around?"

Miss Bowden was older and unmarried. While she never revealed her age, Annabelle assumed she was at least 50. Her clothes were polished and neat, and she clearly took pride in her work of keeping house for Mr. Worthington. Her silver hair and wrinkled hands showed a lifetime of devotion to this family.

They began the tour in the main home, working their way through the galleries and sitting rooms. A maze of a house, Annabelle was worried she would get lost should she ever explore the home on her own.

Attempting to pay as much attention to Miss Bowden as she could while she gave the tour, Annabelle still got lost in the beauty of the home. Plants and flowers were everywhere indoors, and tapestries and prized artwork covered the walls. The beauty of the home was incomparable. Windows were trimmed with gold and the ceilings were all at least twelve feet high.

It was a country home with stone walls and many fireplaces, but some rooms had an aristocratic essence with wood-panelling and expensive furnishings. Paintings of Heaven graced the ceilings of the ballroom and expensive wallpapers covered the bedrooms. The library was home to thousands of books, all of which Annabelle wished to read and the dining hall had tile floors and a table that looked a mile long from where she stood. It was all too much to take in. Too much, too quickly.

"Well that finishes the tour, ma'am." Miss Bowden concluded. "All that is left is to show you to the workers' quarters."

Up a stone spiral staircase that began in the kitchen and lead to the workers' quarters, Annabelle diligently followed the woman, afraid of making a wrong turn.

"Here is your room," she said motioning the door open to reveal a room with a large bed and a fireplace.

"This is mine?" Annabelle inquired. "Who do I share quarters with?"

"No one, dear," Miss Bowden explained with a chuckle. "This is all yours. Mr. Worthington is kind enough to give each of us our own living space."

Stepping inside the room, running her fingertips along the bedposts, and then the mantle above her fireplace, Annabelle felt tears come to her eyes looking back at Miss Bowden and whispering to herself. "This is mine."

"Yes, dear," Miss Bowden replied, mistaken in thinking that Annabelle was asking a question. "You may have time to unpack tonight, but for now, Mrs. Kennelworth, Mr. Worthington's sister, and the mother of the children, would like to meet you. Brush yourself off and follow me downstairs."

Too fearful of her uncertain situation to not oblige, Annabelle shook the loose dirt from her dress, placed her suitcase on the quilt-covered bed and followed Miss Bowden down the staircase towards Mrs. Kennelworth's parlor in the west wing of the home.

Unsure of whether to knock on the door, or walk in, Annabelle waited for Miss Bowden to give direction.

"Goodness, child," Miss Bowden said. "Well, go in, won't you? She is expecting you, you know, and she detests when the help is late."

Her small hands gently wrapped around the doorknob as she pushed the large wooden door open to the parlor. The flower covered walls and exquisite furnishings told Annabelle everything she needed to know about Mrs. Kennelworth before even laying eyes on her. She was a woman of good taste and a clear high society upbringing. She sat, perfectly poised, in a chair by the window. With dark brown hair pulled behind her head, pearls draped along her neckline and an elegant evening dress on, Annabelle knew right away that looks were important in this household. Mrs. Kennelworth did not possess natural beauty with her small eyes and larger than normal nose. While not distinctly unattractive, she would not stand out in a room. Annabelle wondered if this was why she surrounded herself with things of such beauty.

The layout of the room created a maze of tables, chairs, and statues for Annabelle to dance through before she came into the presence of Mrs. Kennelworth.

"Ma'am," Annabelle began with a small curtsy. "I heard you asked for me."

"So, you're the new governess?" She responded with her head held high and an accusing eye studying Annabelle. "A little too pretty for my tastes, but my husband isn't here, not that you would be a threat to me anyway."

Annabelle just stood still, unsure of what to say.

"Well sit down, my dear."

Pulling a chair away from the table, Annabelle lowered herself into a seated position. Certain to keep perfect posture, she sat straight and gently laid her hands in her lap.

"I am pleased you arrived so quickly," Mrs. Kennelworth said. "When that other good-for-nothing governess died, I had absolutely no clue what to do. She wasn't worth much, but she at least took care of the children. My brother was firm that another governess was to be hired before his return next month. He left today for Paris."

Still unsure of how to respond, Annabelle simply said, "It is a great honor to be working for you, ma'am."

"I know it is. We are one of the finest families in the country," Mrs. Kennelworth shamelessly replied. "You will take charge of the children beginning in the morning. The servants are burying Catarina, or whatever her name was, on the edge of the property in the morning, and since the children had grown somewhat attached, I do not wish for them to be there. I am just thankful she has no family. That makes my job of getting rid of her much easier."

Annabelle had to fight back tears during Mrs. Kennelworth's words. She was boiling over with rage at the way she spoke of her friend, and of sadness, knowing the burial Catherine was destined for. Surely, she deserved better than this.

"You just cannot find reliable help these days," Mrs. Kennelworth continued with a wave of her hand and a roll of her eyes. "I just pray you do not meet an untimely death so soon. My brother would not have it if two governesses in my charge were to die in his home. It would be the end of me."

"I am sorry for the trouble that has been caused, ma'am." The words of respect escaping her lips tasted like vinegar. "I hope my presence can ease the stress caused by the situation."

"Never mind. Be downstairs tomorrow for breakfast and you will meet the children. If you are late, you will not eat. Am I understood? I have no compassion for tardiness."

"Yes, ma'am," Annabelle shyly stated. "I will be ready for breakfast in the morn."

"And do wear something nicer," Mrs. Kennelworth hissed motioning her hand over Annabelle's dress, as if she had a need to point out a single flaw. "We are a fine family and the help needs to portray this as well. You represent us now and we cannot be seen with someone in such rags. No need to look like a pauper now. Living in this home, no one will pity you."

"Yes, ma'am."

And so, she walked back through the house that had become her new cage. Up the spiral stone staircase that led to her quarters, once she was behind the safety of her own door, she collapsed to the floor in tears. Ripping off her faded dress and throwing it on the floor, she leaned against the cold stone wall and let the water flow from her eyes. All her pain and anguish over the loss of her friend, and the loss of her safety and certainty escaped her through cries of pain and tears of heartache. She lay on the floor all night, almost frozen, lost in her emotions. Leaving one form of hell for what seemed to be another, far worse, was only the tip of a very large iceberg of emotion that clouded her thoughts that night. She got no sleep, and she had no peace.

When the sun rose the next morning, Annabelle rose with it. August was underway, and the air was fresh and crisp in the morning, without a cloud in the sky. While a slight breeze danced across the fields in the yards, Annabelle opened a window to let the world in. No sooner after she did this did a small goldfinch land on the edge of her window and begin singing a song. Annabelle sang along with a small smile while she readied for the day.

"Why thank you for this bit of cheer, little one," she said, taking the bird onto her index finger. She lifted it closer to her face and looked into its eyes. "Now go and be free. If not for yourself, for me."

And the goldfinch dashed off her finger and through the air. Back out the window, the small bird landed at the top of a large cedar at the edge of the gardens. The tree looked as if it had stood the test of time and lived a long and fulfilled life so far. Annabelle closed her eyes and took a long breath, as if she was embracing the bird's spirit of finding a home, and finished preparing for the day, hoping her second impression of Mrs. Kennelworth would be better than her first.

The stone hallways and staircase looked pretty in the morning colored with golden light. Their beauty was unmatched with the light pouring in from the iron-strewn windows. As Annabelle descended the stairs leading to the dining hall, she could not help but feel that this was the first time the estate felt warm.

"Good morning, Annabelle," rang Miss Bowden from the bottom of the staircase. "You look chipper this day."

"Good morning, ma'am," Annabelle answered. "Yes, I slept quite well and feel refreshed after my journey yesterday."

"I am happy to hear it, dear. Now go on and find your place at the table for breakfast. Misses and the children will be waiting on you if you do not hurry."

"Of course," Annabelle walked through the kitchen, attempting to avoid the stares of the other workers.

She was new, and they were unsure of her.

After entering the dining hall, she found herself frozen in her tracks. Mrs. Kennelworth sat at the head of the table, and her children sat at the wings beside her. A little boy and a little girl waited with their mother. Staring at the chairs, Annabelle could not decide where she was to sit.

"Well, good morning Miss Faraday," Mrs. Kennelworth greeted. "It is Faraday, correct?"

"Yes, ma'am."

"Well sit, dear. No need to stand and watch us eat breakfast."

"Where should you like me to sit, ma'am?" Annabelle inquired.

"Next to Lucas will be just fine," Mrs. Kennelworth replied motioning to the little boy. "Lucas is a family name. Named after his great uncle on my mother's side. He fought in the revolution you know. On the side of England of course."

"Very well, ma'am." Annabelle retorted, again unsure of how to reply to Mrs. Kennelworth's ramblings. As Mrs. Kennelworth turned her head to address her daughter, Annabelle saw little Lucas stick his tongue out at his mother. She let a faint smile come upon her lips but was sure not to say a word. His sister was not so lucky, however, because she couldn't help but giggle.

"Now stop that!" Annabelle heard right before the crack. As her daughter held her face, already turning red from Mrs. Kennelworth's strike, Annabelle was back in Auburn, looking at the faces of the little girls she so loved, after her face had survived many a similar ordeal. Lucas' face went blank as guilt spread over him like a wildfire. He had clearly not intended for his sister to be struck.

"Sorry you had to see that, Miss Faraday," Mrs. Kennelworth stated with no sincerity. "But children must be disciplined if they are to grow up to be respected in society." She then smiled at Lucas, who was still paralyzed with fear from the anger emanating from his mother.

"And that is Isabelle, over there," she said while waving her hand in the direction of her daughter dismissively.

"Hello, Miss Isabelle," Annabelle greeted, a red mark now forming on the little girl's face where the remnants of her mother's anger remained. Her words brought a smile to the girl's face, a look that seemed rare. Annabelle's hopes of a more cordial second meeting were dashed with this breakfast.

Annabelle quietly ate her breakfast and prayed that the children would eat quickly so they all could escape this situation.

After surviving the increasingly uncomfortable meal, the children were left in Annabelle's care for the day. Lucas, only seven, had a dark shade of blonde for hair and crystal blue eyes which his mother credits his father for. Isabelle, at nine, had long chocolate curls and brown eyes. She had a sweet smile and a quiet demeanor, while her brother was only shy for a moment after meeting you and was quick to misbehave when his mother's back was turned. Annabelle already knew one of his favorite pastimes was making silly faces behind her back.

As breakfast concluded, Annabelle took the children to their study where she would spend her days watching after them. The study was on the third floor of the home and was larger than any of the classrooms Annabelle had seen at Auburn. She stood in the door for a moment gaping at the scene in front of her, as the children entered, making themselves comfortable. Along one wall were bookshelves, floor to ceiling, with more books than Annabelle could ever dream to read in her lifetime. She walked over to the wall and ran her fingertips along the spines, taking a moment to touch each one of them on the shelf just to make sure she was not dreaming. Floral designs covered the remaining yellow walls with expensive paintings hung on top. A grand piano sat in the corner next to a window, living up to its name. Sunlight covered the room as long maroon velvet curtains framed each of the windows facing the south side of the house.

Annabelle had not seen a piano so large in years. Her mind strayed back to the one that used to make a home in her parents sitting room. Her mother spent every Sunday afternoon teaching her how to play while singing along as Annabelle's fingertips danced along the keys. Her hands hovered over the keys for a moment as her soft skin took in the light that poured from the window. She took a deep breath as the warmth covered her skin. A small smile tugged at her lips and a tear traced down her cheek with the memory lingering in her mind as she turned to the children who were seated on the couches in front of the fireplace. A large globe sat next to the door displaying the world as it was known.

Lucas noticed Annabelle's gaze on the object and cheerfully jumped off the couch and ran to the globe. With a swift move of his hand, the globe started spinning feverishly. A bright smile graced his face as Lucas turned back to see Annabelle's caring eyes smiling at him. She already loved these children. They were inherently good and sweet. She almost wondered how with the mother they had, but Annabelle quickly pushed that thought away. She had just met the woman and would not allow herself to pass judgement so swiftly.

She spent her days teaching the seven-year-old Lucas and nine-year-old Isabelle French, reading the Bible to them, listening as they read to her, and assisting them with their writing skills and instrumental lessons. Mathematics and the sciences were taught out of the flood of books on the shelves. The children were also given two tea breaks throughout the day, which was a secret Annabelle held with them, certain their mother would not approve of a break.

After dinner, the children were put to bed with Annabelle singing them sweet lullabies until slumber overtook them. It was the only time of day she could see the mischievous Lucas completely at peace. Isabelle was always last to fall asleep between the two, taking a couple of minutes to speak to Annabelle without her brother's curious ears listening in on the conversations.

"Do you like it here, Miss Faraday?" Her small voice called out from the darkness as Annabelle was about to close the door one night.

"Why yes, my dear," Annabelle replied, crossing the floor and taking a seat on the end of her bed. The only light in the room came from a candle that was lit on the table next to Isabelle's bed. "Why would I not?"

"I just wanted to make sure," she said with a gentle smile. "I enjoy it much more with you here."

Annabelle felt tears threaten her eyes. She leaned down to kiss Isabelle gently on her forehead and gave her a quick smile before exchanging goodnights. Maybe this experience would not be so bad. Maybe her cage was not a form of hell so long as she had these children to look after and bring er joy. She pondered the thought as she closed the door quietly and resigned to her quarters for the night.

Two days later, Mrs. Kennelworth took the children to the marketplace to shop and Annabelle was told she would not have to go along with them. After diligently pleading with the children to behave for their mother and praying Lucas would not cause too much ruckus, Annabelle made her way to the gardens in search of a friend.

Weaving through the flower bushes and ivy growing up the garden's walls, Annabelle had found who she was looking for.

"Jonathan Conaway, is that correct?" Annabelle inquired from one of the many landscaping staff at Arrington.

"Yes, Miss Faraday," he replied while dropping his tools to the ground and standing to bow to her, his tall and thin frame still towering over her. He had a worn face and shallow eyes, a result of a long life that had not treated him particularly poorly, but not particularly well either. "What can I do for you, miss?"

"Mr. Conaway, it is my understanding that you assisted in the burial of the late governess, Miss Catherine?" Miss Bowden told her who was charged with Catherine's burial, and Annabelle had a request for the man.

"Why yes, ma'am," he answered. "Why do you ask?"

"Could you please show me to her place of burial?" Annabelle responded after breathing a sigh of relief.

"I am not sure the master would like it, miss," replied Mr. Conaway as he cast his gaze downward. "He would scorn me good if I were to leave my work."

"I promise it will be quick!" Annabelle rushed, desperate to see the resting place of her fallen friend. "You need only point me in the direction and I can find it myself from there. I need to know where she was laid, sir. I will take the entire punishment should anyone find out and grow riled."

After watching Mr. Conaway ponder the thought for a moment Annabelle made one last desperate plea.

"Please sir," Annabelle began as tears fought to fall from her saddened eyes. "She was a sister to me. I knew her for years and my soul needs to know that she was buried properly. If she could have not been well treated during life, I need to know she was respected in death. I am desperate for peace."

With a long intake of breath and an even longer sigh, Mr. Conaway acquiesced.

"Of course, miss," he reacted softly as his drew his eyes up to meet hers. "We must be quick though. I will escort you the entire way there as long as you can find your way back. If I should be gone for longer than a few moments, someone will surely know I have left the premises."

"Absolutely!" Breathed Annabelle. "Thank you so much for your kindness, sir."

"Very well," Mr. Conaway began as he turned his back and walked out of the garden. "Let's be off."

Annabelle followed behind diligently, taking care to notice every tree and every turn her steps took. She memorized the route not only to find her way back to the estate, but to be able to visit her friend again. The thought of Catherine being alone for any length of time tried Annabelle's spirit, but she conceded that all would not be bad as long as she could visit sometimes, so Catherine would not always be alone.

After over a mile of walking Annabelle knew she had come to her friend's resting place once she noticed the rectangle of fresh dirt laying in a sea of green grass. Tears flooded her eyes as she took in as much air as her lungs would allow and let it out slowly. Peace. That is what this place was.

"She was a sweet girl, miss," Mr. Conaway broke the silence. "Always smilin' with the kids and such. It was a shame to see her gone so young."

Annabelle lifted her teary gaze to the aging man who had taken his hat off in respect.

"She was family here, miss," Mr. Conaway continued, looking Annabelle in the eye. "I can see your heartache in your eyes, but she did not die unloved, miss. We staff, we are a family. She was loved until her dying breath, and she is loved still. Like a daughter to me, she was. We made sure to take care of her and put her here, where she could be surrounded by sunlight and flowers."

Annabelle's tears fell as the man's face grew pained through his own grief. Finally taking a moment to study the area, Annabelle's heart was warmed by the sight of rose bushes and trees that housed beautiful birds who could sing to Catherine. She saw weeping willows in the distance and warm sunlight bursting through the branches. It was a place worthy of Catherine. Annabelle was sure the beautiful blonde-haired girl with joyous eyes was looking down from Heaven with gratitude for those at Arrington who gave her such a splendid place to call her own.

"She always had a smile, even in her last days, she would smile," tears began welling in Mr. Conaway's eyes, but he did not cease. "We all cried for her, and while she may have not been treated the best by the master and his family, they were never outwardly cruel in a physical sense. The master's sister can be harsh with her words, but Miss Catherine did find happiness here. She was loved, and a piece of us was taken when she was, so please, miss, do not let your heart hurt for long. She loved you and spoke of you often. How brave she thought you were and your beauty and intelligence. She would want you to find the same happiness here she did."

With that, Mr. Conaway wiped his eyes and bowed his head. Annabelle could not take her eyes off the brown rectangle in front of her and did not even notice Mr. Conaway turn and begin the journey back to the main grounds of Arrington. More tears came but would not fall as Annabelle held an unbreaking stare at her best friend's new home. She had found happiness. She had a true home.

And so, with tears in her eyes and the memory of her sweet friend's beautiful smile filling her mind, Annabelle made her way back to Arrington, determined to make this new situation work for her benefit, if not for herself, then for her lovely friend.

CHAPTER 3

As the days past Annabelle began to feel at home at Arrington, or more at home than she had felt at Auburn. After two weeks, comfort fell upon her as she became familiar with her surroundings and day-to-day responsibilities. She especially loved the children. While little trouble makers, they both possessed hearts made of the purest gold. One of her favorite times of the day was right before lunch, when she was able to read a story to the children, or rather, perform it. When *the Nutcracker and the Mouse King* was on the agenda she performed it with similar fervor and the same voices as she did for the girls at Auburn. Isabelle and Lucas loved her acting, but some days, her favorite time of day damaged her heart with the pain of loss. She wondered what her girls were doing, whether or not they missed her, and she said a little prayer.

"Protect my girls," Annabelle prayed. "Please, Father? Keep them safe and gift them with the greatest forms of happiness in this life."

One Thursday afternoon, Annabelle was in the middle of one of her grandiose performances when black boots made their way up the stairs. As she came to the part where the mice and nutcrackers fight, she pinched Lucas' sides as she described the sword fight. He shrieked and jumped off her lap. As he landed he began to giggle incessantly and asked her to continue the story. His laughter brought a smile to her face. An expression she had not known well since arriving at Arrington.

The click of the heels stopped at the doorway to the children's study. The unfamiliar tone of the shoe made Annabelle turn from Lucas to face the doorway. Much to her horror, she found herself looking upon the man who rode past her atop the black steed the day she ventured to Arrington weeks earlier.

"Hello, sir," Annabelle said as she bowed, breaking the much too long silence.

"Hello madam." The man responded. "And who may you be?" He questioned pridefully, already having received news from his sister of Annabelle's position.

"I am your governess, sir." Her eyes met his and her stare was sure not to break. It began soft and sweet, but as the conversation grew hostile, so did the fire in her eyes.

"Well then, my lady, your services will simply not be needed in this house," He countered with a sly grin. "My governess left years ago, and I am sure I am not in need of a new one." His sarcasms were not met with welcome from Annabelle, still mortified from their last meeting.

Annabelle was unamused and quipped back, "Why sir, are you not entertaining? Are you sure you are not in need of a governess to educate you? From our last meeting, it was clear to me that your communication with others could use much work."

Feeling slighted and filled with anger, the man probed in a stern tone, "Do you not know who I am?"

To which Annabelle quickly bantered, "Of course, Mr. Worthington. I would not offer my services to just any one. Only those I have been forced upon."

"Forced upon? You make it sound as if life in this large house is filled with misery." Her tone and freeness of speech intrigued him. Mr. Worthington was determined to be angry with her comments but could not find the anger inside of himself at the moment. It had all drained away and had been left with curiosity and amusement. It had been too long since someone sparred with him through words.

Meeting his softened tone, Annabelle allowed her gentle demeanor to overtake her again. "I am sorry Mr. Worthington. You have a beautiful home. Few are so lucky as I, to live in such a place." Her eyes fell from his to the floor.

"Let us hope you last longer than the last." Annabelle was thrown over the edge by his disconcert with Catherine. Where his fury had depleted, hers had grown into a wildfire.

"Do not talk about Catherine," Annabelle snapped as she rose from her seated position on the floor.

"Who do you think you are to talk to me this way?" He answered, stepping towards her as his brow furrowed.

"Sir, I am your governess, and you may send me back to Auburn at your leisure, but I will not sit here and listen to you make disparaging comments about my friend," Annabelle replied. She was fierce in her words as heartache at the very thought of her lost friend crushed her heart once again in a storm of grief and pain. "I knew her for years, and she held a place in my heart."

Mr. Worthington stepped back to the doorway, and stood completely still, watching tears fill Annabelle's eyes as she remembered her friend.

"She loved daisies, and summer breezes. The colors of Autumn and making piles of leaves for the young girls to run through," Annabelle rambled sternly, fighting back every tear, unaware her voice was rising as she recounted her favorite qualities of her lost friend. "She was only sweet. Nothing sour in her, and she was the most beautiful human I have ever met, so do not talk as if she was not important to someone, Mr. Worthington, because she was very important to me."

A stunned look on his face at the power behind her words, Mr. Worthington could only look upon her with sympathy and admiration. "I am very sorry for your loss, Miss Faraday."

"Very well." The only answer she gave as Lucas walked over to Annabelle and stood next to her, leaning against her legs, looking to give her any form of comfort.

Mr. Worthington walked away with a quizzical look on his face. He wanted to be angry, or he thought he did, but could not find the emotion in him. He had fired servants for much less and had little appreciation for his workers in general. They served a purpose, but most were more trouble than they were worth in his eyes, and Miss Faraday looked as if she herself, would give him more grief than most. Shocked at her tone when speaking to him, he was able to find anger to unload onto his sister, who he believed should have tamed her the second she entered Arrington.

"Do you realize the way your governess just spoke to me?" He berated as he stormed into his sister's study while she sipped her tea. "How could you allow such a person into this place? And why did you not tell me she knew the last governess?"

"Dear brother, she came from the same place as the last governess, Catrina, or whatever her name was," Mrs. Kennelworth began, waving her fork in the air and not looking up from her plate. "Are you not supposed to be the educated one in the family? Surely you could have pieced that puzzle together."

Pacing back and forth, Mr. Worthington replied starkly, "well if she speaks to me once again in such a way, she will not be the only one without a roof over her head. You and your children, too, will be without a home and forced to return to London."

Jumping out of her seated position and dropping her plate to the floor, his sister barked back at him, "you would not send us back to him. We are family, you could not do that to me nor my children. Surely you are no that cruel."

"Do not test me, dear sister. I can promise you will not appreciate the answer."

And with that, Mr. Worthington disappeared from the room and out into the fields.

Truth be told, Annabelle would not have minded if she were to be dismissed. She was not happy in the cold house with such woe-some employers, and she longed to see her girls more and more each day. She had not seen Emma since her work began and a letter had not yet arrived, not sure that it ever would, being so far out in the country. Her world was grey, and with the arrival of Mr. Worthington and his seeming disregard for human emotion, it could only get worst from where she sat.

****

"Grandmother," the girl asked. "Did Annabelle get in trouble for her actions? Surely you would never allow someone to speak to you that way. Mrs. Kennelworth did not tolerate it, I'm sure."

"Yes, my dear," she answered, having moved to a couch near the window to absorb the sun's warmth. "She was withheld her supper that night."

"But why? She only told the truth. He should not have talked about her friend in such a manner."

"I believe the reason was described as inappropriate behavior," she answered thoughtfully. "The true reason is that Mrs. Kennelworth was unhappy that her brother was angered with her because of Annabelle's words. She probably should have had a little more respect for Mr. Worthington."

"But he was not nice to her!" The young girl scowled.

"Manners, child," she quipped. "Niceness has nothing to do with it. She was below him and therefore should have respected him more."

"Well, I like her just the way she is," the young girl answered quickly with a smile, lifting her chin as high as she could.

"I do too," she replied with a sigh and a small smirk. She motioned for her granddaughter to join her on the couch by the window as she continued the story.

****

"Ma'am, I am sorry for the way I behaved today and will not fight my reprimands."

"Good," Mrs. Kennelworth replied before marching off to her quarters on the other side of the house. "Do not let it happen again or I will not think twice before dismissing you."

She walked up to her room and laid in bed, trying to silence the complaints of her stomach. Hunger would not get the better of her tonight.

Annabelle spent the night in bed recounting the day as the moon slowly rose and painted the walls in a glowing light. More than she had in years, Annabelle felt guilty for feeling so miserable. She knew the girls at Auburn would relish an opportunity like this, but she could not help but feel lost and alone in the large halls of Arrington. The stones got no warmer, and winter was creeping up on her as September began. She wrapped herself in blankets, too tired to light a fire, and hoped the morn would be better company.

Days past since her original meeting with Mr. Worthington and Annabelle thought she was safe from the contempt of the man. Maybe he had decided to leave her to the children and allow her to do her job in peace. Her wish, however, was not granted. Almost a week after she formally met the man, his very existence disturbed her once more.

In the darkness of night as Annabelle laid in her bed, ready for sleep, she woke in a panic at the sound of the door rattling. Throwing herself under the covers, she said as many prayers as she could think to speak as sheer fright fogged around her in a thick aura.

"Our Father, which art in heaven, Hallowed be thy name," Annabelle whispered. "Thy kingdom come, thy will be done in earth, as it is in heaven. Give us this day our daily bread. And forgive us our debts, as we forgive our debtors. And lead us not into temptation but deliver us from evil: For thine is the kingdom, and the power, and the glory, forever. Amen."

Her breathes increased and sweat grew on her brow from the stress. Her nightmares had finally come for her and she could not think clearly enough to find a suitable place to hide.

Her fears escalated when she heard the door creak open. She couldn't shut her eyes but did not want to see what would happen next. She forgot where she was and could only make sense of the fact that she was not safe. White sheets were ripped from her, to which she thrashed in response, sure to fight anyone who had come to hurt her. Her breathing slowed, and her heart calmed after almost exploding out of her chest when she saw who was standing over her.

"Goodness, child," Miss Bowden stated stumbling back with confusion. "What on God's Earth are you doing? I was knocking but received no answer."

Annabelle quickly tried to compose herself and sat up in her bed. "I am sorry ma'am, I did not know who was at the door so I…"

"That is why you answer it, my dear," Miss Bowden interrupted, looking down on her quizzically. "I am here to deliver a message to you. Mr. Worthington would like to see you in his study. You are to wear your best garment and visit with him as soon as possible."

"I'm sorry ma'am, but I am ready for bed," Annabelle replied, pleading to be left in peace to regain her breath and composure.

"Not after that performance you're not," Miss Bowden answered quickly. "And there is to be no argument." She chastised.

So, Annabelle rose from her bed and saw Miss Bowden out of her room. She quickly shut the door behind her and slid down the wood onto the floor. Grasping her temples in her hands, she breathed as hard and as slowly as she could, filling her lungs to the maximum with every breath, pushing away her nightmares and memories, until she was composed. She then slipped into her navy dress with the lace at the collar, hems and sleeves. With hair pinned behind her head flowing down her back in natural curls, she made her way down to Mr. Worthington's study. Annabelle would not spend too much effort on the male after the panic that swept through her because of his demands.

The estate became warmer with the night, she noticed. Not as warm as it was with the light of the morning, but warmer than the cold air of afternoon. The light of the fireplaces and candles colored the walls in embers and gold. The darkness did not scare her as long as some semblance of light existed, for the cold of the darkness could not thrive in the heat of the fire.

As she was about to knock on the door to the study, it swung open in front of her. Mrs. Kennelworth had fury covering her face as she stormed out of the room. Across the room, Mr. Worthington held his head in his hands as he settled into a chair by the fire.

"I know you are there, Miss Faraday," he began, now pinching the bridge of his nose in agitation. "Are you waiting for an invitation?"

Annoyed at his unawareness of the hour and his harsh words towards her in the first seconds she had been in his presence, she bluntly replied, "Yes sir, indeed I am, and I will not be so rude as to enter without one."

Without moving from his chair or even turning his head, he replied shortly, "and what do you think Miss Bowden did when she summoned you?"

"That was an order sir, but I am waiting for an invitation from the master of this study." She would not be trifled with after his order rose her from bed in a panic. Her emotions were unclear, but anger was surely one of them.

His voice grew soft as he then, without moving, asked in an unpleasant tone, "won't you come in, Miss Faraday?"

Shocked after not receiving the rebuke she had been expected, Annabelle obliged and walked over the threshold into Mr. Worthington's study.

The study, lit by the light from the fireplace, was not as large as Annabelle expected it to be for such a rich man, and instead of being covered in tapestries and expensive paintings, family portraits covered the wood-paneled walls as a grand piano sat in the corner of the square room and three chairs made a home in front of the fire. Books littered the shelves and side tables and papers covered the desk in the corner. Neat was not a word Annabelle would have used to describe this particular room.

In the largest chair, made of brown leather, sat Mr. Worthington, now only a silhouette as his face did not look to the light of the fire.

Noticing she was standing in front of him, Mr. Worthington motioned for Annabelle to sit down without speaking a word. She could see he was a man of intelligence, only speaking when he felt it necessary and had something to say. His gaze followed her as she made her way to the seat. The reflection of the fireplace in his eyes looked as if a green dragon was spitting fire. Intense and watchful.

"Miss Faraday, we seem to have gotten off on the wrong foot," he stated bluntly, his eyes burning through her as he relaxed and sat back in his chair.

As if her entire vocabulary had been stripped from her, Annabelle did not come up with a quip or a sarcastic reply that she had become so fond of since meeting the man. All she could muster, staring at him in the fire's light, was a soft, "yes, sir."

"What, no beratement?" Mr. Worthington asked in a sharp tone as his eyes narrowed towards her. "I was so looking forward to being made a fool in my own home."

"Well sir," her vocabulary now swiftly returning to her, "I have found that most men are fools for years before I have the pleasure of pointing it out to them." She immediately regretted her words as she saw his eyes narrow further and his right hand begin to twitch on the arm rest. This man brought out the worst in her. Her sweet demeanor always went into hiding in his presence.

"Is that so?" He asked precise and taciturnly. "Miss Faraday, I cannot help but think that you do not consider your fate when you open your mouth to speak. I have fired servants for much less than words."

"My fate is none of your concern Mr. Worthington. If my performance as a governess is not up to par, feel free to send me back from whence I came, but I am the best Auburn Academy has to offer, so I would consider your options before striking me out." She rarely let pride overtake her, but with so many emotions clouding her mind, Annabelle almost wanted to push Mr. Worthington to his edge, just to see what would happen. Maybe he would release her back to Auburn. Maybe he would decide to treat her with respect. Maybe he would strike her. She was still unsure.

"You must think very highly of yourself," he replied, dropping his left hand from his chin and on to the arm rest.

"No sir, I only know my ability as a governess."

Annabelle's eyes met his as she sat high in her chair with her hands gracefully laid in her lap. Her posture was perfect, and Mr. Worthington took notice of her poise. She was much more than a governess, and his

curiosity was piqued. He wanted to know her story, for no other reason than to understand how it was that she ended up on his doorstep. Little did he know, Annabelle was not the kind to let anyone in. Not even Emma knew her story, and she fully intended on keeping it that way.

"What brings you to Arrington?" Mr. Worthington asked, narrowing his eyes at Annabelle.

"Sir, I believe you already know the answer to that question," Annabelle began with a glint in her eyes. "I believe it was a prideful man on a black steed who requested the best Auburn had to offer. Are you disappointed that you ended up with a woman such as myself?"

"Femme insupportable, (insufferable woman)" was all Mr. Worthington could muster to say in that moment. He did not realize how well Annabelle understood French, however, because her comeback was quick and spit with fire.

"Homme cruel et sans cœur, (cruel and heartless man)" she fired back at him. His eyes widened with disbelief as he realized she had understood his words.

Her eyes pierced through him. Not even Miss Haskill brought out such fury in her in such a constant.

"Excusez-moi, (excuse me)" she whispered as she stood and bowed to him, making her way out the door.

"I do not recall giving you leave to exit, Miss Faraday," his thunderous voice echoed behind her as he stood, his back to the fire, making his body a glowing silhouette.

"And I sir, do not recall asking your permission. You have brought me here to care for the children, but if I do not return to bed, I will not be able to properly care for them in the morning. My job here does not require me to make conversation with you in the late hours of night." She turned and walked out of his study, certain she would be released the next morning for her behavior.

She said a quick prayer before readying herself for sleep.

"I am sorry, Father," she began, tears leaking into her eyes. "I know we are called to be good and kind. I do not know where these emotions have found room in me to brew and grow, but I feel ill just knowing they have found a home in my heart. Please rid me of them. And please, care for my girls. I do worry very much about them."

A few tears slipped through her eyelids and down her face as she quickly wiped them away. Changing out of her dress and into her nightgown, Annabelle crawled into bed wondering how she would apologize for her behavior the next morn. Even if she was released, she still had to apologize.

****

"Why should she apologize, Grandmother?" A little voice called out, interrupting her story and causing her to shift her gaze to a wondering face seated next to her.

"Darling Grace, she felt poorly for her actions, so she felt the need to make things right with the gentleman."

"But he was cruel to her!" The girl exclaimed before a look of shock overtook her face at the volume of her words, causing her to hang her head in shame. "I am sorry for my outburst, Grandmother," she muttered quickly.

"Oh, my dear, you have a fire in you," she replied. "I will forgive you for such a disruption as long as you promise never to let your flame dwindle."

"I promise," the light returning to the small girl's eyes.

"Now child," she began, shifting her weight on the seat to better face the young body next to her. "Was she not cruel to him as well?"

"Maybe, but they had not been kind to her since she arrived."

"They are not called to be kind, my dear," she responded. "Annabelle was called to follow orders. Her strong head and gentle heart were clouded with so much hurt that she forgot herself for a moment, but there is not always forgiveness for our mistakes."

"God always forgives us, does He not, Grandmother?" The little girl asked, a confused and worried look overtaking her face.

"Why of course, Darling," she cheerily replied quickly, not wanting her granddaughter's faith to waiver. "The problem comes when we try to forgive ourselves. Annabelle knew God would forgive her actions, but whether she could forgive herself for letting her emotions control her was another battle. She was a strong girl, but her expectations for herself were higher than most anybody."

"Grandmother, what happened next?"

****

Annabelle rose the next morning to sunlight on her skin. A smile crept at the corners of her lips, threatening to spill over her face as she lay tangled in the blanket, absorbing the golden light showering over her. The songs of the birds filled the silence and pulled Annabelle out of her reverie and back to the real world.

After preparing herself for the day, Annabelle descended into the kitchen. Her anxiety was slowly growing the longer the day drug on. Worry clouded her mind as thoughts about her future danced through her head. All she could do was pray for the courage to form a coherent apology to Mr. Worthington.

"I can do this," she chanted in her head continuously.

She was brought out of her trance by the voice of the head cook, Miss Elta Nettles. A boisterous woman with a thunderous laugh. Some of Annabelle's favorite moments were sitting in the kitchen sneaking a taste of the food before it was served to the household. She ate most of her dinners in the kitchen, sitting on a stool in the corner as the cooks and their assistants buzzed around the room. She adored the stories the group would tell and could not help but smile each time the middle-aged woman with a gift for food would find a story particularly entertaining. Annabelle only ever ate with the family when she was summoned, which had only been a total of four times in her entire tenure.

Each time she endured Mrs. Kennelworth's cruelty towards her and the children.

Needless to say, she was much happier in the kitchen.

The women in the area were lucky the walls were stone, or their noise would have surely disrupted the master's meal, and Annabelle knew the wrath of Mr. Worthington and his sister were not anything to be trifled with. Mrs. Nettles would always laugh them off telling stories of Mr. Worthington as a child. She was sure he would never do anything to harm her, no matter how lively she became.

"I raised that boy," the heavy-set woman would state sternly, waving a wooden spoon around to accentuate her point. "If he so much as crosses me, he will know what is coming his way. I do not take disrespect lightly, and the boy knows this." Annabelle would always giggle at the sight of the woman with gray hair falling out of her bun, twirling around the kitchen, laughing off any threat to her livelihood.

Apparently loved by Mr. Worthington's parents, and even the man himself, Annabelle was sure she even saw Mr. Worthington smile at Mrs. Nettels once when he came to the kitchen to choose the meal for the night. She was entranced by the sight and almost thought she was dreaming. This was the first time Annabelle hoped he may not be as harsh as she thought. Not that she did not still think of him as cruel, just a little less so. For someone with such a beautiful smile could not be completely cold hearted. Love would have taught him how to smile such a smile. Happiness too. This man had known both, no matter how much he tried to hide the fact.

Pulling herself from the thoughts plaguing her mind, Annabelle took a seat in her special spot snug in the corner of the room and watched in awe as the ladies got to work preparing the meals for the day. Just once did she rise from her position, only to reel in Lucas, who ran around the kitchen causing trouble. With a soft smile on her lips, she saved him from Mrs. Nettles' ire as the woman was chasing the young boy with a wooden spoon, chanting on and on about how she was too old to deal with such disruptions. She was just about to strike the boy on the rear when Annabelle scooped a giggling Lucas into her arms and spun away and out the door.

"You are lucky such a woman was here to save you, boy!" Mrs. Nettles voice faded as Annabelle walked down the corridor towards the dining hall. "Stay out of my kitchen until you learn not to touch!"

Annabelle chuckled lightly at the words, for she knew Mrs. Nettles adored all children, and had she not been running late for breakfast this morning, she would have humored the young boy instead of chastising him.

"Now my dear Lucas," Annabelle began lowly, as to not have her voice echo down the halls. "What on Earth were you doing in the kitchen at this hour? Surely you know better than to disrupt Mrs. Nettles whilst she cooks."

Raising a wooden ship that fit perfectly in his small hand, Lucas' response was simple.

"I had to show everybody my new ship!" He began as his voice bounced off the stone on the walls. "My father sent it to me from London. He stays there while we are visiting with Uncle Sheridan."

A smile graced his face as he looked back down at the object and began to fiddle with it once again. Annabelle was awed at his simplistic look at life and so a smile graced her face looking at the young boy huddled in her arms, blissfully happy because of a small wooden boat, or ship as he would have quickly corrected had she spoken the word aloud.

After a few moments she returned the boy to the ground and began walking alongside him as they ventured nearer to the dining hall. All Annabelle could hope for was her scolding for the previous night to be held in private. She did not wish to have the children witness such malice or watch as Mrs. Kennelworth's face contorted into smugness witnessing the moment. She hoped Mr. Worthington would allow her to hold on to the smallest bit of her pride by berating her behind closed doors.

Pulling Lucas to a halt outside Annabelle bent down to the young boy's height and gazed into his eyes sternly.

"Now, my dear Lucas," she began in a gentle tone, but seriousness shone through her stony eyes. "I expect only the best of your behavior this morn. Are we understood, young man?"

The young boy, clearly unsuspecting of such a demand, only widened his eyes and stiffly nodded.

"Yes, Miss Faraday," he whispered. "Have I done something to upset you? I am very sorry if I did! I promise I did not mean it! You are my favorite governess. I enjoy you more than even Miss Catherine. You will not leave as well, will you? I can be better! I am sorry for not being better. I know I upset mother, but sometimes I get carried away and do not understand why I cannot laugh when other adults are around. You smile all the time and –"

"Lucas!" Annabelle hushed the young boy who was speaking quicker than he could breathe, and whose eyes had now filled with tears. "Calm down, young one." She cooed him while pulling the lad into her arms and wiping his tears with her sleeve. She would never willingly be the cause of tears to enter the children's eyes. Such high emotions made her worry about the young boy. He did not want her to leave, he did not want to lose someone like he had lost Catherine. He was much too young for such sorrowful thoughts to be running through his small head.

It was only when his breaths eased, and his sniffles stopped that Annabelle pulled away and looked at him with determination. "I am not leaving you Lucas. I only ask you be on your best behavior during breakfast, and we can smile as much as you wish once we go upstairs to learn for the day." She ended her request with her own smile, gentle and kind, to show him she was serious. "Now, come little one."

Annabelle stood, holding her hand out for Lucas to take. "Surely your stomach must be causing a ruckus underneath your skin. You have yet to feed it this morn."

With a giggle the young boy took her hand and walked with her the rest of the way into the dining hall.

CHAPTER 4

As Annabelle and Lucas entered the hall, Lucas promptly let go of her hand and trotted over to his place at the table. Clanking was heard as Lucas place his toy on the table next to him. Annabelle winced at the sound, understanding what was to follow quickly.

"Lucas!" Mrs. Kennelworth snapped as she dropped all her utensils onto her plate with a crack. "Do not leave that dastardly contraption on the table. I have surely raised you better than this."

Annabelle had never seen the vibrant boy look so small as tears grew in his eyes and he muttered, "I am sorry mother. I only wished to show you the gift father sent to me from London." As the last words slipped through his lips, he bent down and stared at the table, slowly eating bits of his meal.

Mrs. Kennelworth swiftly plucked up her utensils and once again began to eat her meal, only with a new vigor and violence to her actions. It was as if she was attempting to cut through both the plate and table with her fork and knife. "Do not mention that man to me," she spat. "You listen to what I tell you, for he is not here to say otherwise. Understood?"

Both children slowly nodded their heads. Annabelle did not move from her place near the door for she was contemplating her next move. It was quiet in the hall until Mrs. Kennelworth slammed her glass back down to the table after taking a drink of her water. At this, Mr. Worthington had finally had enough, and snapped himself.

"Dear sister," he stated with the highest form of sarcasm. "If you wish for me to purchase a new table, you can simply say so. No need to destroy the one I already possess by sawing through and shattering glass atop it. Not that I would listen, but in most instances, I personally prefer words to actions."

Annabelle bit back a laugh as Mrs. Kennelworth flushed the brightest shade of pink on her pale skin at her brother's remarks. When the man in question glanced up to look at Annabelle, he felt his lips start to twitch upward as he saw her entertained expression. The feeling, however, was quickly replaced when the previous day's events flooded his memory and his lips fell into a frown.

Annabelle could feel his eyes on her as she stubbornly gazed upon the children smiling at their mother's beratement. She would not meet his eyes and was trying to steady her breathing when Mr. Worthington spoke.

"Miss Faraday," he began, a slight edge to his voice, "how nice of you to join us this morning. Would you please sit?"

Annabelle quickly looked up and got lost in the piercing gaze of the man. "Thank you for the invitation, sir," she tentatively began. "I am content eating my meal with Mrs. Nettles in the kitchen. However, I would like to request an audience with you at some point today if you have time."

"Of course, Miss Faraday," Mr. Worthington spoke sharply. "If you insist. You may meet me at my study once this meal has ended."

Annabelle simply bowed her head and walked out of the room without a second glance. All she could do to calm her nervous heart was to place her hand above it and breath as slowly as steadily as she could force herself to in that moment.

After the meal was completed, Mr. Worthington walked through the halls to his study, to find Annabelle seated in a chair next to the door to his solace. His study was the one place that was his. It was almost sacred.

"Miss Faraday," he stated as her eyes rose to meet his. He opened the door to his study and motioned for her to rise and enter. "Please come in. If I remember correctly, you are very particular about invitations."

Annabelle ducked her head as she rose, attempting to hide the small smile that graced her face. She could not decide if it was because his voice held a playful tone, or because he remembered the details of their last conversation. Walking past him, she began to feel more at ease. His mood could change very quickly, but she would take his happiness where she could get it.

"Of course, sir."

Once inside the study Mr. Worthington sat comfortably in his chair beside the fireplace, while Annabelle slowly lowered herself onto the seat she sat in the day prior. Perfectly poised with her hands placed gently in her lap, Annabelle just stared at Mr. Worthington, as he stared back. Perching his elbow on the arm rest of his chair, leaning his head into his palm, Mr. Worthington simply tilted his head and cocked a brow, silently persuading Annabelle to begin.

Clearing her throat, Annabelle swallowed her nerves and began with a rushed, "I am very sorry for my actions the last time we spoke."

When the man did not respond to her statement, she continued.

"It was completely out of line for me to speak to you in such a manner, sir. I am deeply sorry for my rudeness and disrespect. Please grant me your forgiveness."

After completing her monologue, she averted her eyes to her fingers that still lay in her lap. Mr. Worthington let her stew in her nerves for a few moments until he leaned forward in his chair, propping his elbows on his knees and lifted Annabelle's head to meet his own.

"You are forgiven, Miss Faraday."

The sigh of relief that she breathed was very audible, causing Mr. Worthington's lips to quirk up into an almost miniscule smile, but Annabelle saw it, and responded with a gentle grin of her own.

****

The young girl perched herself on the edge of seat as she listened to her grandmother intently.

"But why did he forgive her so quickly, Grandmother?"

"Why, my dear, I am not sure he even knew at the time," the woman replied softly, amused by the young girl's confusion.

"That is no good answer," she pouted, crossing her arms over her chest tightly. "Boys are confusing sometimes."

"Child, please behave as a lady would," the grandmother chastised lightly, motioning to the girl's aggressive pout and crossed arms. Noticing her grandmother's movements, the young girl quickly averted her body back to a graceful stance and mumbled a soft apology. "Emotions are real, and we are always allowed to feel them, however, a little self-control and grace is always appreciated."

****

They sat in silence for a few moments before Annabelle found her voice and spoke.

"Sir," she took his raised eyebrows as permission to go on. "Is there anything else you need to speak to me about? The children should be waiting for me and I would hate to be late for them."

"You can leave, Miss Faraday, only when you tell me where you come from."

Confused by his question, Annabelle opened her mouth to speak, only to be cut off by him clarifying himself.

"You sit with the grace of an angel and speak at least three languages, as I have heard you teaching the children French and Italian, and I am assuming English was your birth language. You read remarkably well, far better than I could have found from any other country governess. You handle yourself with poise and speak eloquently. You are an anomaly. I know you did not grow up in this life, so I wish to know where you came from."

Annabelle started to sweat as she was afraid her secret would get out. Noticing her distress, Mr.

Worthington spoke gently to her.

"I do not wish to cause you stress, Miss Faraday. You are remarkable with the children, please do not think I have not noticed, and I quite like our verbal sparring when I can aggravate you enough. For the life of me I cannot find out why I cannot stay displeased with you, but in this moment, I only wish to know more about this young lady who now calls Arrington home."

Annabelle relaxed a little and spoke softly, her next words carrying an edge. "This place is not my home, sir."

Now his turn to be confused, Mr. Worthington raised his eyebrows in question.

"I do not wish to sound ungrateful, for you have given me much more than I could have ever imagined, living in Auburn, but this is not my home. My family perished when I was younger and now I do not even remember where my home is, but this is surely not it."

Looking into his eyes, all she saw was pity. She knew he had both parents, alive and well, living in France, for Miss Bowden had told her so, but she did not want anyone's pity.

"Please sir, do not look at me so," she spoke with a smile, trying her best to muster a twinkle in her eyes. "I have made peace with my fate and the emotions no longer plague me the same as they used to." The lie twisted in her heart. She felt uncomfortable lying, but especially lying to this man. "But I do not believe I will think of any other building as my home. The place where I was happiest with my family is home, and my home, while I may not remember where on Earth it is, lives on quite vividly in my memories."

The look on his face watching her speak could only be described as amazement and awe. This girl had been through so much, much more than he currently knew about, and here she was, strong as ever, smiling at him. How such a woman could smile such a peaceful smile after such words left him wonderstruck. So wonderstruck he did not even feel his lips move to create a smile of his own. He only realized how his muscles had betrayed him when her eyes glanced at his mouth and her own smile grew tremendously.

****

"Dear child, what do you think of the story so far?" The grandmother questioned.

"Grandmother," the young girl began with a shy smile. "Are they friends now? Does lovely Annabelle not dislike Mr. Worthington? He seems to be a bit of a grump, but he is not so bad."

With a chuckle the grandmother simply smiles and nods at the young girl.

"Yes, my dear. They are slowly growing fonder of each other. They were finally able to exist in the same area without violent bickering, which can be seen as great improvement."

****

With his curiosity now piqued, Mr. Worthington had been running into Annabelle more frequently as she went about her daily duties. These encounters did not go unnoticed by the young maiden. She would release a chuckle every time he would sit in on her lessons and attempt to interact with his niece and nephew. He popped by only once a week, but over the course of three weeks the pattern was known, and his presence was expected.

He was not terrible around children but was not particularly gifted in the area either. He would not humor the children by laughing at jokes that made no sense and would always correct them every time they were wrong, but Annabelle and the children had begun to grow fond of his surprise visits. With each passing day, he became more comfortable around the children, and Annabelle thought, severely less pompous.

"Annabelle," Isabelle murmured while walking up to the young lady. Mr. Worthington had been gone on business for a week and his visits were missed. Annabelle did not understand how she allowed him to weave his way into her life, but the infuriating man had done it and had the nerve to make her miss his presence.

"Annabelle, can you please play the piano for us?" Isabelle asked, almost in a whisper from fear of being rejected.

"My dear Issy," Annabelle began. "You know I do not play the piano, my dear."

"But you do!" Lucas chimed in loudly. "I watch you dance your fingers across the keys all the time! You just never press them down to make the music." He finished his sentence with his arms crossed and a pout on his lips to show his disagreement with her actions.

"Children—" Annabelle was swiftly cut off by chimes of "please" and hearty begs coming from the mouths of the children.

The idea of playing the piano stressed Annabelle's nerves. Since her fright in her chambers weeks earlier, Annabelle had been very cross with herself and strayed from anything that could remind her of her terrors. She did her best to stray from anything that brought the memory of her parents to the forefront of her mind to keep her sanity intact, and she knew the piano would crumble her hard work. Even with all this logic crowding her mind, Annabelle could not deny that she longed to touch the keys and hear their songs once again. The smiles she would surely bring the children would only be an added bonus, but she was not sure she could afford the risk.

"Annabelle," Lucas walked right up to her, breaking her out of her tense thoughts. "It would count as both a birthday and Christmas present if you would please play the piano."

His eyes were big, and his lips were quivering and all of Annabelle's resolve shattered under the gaze of the small boy in front of her. She had seen how their mother had treated them since she arrived, and with all her heart, she longed to balance some of the sorrow they endured with any form of joy she could bring. She would take the risk for them.

Silently rising from her seat near the fireplace, Annabelle walked to the piano as slow as molasses. The children lit up like fireflies in the summer as she took a seat on the piano bench and stretched her fingers, readying them for the task at hand. Taking a quick look out the window at the sun brightened day and the sky that resembled a window into the heavens, Annabelle sighed. Her body was ready to play, but she was not sure her mind was, and she was almost sure her heart was not.

Laying her fingertips against the ivory keys, Annabelle made sure to stray away from any songs that her mother would play during her childhood frequently. She was already fighting off memories and did not need to be the reason more reemerged. Soft music filled the room as she reacquainted herself with the instrument. The children were entranced by the complexity and beauty of the piece she was playing, but

Annabelle did not notice their awestricken faces fore she was lost in the notes flowing out of her fingers. With eyes shut and body swaying, Annabelle created the most beautiful sounds Arrington had heard in years. She did not even notice the windows or doors of the room open, allowing her music to bestow a trance upon the halls and grounds of the estate.

The sound floated through the halls of the estate, bouncing off the stone and drifting into whichever ears were willing to hear such a sound. One man, walking down the hall with a distinctive click to his boots, halted as he heard it. The broad man stood in the doorway to the kitchen, having just released his horse to the stable hand. He was looking forward to bathing and stowing away in his office for the night to recoup from his laborious travels, but a song pulled his heart to follow.

"Nettie," Mr. Worthington began monotonously, seemingly in a stupor. "Where is that sound coming from?"

His question was answered with a quick crack of a spoon to his backside.

"What in all that is holy was that for, Nettie?" Mr. Worthington all but shouted at the sudden impact his derriere felt. The stout woman felt no remorse for her actions and was quick to explain her ire.

"Why yes, Master Worthington, I am very well, thank you," she began, dramatically swaying her arms through the air to dramatize her sarcasm. "It is so nice to have you back after such a long week. I am so pleased you thought to ask how I was considering I practically raised you!"

Her voice steadily got louder as her rant continued and just as she was about to strike the grown man once more, he chuckled softly and pulled the woman into a tight embrace, twisting the spoon out of her hand for self-preservation at the same time. With a quick kiss to the forehead he murmured to the woman,

"Nettie, I am so glad to hear you are doing well, and I missed you very much as well. Although your duck is no comparison for a recipe I tasted on my travels."

As he saw the woman about to explode, he spun out of the embrace and headed for the stairwell. The woman decided to let him live one more day and forget his comment about her duck, for she had not seen him so jovial in years. She stopped him quick as he was about to bound up the stairs.

"I believe the source of the noise you are searching for is coming from the room the children are taught in, Sheri."

She smiled to herself as Mr. Worthington visibly scowled at the nickname from his youth. Few people existed in his life that he could lower his stone walls in front of, and he would forever be grateful that Nettie was one of them, especially with his parents in Paris for the last two years. Everyone wanted something from him these days after taking over his father's business at age twenty-five, and he found himself missing the days of youth more and more, where little was expected of him, and little was taken. Now was not the case. Every action he made was analyzed by society, and every person he encountered wished to associate with him, for no other reason than his rank.

His thoughts on the subject halted as his boots came to a stop outside the door of the children's study, the door wide open. It was here that he saw Annabelle, bathed in sunlight, swaying with the beautiful music that was created at her hands. He was swiftly proven wrong in thinking that the young woman had no more surprises for him, for she could play better than his own mother, who played the piano at least an hour a day during his childhood.

A natural at the instrument, Annabelle was so lost that she did not hear the clicks of his boots disrupt the tune of the music but did notice the hushes and giggles sounding from the corner of the room. Broken out of her trance, Annabelle came face to face with the man she had such conflicting emotions about earlier in the day, huddled in the corner, with a young boy and young girl on each knee, watching her, examining her, as she played.

"Beautiful," was the only word that slipped passed his lips as he made eye contact with Annabelle. Her yellow curls shining like a golden halo in the light of the sun, but her face in the shadows as she returned his gaze. The children clapped for Annabelle in the background, but neither adult heard the ruckus as they stared at each other. His mind could not decipher if he was complimenting her about her looks, her forte at the piano, or both, but he did not mind either way, for either statement would be true.

Annabelle twisted her gaze to her fingers that still lay upon the keys and whispered, "my mother taught me."

Mr. Worthington opened his mouth to respond but was cut off as one of the house staff announced that the day's meal was ready. Lucas and Isabelle flew off their uncle's lap and pulled Annabelle out the door and down the hall by her hand, excited for Nettie's food. All Mr. Worthington could do was watch her go as she trailed behind the children out the door and down the hall.

✳✳✳✳✳✳✳✳✳✳✳✳✳✳✳✳✳✳✳✳✳✳✳✳✳✳✳✳✳✳✳✳✳

"Grandmother," the young girl enquired from her grandmother, "was Annabelle a better piano player than you are?"

"Darling, I am sure she could play circles around me," she responded cheekily. "These old fingers can hardly play a hymn these days, let alone a classic masterpiece."

****

Annabelle's anxiety grew as the day went on. Clouds rolled through the countryside, mirroring her emotions, signaling unpleasant weather on the horizon. Playing the piano was clearly a mistake because now she could not get the image of her mother playing out of her head. This image played in her head over and over again, twisting and turning through her mind until she was a mess with memories. Her parents' smiles, her mother's laugh, and her father's kisses. These images always led to a stinging and raw pain in her heart. She fought it all day and was extremely restless by the time she emerged in quarters to prepare for bed.

A storm was brewing through the air as Annabelle readied herself for the night. She especially disliked storms. The cracks of lightning and roars of thunder always brought on her worst nightmares. When she lived at Auburn she would not even sleep on the night of storms; instead staying up all night with a candle next to her bed and read her Bible while she tried to block out the violent winds ripping outside her window. She did not want to wake in a panic and scare her girls. More so, she did not wish for anybody to have questions she was not ready to answer.

Being the first storm since she arrived at Arrington, Annabelle was vexed as to whether she should allow herself sleep or not. Exhausted from the months spent at her new residence, she knew she could not forego a night of sleep, and only hoped to have her own quarters would muffle any disturbances that may occur throughout the night. She would also let the fireplace burn on full light, not only for heat, but with the hope that if the room was illuminated from the flames, the lightning would not affect her so.

As night began to fall Annabelle changed into her sleeping dress. The dress, white, thin, and sleeveless, covered her entire body except for her head, just below her neck, and her arms. It draped to the floor and did not conserve much warmth. If it were not for the fire, Annabelle was certain she would freeze.

During her winter nights at Auburn, the girls would huddle together to keep warm and Annabelle rarely allowed herself to wear only a nightgown to sleep. In this garment, her left shoulder blade was on display for all to see, as was the over four-inch scar that ran vertically, beginning at the top of her back and down the blade. A nasty reminder of a previous life, Annabelle made certain none of her girls saw the scar.

Now with her own room, Annabelle felt less anxiety about the mark, sure no one would see it, and was able to wear her nightdress to sleep. She reached her right hand behind her and traced the fading scar as she squeezed her eyes shut tightly, trying to keep her demons at bay. As her candle beside her bed dwindled, Annabelle crawled into bed praying sleep would come quickly tonight.

Darkness crept in and the wind howled from outside of Annabelle's window as the thunder rolled through the air. The fire embers burned slower, cloaking the room in gloom. Between her tosses and turns under the blanket, Annabelle groaned with annoyance from lack of sleep. It was then that within seconds

Annabelle found herself hyperventilating on the ground, hearing a sharp scream, and succumbing into a vicious panic as the blankets from her bed floated down around her.

A crash had come through her window, destroying the glass that had once shielded her from the bitter cold waiting for her. Lighting cracked through the clouds, illuminating the room for the briefest of seconds and the panic in Annabelle's body grew. She threw her hands to her ears to block the cries of thunder and shut her eyes as tight as possible to hide from the shards of light that pierced the sky every few seconds.

In such a state, she could not help her mind from drifting back to her parents, and the similar crashing and screams that occurred that night. Looking past her tear blurred vision, Annabelle dove underneath her bed and let out shouts of fear and pain as she shook with a determination and a violence that could hardly be rivaled. She kept her eyes shut and closed off her mind to the world, as the scene from that night replayed in her mind relentlessly.

The crashes and screams. The tear stained eyes and the fear. The leaves and twigs snapping underneath her feet as she made the choice to live. The guilt.

Broken from her trance by a piercing cry, the same one she heard moments before, Annabelle began thrashing and throwing her limbs in every direction as rough hands ripped her from underneath the bed and shook her, attempting to force her eyes open. She had not noticed the door open, or the light suddenly fill the room, pulling her from the pit of her darkness. Unable to think or breathe, Annabelle crumbled to the floor in fear and exhaustion.

The rough hands that had pulled her from the bed moments earlier were now rubbing smooth circles on her back as a deep voice hummed to her, hoping to steady her breathes.

Annabelle, now able to comprehend her surroundings, slowly opened her eyes only to look upon Mr. Worthington, kneeling next to her, rubbing her back. Her eyes were swollen, red, puffy, and tired. Her lungs felt as if they were on fire, and a fearsome migraine was surely on the way. Her throat was still constricted, and she could not find it in her to do anything other than to look into his eyes. She was vulnerable, cold, and heartbroken, and he looked upon her with his usual strength, but with a hint of worry in his piercing eyes.

"Annabelle," he whispered slowly as he looked upon her terrified eyes. "What happened?"

Her only response was to continue to gaze deeply into his eyes, as if questioning how he got here, and how she found herself in his grasp.

Their stares were only broken by the wind whistling through the now broken window sending a chill through Annabelle's body.

Noticing her shivers, Mr. Worthington pulled one of the blankets from the floor next to her and wrapped her in it, but not before noticing the mark that decorated her back. Jagged and sharp, Mr. Worthington could not even think of a reasonable explanation as to how the mark was formed.

Staff were now crowding around her door, having heard the window break and the following screams. She could see the looks in their eyes as Mr. Worthington pulled her up from the floor and into his arms. She quickly relaxed and took her first deep breath since she first heard the crash. Feeling her lungs fill completely with oxygen, she allowed her eyes to flicker closed, ignoring the stares from the crowd around her room.

He laid her still body down onto the bed and sat on the edge next to her as she twisted deeper into the warmth of the blankets. She was soon cocooned into the sheets similar to a child searching for warmth in the arms of a mother. It was as if the blankets could keep her fears at bay and fight her monsters for her.

It did not take Mr. Worthington but a moment to notice the crowd, and his steel eyes appeared once again as he scolded workers for their presence at this moment.

"Back to bed, all of you!" He barked. "And I will not hesitate to dismiss any one of you that does not perform at top capacity tomorrow, because of this little midnight walk."

The servants quickly dispersed, all expect for two. Miss Bowden and Paul O'Connor, a middle-aged Irish man who served as the Estate's main gardener. Mr. Worthington had nodded his head at Paul to inspect the window as Miss Bowden began making a new fire in Annabelle's fireplace, hers having dimmed through the night, more so from the wind whipping through the room.

Having regained her breath and warmth, Annabelle allowed her eyes to open once more, looking upon the scene around her.

"I am sorry for such trouble, sir," Annabelle mumbled to Mr. Worthington. Upon hearing her voice, he diverted his attention back to her. His eyes grew a shade softer as he spoke.

"Do not be, Miss Faraday," he began, with a forgiving tone that Annabelle almost didn't recognize. "What happened to ail you so?"

"I do not know, sir," Annabelle spoke softly. "I just remember hearing a crash, and a scream, and then seeing you next to me. The rest is just a blur of sounds and colors."

"Annabelle," he began, forgoing formalities for a moment and only whispering her name. "Those screams were your own."

Attempting to sit up at the news, Annabelle felt a rush of pain echo through her head, a clear side effect of her headache, and slowly sank back down to the comfort of her pillows, clutching her temples in her hands, groaning numbly.

"Take it easy," said Mr. Worthington, moving closer to her while pulling more blankets around her cold form.

"Excuse me sir," Paul began, walking up to where Mr. Worthington was seated holding a rugged piece of wood in his hand. "It appears the wind blew this branch through the window, causing the crash."

"Thank you, Mr. O'Connor," Mr. Worthington replied, his eyes never leaving Annabelle's form. "I want that tree cut down and disposed of in the morning."

Annabelle shot up from her bed quickly and glared at Mr. Worthington as he gave Paul directions.

"You cannot do that!" She snapped, not caring who she was speaking too, but quickly holding her head in her hands from the pain.

Mr. Worthington noticed the sudden movement as held her wrists, looking intently into her eyes to make sure she was okay.

"And why not, Miss Faraday?" He replied with clear annoyance lacing his tone.

Looking up through her sprawling hair and small hands, Annabelle replied softly, "that tree is someone's home."

"Yes, but it is not my home, so why do you seem to think this should affect my life choices?" Mr. Worthington chastised. "Their home damaged my own. Do I not have a right for retribution?"

"Just because they are not you, sir, does not mean that are any less important to the world," Annabelle replied quickly wincing at the pain spreading through her head. "These creatures that call that tree home are important to someone and should not have their home destroyed simply for a whim of a crank of a businessman who cannot seem to find empathy in his heart."

"Ignoring your harsh tone towards me because of the event you have just been through, Miss Faraday, who, may I ask, are these animals so important to that I should alter my plans? I do not take kindly to my things being destroyed every time the wind blows."

"They are important to me, sir." Annabelle looked at him with clear and sad eyes. "The birds sing to me every morning."

A moment of silence passed through the room as Paul and Miss Bowden looked at the exchange, unsure of what to do or say. Mr. Worthington did not give them a chance to try, as he replied with a softer tone and empathetic eyes, his gaze never breaking from Annabelle's.

"Very well, but that branch which so violently destroyed the window will be cut down in the morning. You may keep the rest of the tree, however."

A small smile pulled at Annabelle's lips as she sat back in her bed, nodding her head gently towards him, replied with honest and clear eyes.

"Thank you, sir."

Miss Bowden left to prepare the empty room next to Annabelle's on Mr. Worthington's orders. Once she alerted him the room was ready, Mr. Worthington picked her up out of her bed and carried her to the room next door. Annabelle was ready to protest, but a stern look from the man shut her mouth quickly. She would accept this help whether she wished it or not.

He gently placed her form on the bed and sat on the edge while Paul began to make a fire and Miss Bowden lit a candle on the night table.

"Get some rest, Miss Faraday," Mr. Worthington began, moving on from the moment they shared so little time ago. "You can certainly not be an effective governess in this condition. You are to take the day tomorrow. I will inform my sister that she will be forced to care for the children."

"No, sir," Annabelle rushed. "I can assure I will be alright by morn. Mrs. Kennelworth will not be pleased."

"Last I checked, Miss Faraday, this is my home, and you are employed by me," Mr. Worthington interjected. "My sister will not question my decisions, and I should expect the same behaviors from my staff."

He turned his head to Miss Bowden and Paul and with a nod of his head, motioned to the door. They took this moment to leave the two as they ventured back to their own individual quarters for some for rest.

"Yes, sir," Annabelle bowed, not willing to argue with man, only wishing to be left alone to sort through her emotions. "I will take the day. I apologize for my outburst."

Mr. Worthington rose from his place on the edge of her bed and began walking to her door.

"All is forgiven," were the last words he spoke before exiting the room and closing the door as softly as possible, minding Annabelle's headache and stressful night. With an exhale, Annabelle put out the candle next to her bed and basked in the warm light of the fire as she attempted to fall back into slumber.

When Annabelle rose the next morning, her mouth was rough, and her face was stained with dry streaks of tears. All her muscles ached, and her mind was fresh with worry. She did not wish to face the day, and she held no desire to face the questions that would accompany it, especially in such a state. Few hours of slumber graced her body and even fewer were restful.

Annabelle pulled herself out of bed slower than molasses and crept along the room that was so unfamiliar. The only thing that brought her comfort this day was seeing her birds dancing through the breeze outside the windows. Their blurred forms twisting and turning behind the waves of glass brought the slightest of smiles to her face. She was not willing to let a scare ruin her demeanor. In some ways, she needed people to see her as she presented herself; gracefully, kind, and happy. Should she show them the inner workings of her heart, she feared they would see her pain and regret. Another judgmental stare she could not survive. She blamed herself enough, she did not need the accusations of others.

Turning away from the window, Annabelle ventured to her own room to see if the window had been fixed. She also needed to ready herself for the day. She knew she would not be caring for the children, but she would not allow herself to sit and rot throughout the day. A plan formed in her mind and the determination to see it through pulsed through her veins, hotter than fire.

Entering her room, Annabelle was pleased to see the glass had been swept and disposed of before she returned. The window was not yet fixed, but the branch was gone from the tree. Annabelle felt a twinge of heartache at the sight but felt a deep uncomfortable emotion fill her when she saw that Mr. Worthington had indeed kept his promise and had left the rest of the tree standing. She was rooted to the ground with her shock ridden face losing track of time as she could not process the fact that such a cruel man was capable of keeping such a promise. A man's word was everything in society, but she did not think he would care if he kept his word to her. She simply did not know what to make of his tender moments. Brushing all thoughts of Mr. Worthington from her mind, Annabelle quickly readied herself for the day, thankful that the chill of night was no longer lingering in the air and made her way to the kitchen.

Upon entering the room, Annabelle was bombarded with what she was sure was the tightest hug she had ever received in her life.

"Oh my goodness, Dear," Mrs. Nettles' voice was laced with a thick and heavy form of worry. "What on Earth happened last night? I heard your scream all the way in my cottage past the garden."

Annabelle had forgotten that the woman had been gifted a cottage. Mrs. Nettles had invited Annabelle over more than once for early morning tea. Her humble abode lived beyond the garden almost hidden by the trees at the forests edge to the west. The east side was where Catherine was buried.

Mrs. Nettles squeezed Annabelle as hard as she could, as if a hug from her would make her pain dissipate, and while the pain still existed after the embrace ceased, Annabelle had forgotten about it for that single moment.

Once the aging woman pulled away she looked deep into Annabelle's eyes. It was as if she was attempting to gaze upon the purest form of her soul, but Annabelle had walls that had survived for years, and she was certain one look from Mrs. Nettles would not be her downfall, even when she narrowed her eyes and clenched her jaw, as if she knew Annabelle would not be so easy to crack.

"Where has my sweet Annabelle gone?" She asked with so much conviction and caring that Annabelle felt the first crack in her resolve. "What troubles you so, my dear. You can surely trust us."

Annabelle gave a response that she hoped would squelch Mrs. Nettles curiosity. She was not ready to let someone in and was not certain whether she ever would be. "I did not get enough sleep last night because of my terror, Mrs. Nettles. I promise my smiles will return tomorrow morn."

Mustering up as much of a smile as she could, which to Mrs. Nettles looked pained and incredibly forced, Annabelle bowed her head shortly as she retrieved a plate of food and strode to her corner slowly. It was later in the morning than when she normally ate, so her corner was clothed in darkness. Annabelle's heart hung heavy acknowledging that she was indeed used to this and the darkness not only did not bother her as much as it used to, but it was slowly swallowing her up completely, and she had no clue how to save herself from drowning in the depths of it.

****

"Mr. O'Connor," began Annabelle as Paul lifted his eyes to meet hers. "May I please have any small twigs that may come off the branch that broke my window last night?"

"Why, of course Miss Faraday," Paul replied, to which a smile brightened the young woman's face. "May I ask whatever for?"

"A cross," she simply replied. "I mean to make a cross. You would not happen to have any twine to secure the branches together, would you?"

"M'lady," Paul slowly retorted. "If it is a cross you wish, let me have one of my apprentices use an axe to cut you one from the branch. It will only take moments and we can easily secure it with a nail or two. It will be much sturdier than one held together by twine and twigs."

"I could not ask for such a thing, sir. I truly do not mind building the item myself, I only lack the supplies needed to do so."

"Nonsense, dear. The boys and I will be happy to do it for you." He rebuffed with an easy smile. "The property has been brighter since you have called Arrington home and we are a family here. Be certain that we would be honored to make you such an item. It is well known how deeply you treasure your faith, dear. Please just let us do this for you?"

Annabelle felt tears burning behind her eyes at the thought of being a part of a family again and in that moment, her mouth could not find the strength to say no. With a whispered "yes" and a faint nod of her head, Annabelle gave the man a last smile before she left the stable, hearing Mr. O'Connor promise to have the cross ready by lunch for her to do what she will with it.

On her second visit to the kitchen of the day for her lunch, Annabelle made sure to wait until most of the staff was completed with their meals before entering. She could not face more questioning looks from those who called Arrington home. She entered the kitchen quickly, quietly, and quaintly. Eating her meal faster than she had in the morning, Annabelle disposed of her plate and left the room without a word, ignoring the quizzical start of Mrs. Nettles as she began making early preparations for the final meal of the day.

As she walked out of the kitchen and into the garden, Annabelle began to roam the grounds, venturing to the barn where Mr. O'Connor and his apprentices worked. She was antsy about her cross and wanted it in her hands soon, so she could give it a home.

Peering around the door of the barn, cautious to not interrupt anything, Annabelle was met with Charlie, a sixteen-year-old apprentice of Mr. O'Connor. He was also the man's son who was learning the trade to take over for his father once he was unable to continue his work.

"Hello Charlie," Annabelle greeted with a smile and a nod as her feet slowly crept into the building. Once she received a smile in return, she continued the conversation. "Do you happen to know where your father is? He was going to make something for me quickly this morning."

"Are you questioning about the cross, Miss Faraday?" Once she nodded in reply, Charlie began shuffling around the barn until he found the item. "I hope you do not mind, but my father had me make the cross for you."

He handed her the cross gently, as if he knew how important the two flat pieces of wood held together by two sharp pieces of metal were to her.

"Goodness, no, Charlie," chastised the young woman. "I know your work is of high quality and I am honored that you have seen it fit to take time out of your day to complete such a task as a favor for me. I am eternally grateful for this gift. You truly do not know what this means to me. Thank you for completing it so quickly."

"It was my pleasure Miss Faraday," Charlie replied to her bright and kind smile. "I will not ask what you will do with it, as I can see it has a great personal meaning to you, but please know that if you ever are in need, you may always come to my family for assistance."

"I do know that very well, Charlie," replied Annabelle in a soft voice. "Thank you again, so much."

With a nod of his head, Charlie went back to work, and Annabelle made her way back to the kitchen. She hoped to bring a satchel of water and some biscuits for her journey. It would not be a long one, but she would spend the better part of her day in this place.

As she crossed the threshold, Annabelle noticed all the workers had become incredibly hushed. She chose to think the cause was her entrance and was about to inquire about the biscuits with Mrs. Nettles when a voice sounded behind her causing Annabelle to spin so quickly her balance was thrown off and she almost tumbled over, regaining her center of gravity at the last moment.

"And what exactly do you think you are doing, Miss Faraday," Mr. Worthington inquired as he entered the kitchen, watching Annabelle throw her hands quickly behind her back. "I thought I told you to take the day."

"Sir, I am venturing to the edges of the forest, and you told me not to care for the children today, not to be confined to my quarters," Annabelle began, attempting to skirt around her true intentions. "There is a beautiful meadow, and I felt that some fresh air would do me well in my current state."

"Is that right," he replied, tilting his head to see behind her back, only to have her twist to continue to hide. "And you thought that this strenuous journey would do you more good than spending a day in bed, recovering from the night?"

"Yes sir, so if you please," replying shortly as she began moving out to the gardens.

"Nonsense, Miss Faraday," he stated quickly holding up his hand to silence her. "I shall accompany you. I do not recall such a meadow on my lands and would be pleased to see such a sight. Tell me, when have you had time to find such a place?"

Aggravated by his accusations, Annabelle tersely replied "the day Mrs. Kennelworth took the children shopping with her, sir. She gave me the day to do as I pleased, so I roamed the grounds. Now if you will excuse me…"

An amused smirk played on Mr. Worthington's lips as he watched Annabelle become agitated. He had already decided she would not be venturing out to the grounds alone today, she just had no knowledge of that little fact.

"Of course, Miss Faraday," he replied. "By all means, lead the way."

Her eyes sharply rose to his as she took a heavy intake of breath. She would not win this argument and had to accept this, something she was never good at. With her lips tightly locked into a thin line she tensely replied, "very well, sir. Please follow me."

She then turned with Mr. Worthington on her tail and ventured into the gardens and across the grounds to her friend's resting place. No conversations were had during the journey, but the two would steal glances of curiosity every now and then. Annabelle wondered why he forced himself to join her, and Mr.

Worthington wondered where this girl, who was so much more poised than some of societies highest and more educated than some of the best governesses, came from.

They accepted this silence and left one another to their thoughts as Mr. Worthington followed her footsteps through the tall grasses to the edge of one of the many forests that graced the grand estate. He never did see what Annabelle was clutching so tightly in her arms on their walk, but not without trying. She held it close to her chest with both arms wrapping tightly around the object, obstructing his view completely. He wondered whether he should ask about it but decided she would only chastise him should he decide to do so. He was not one to turn away from a verbal spar with the fiery girl with a sweet demeanor, but something told him she needed this silence. She needed the peace this place would bring.

CHAPTER 5

Arriving at Catherine's meadow, Annabelle noticed the rose bushes were no longer showered in reds and pinks, but were bare and covered in thorns, brought on by the coming winter. The weeping willows have lost their lush leaves with the cold air. Even barren by the cold, the meadow was still draped in peace.

Annabelle's only consolation came from the sun that warmed the bristling grass she walked upon as she entered the meadow. The area was not nearly as lovely as when Annabelle first came to Arrington, but grass had begun to grow upon the place where Catherine lay.

Mr. Worthington had trudged the journey in silence, his mind drifting to the woman walking just paces ahead of him, until they finally reached their destination. Near the edge of the trees he stood, only watching, as Annabelle neared the fading gravesite.

It was then that Annabelle pulled the cross she had hidden behind her back out. She was sure that the wood could hold up underneath the cover of the surrounding trees. The weather would not bother Catherine's place here. Mr. Worthington did not dare utter a word as Annabelle walked towards the plot and began pushing the wooden cross into the Earth.

After a few minutes of struggle to force the item deeper into the frigid and stiff dirt, Mr. Worthington left the meadow for a moment. Annabelle thought his reason for leaving was that he simply did not see the point in her actions, but when he returned a moment later with a large branch, Annabelle grew incredibly confused.

"Here," he began as he crouched next to where Annabelle was kneeling on the ground. "Let me help you."

Annabelle merely nodded and moved away from the man as he took the large branch over his head and brought it down heavily on the cross. Annabelle watched in wonder as the wood pierced the ground deeper with every downswing of Mr. Worthington's arms.

After several swings he ceased and looked towards Annabelle. "Do not worry, Miss Faraday, the cross should not move from this position. You will always be able to find your friend here."

Annabelle nodded slightly. She was taken aback by the man's actions and did not understand how to tread this new situation. She was searching for words to break the stiff silence, only to be relieved from the task by Mr. Worthington.

"I must say, Miss Faraday," he began, looking down at the cross that marked her friend. "I do admire your fierce trust in God. Tell me, how can you continue to put such value in something as fickle as faith?"

Shooting her head up, Annabelle's eyebrows furrowed into deep creases as she digested his words. "I am sorry, sir," she began. "Are you telling me you do not believe?"

"How could I, Miss Faraday?" His deep voice echoed through the meadow, carrying pain and heartache in its path. "The only time I put value in such things, your God let me down in the truest form."

"My God?" Annabelle recalled. "I hold no ownership of God. Faith is there for everyone, it does not discriminate who can believe."

"Maybe so, but it is my choice not to."

"Sir, forgive me, but you sound bitter," she began, ignoring the feeling of hypocrisy that settled in her belly. "We know not, God's plan for our lives, so how shall we know if God has let us down?"

"I prayed one prayer, Miss Faraday," his solemn voice continued. "A young boy prayed for his hero, his grandfather, to be allowed to live, and your God let me down in the truest form. Watching someone you love dearly be lowered into a cave of dirt, never to rise again, scars a young boy more than most would imagine."

"Sir, I have known loss," Annabelle treaded lightly, wary of the direction the conversation could take.

"But my faith is not lost, even when my heart is in pain and my mind is confused, my faith holds strong.

Maybe it is because I have to believe that everything serves a purpose and awful things do not occur with no consequences. I have to believe this life means something more, even if I do not know what."

"As I said, Miss Faraday," Mr. Worthington began again, lifting his eyes to her. "I admire your faith; however naïve it may be."

He then took the branch back out of the meadow, as if not wishing to further disturb this tranquil place. His back disappeared beyond the trees before Annabelle could comprehend the slight insult he directed towards her, as if calling her simple minded. She was not quick enough to think of a retort but was pleased she did not. He was a hurting man, and she knew his ire was not directed at her in that moment, but something much greater than she. Turning back to the cross, Annabelle pushed the last few moments to the recesses of her mind to focus on her purpose for this journey.

"My dear Catherine," Annabelle began, turning her attention back to her friend. "Oh, how I miss you so. I hope the angels are treating you well. I am most certain you will be earning your wings soon, for there is no one I can think of who deserves to be an angel more than yourself. Do be happy. I have no doubts that you are, but please know you are not forgotten here. I promise to visit as frequently as possible."

Annabelle continued her ramblings to Catherine as she plucked all the fallen and dead leaves from where her body lay under the Earth, discarding them to the side to keep the area clean. It was many minutes before Annabelle was done speaking with her friend and rose to return to Arrington. Mr. Worthington had not return, and Annabelle had assumed he had returned to his home until she exited the meadow to find him leaning against a tree a few paces away. His arms rested on bent knees and his head was tilted back, leaning against the bark that protected the heart of the tree.

Venturing closer, she realized that Mr. Worthington had fallen into slumber against the trunk of the tree. Annabelle was in awe of his appearance under the peaceful trance of sleep. His face held no lines of worry or angry scowl. No signs of frustration or impediments visible. As she was walking closer, a snap sounded underneath her foot where she had broken a branch. Mentally, she scolded herself as she saw Mr.

Worthington's nose twitch and his eyes flutter open. A look of confusion passed over his face for a moment. The way his eyebrows furrowed caused a smile to slip on to Annabelle's face as she watched realization dawn on the man, who seemed more like a child in this vulnerable state.

"I apologize for nodding off, Miss Faraday," Mr. Worthington stated as he looked up at the woman, shaking the sleep from his head slightly. While he was in better spirits from their last encounter, he felt a crack resonate in his heart seeing her swollen eyes as her nose and cheeks now held an unfamiliar pink tint. Her cheeks were rosy, but never flushed as they were now. She was emotional, and he foolishly fell asleep. He only hoped the precarious situation she had found him in was the reason for upturns of her lips. If he could, he would always cause her to smile.

"It is quite alright, sir," Annabelle whispered back to him with a thick voice betraying her emotions. "You have done more than enough simply by accompanying me on this endeavor, however we should be getting back to Arrington. The sun is beginning to set, and supper should be completed soon."

With a nod of his head, the man lifted himself from the ground effortlessly. "Very well, Miss Faraday." He looked towards her as he finished brushing the leaves and dirt from his trousers. "I hope you have accomplished all you have wished for the day."

"More so, sir," Annabelle whispered following a subtle nod as she turned to begin her journey back, leaving Mr. Worthington to follow.

The two went on their journey back to the estate's main grounds side by side, not talking much, but simply existing together. Neither would ever admit how much they enjoyed the journey either. Conversation flowed naturally as Annabelle informed Mr. Worthington of the children's education, and Mr. Worthington made Annabelle aware of a ball his family put on every year. It would come in a few months, after the holidays and a short business trip, and Annabelle could only hope to avoid the event entirely.

"My grandfather started the event the year after he built Arrington," Annabelle watched Mr. Worthington talk with pride as he described his familial roots to her. He told her about how Arrington was built and told her about the aspects of the ball that were already planned. He was like a small boy as he smiled when informing her that his parents were travelling in from France for the annual event after Mr. Worthington, his sister, and the children travelled to France for the holidays.

"Ever since they have been spending the majority of their years in France, it seems I see them less and less," Mr. Worthington spoke. Annabelle could hear his vocal cords working hard to hide his emotions. "I am sure the children will be thrilled for the visit, as my parents will be."

Only speaking when needed, Annabelle simply listened. This was the most she had heard the man speak since she had known him, even if it only were a few short words separated by terribly long bouts of silence, she still reveled in it. When they were not conversing, they both looked to the horizon as they walked. The sun was dipping low, twisting into a sea of reds, yellows, and pinks with orange fire burning brightly in the middle. Drifting higher in the sky the warmth melted into deep blue hues that held the stars firmly in the night. The sunset was awe inspiring. Annabelle loved the soft yellows and bright lights of morn, but it was as if the fire burning on the horizon, as each day was on the brink of night, touched her deeper than she could ever understand. It felt as if the sun was scorching her, not only the edges of the Earth.

Her thoughts on the subject were short lived as they found themselves back at the steps of Arrington, awaiting the return to their simple lives. Annabelle looked at her day's travel companion with soft eyes. The man got lost in the pools of color for a moment and almost missed her curtsy. Similar to a fog in the wind, she was gone, back into his home to likely care for the children before bed, even though he told her to take the whole day. Just thinking of her stubbornness brought a faint smile to his face and a chuckle to his lips as he followed up the steps she had graced a moment before.

Days passed since her journey to visit Catherine and Annabelle finally found herself able to succumb to some form of sleep without disturbing the household. The days prior, even closing her eyes in the dark had brought on her worst memories, forcing her to keep a fire burning bright in her quarters to allow herself even the most restless of slumbers. While she slept very little each night, the few hours were better than none, and as long as she could teach the children during the day, she was not very worried of her state of dreams at night.

Life had gone on as she was accustomed to for the next days. Those around her had ceased their questions and worried glances and Miss Bowden no longer treated her as if she was breakable glass. She was settled in life once again and could not hide her joy when a letter arrived from Emma for her. Mr. Longfellow gave it to her as she entered the kitchen to prepare for dinner.

Overjoyed, Annabelle ripped it open in the middle of the kitchen and read it to herself. Mrs. Nettles lifted her eyes from the pot she was stirring to take note of Annabelle's apparent bliss, simply raising an eyebrow at the scene. Mr. Worthington however, noticed both women as he was headed through the kitchen to the dining hall for his meal. He endeavored to sneak a biscuit from one of the platters only to have his hand slapped away by Mrs. Nettles. Annabelle looked as if she did not even take note of the interaction as she was engrossed completely by the words of her friend.

"Now listen here boy," Mrs. Nettles began, placing fists on her hips and glaring at the man, who suddenly looked years younger as he was chastised. "You may own this house, but this is my kitchen. You know that I tolerate nothing less than respect."

Mr. Worthington took a chance, only to see how the woman who he spent many hours a day with as a child, would respond. "And if I decided to obtain a cook with less strict rules?" he began. "What then, Nettie?"

Her face turned red as she scoured the counter looking for a spoon to beat the boy with. "Then you would starve because no cook would tolerate you and since you have not had to cook for yourself in years, surely you would burn down my kitchen. Do not toy with me boy, for I will leave you to visit my sister and have you begging me to come home after a week."

Mr. Worthington paled at the thought of the woman leaving him and quickly engulfed her short frame in a hug and kissed the top of her head.

"You surely know I am completely inept without you, Nettie. I could not survive should you leave."

The aging woman embraced the boy back and instantly forgave him.

"I am well aware, Sheri." She began, using his childhood nickname that made him visibly scowl, before pushing him away. "Now get out of my kitchen before I find my spoon."

Mr. Worthington quickly scurried away with a chuckle, only to be met with Annabelle eagerly reading in a corner, not paying him any mind. His attention piqued, he couldn't help but peer over her shoulder to catch a peek of what brought her such joy.

Little did the man know, Annabelle was very much aware of his presence. Peeking up at his interactions with Nettie when the two were near one another was a constant. She always fought a twitch of her lips and was quick to duck her eyes, not wishing to be caught watching such a moment.

In this moment, however, Annabelle fought a wave of emotions threatening to trample her as she read through her dear friend's words.

"Dear Annabelle,
I am terribly amiss that it has taken me so long to write you.
Please do not worry about me as things have been lovely, but I feel
like the most rubbish of friends having not contacted you sooner. I
dearly hope this letter reaches you in a timely manner. Please do not
think of ill of me because of my behavior.
I miss you dearly and am writing this letter with a purpose. I
have a free day on the first Wednesday of December and was hoping
you and I could meet in the market. I am aware your position as
governess may not allow such a meeting, but I would feel terrible
if I had not even tried to see my beautiful friend. I wish to hear all
about your life as I have so much to share with you as well.

It is simply not the same waking up and having you two beds away humming with the birds. My husband is lovely, and I adore him deeply, but few things can take the place of a wonderful friend, as you have always been to me.

Even if you are not able to meet me, please write back. I have few friends here, as most of the staff is unmarried and almost entirely male. I would welcome any words from you, my dear Annabelle.

Yours,

Emma"

Annabelle could not control the growing desire to see her friend and spent that night and the entirety of the next day lost in her thoughts of how to appropriately ask Mr. Worthington for leave to see her. She had even lost her train of thought while teaching the children multiple times that day.

It was not until night had fallen and the children were put to bed that Annabelle decided on requesting an audience with her employer. She wrung her fingers together as she stood at the door to his study, awaiting her invitation to enter. A knock had already been cast upon the wood, and as she heard his voice sound from the other side, she drew in a harsh breath. Desperately wishing to see her friend, she could only hope he would allow her a day to do just that.

The door swung open, and in front of her, stood Mr. Worthington dressed only in trousers and an untucked shirt, with the top few buttons unfastened. Annabelle was not ready for such a sight. His skin was bathed in the glow from the fire, and his hair was a terrible mess, falling over his forehead in beautiful chaos.

His scowl that marred his lips lessened when he saw the governess shifting on her feet in front of him.

"What may I help you with, Miss Faraday?" His voice was rough from his long day spent looking over business documents and his muscles in his neck and shoulders were tight from stress. As much as he loved his banter with the lady, he was not sure he was in the best spirits for such a challenge.

"May I come in, sir," she questioned in a soft voice. "I have a request I would wish to make to you."

With a risen brow, Mr. Worthington stepped to the side and allowed the woman entrance into his study. She walked in but stood in front of the chair she sat in the last time she was in this room and made no move to sit down. He almost smiled remembering that she insisted upon an invitation to do such a thing.

"Please, be seated Miss Faraday," he spoke as he took a seat of his own.

"Thank you, sir." She gently lowered herself into the seat by the fire and sat with poised perfection as she looked at the man in front of her. Stress marred his features as he slumped back into his seat and let out a heavy breath. He did not speak for a few moments, until his green eyes rose, and pierced her.

"Now, Miss Faraday," he began in a tired voice, "what may I do for you?"

"Sir, I have received a letter from dear friend yesterday," Annabelle began her inquisition carefully, watching the man intently in hopes of judging his mood. His interest, however, was piqued as he remembered the letter from the day before, and her smile as she read it. "She has requested that I visit with her in the village market the Wednesday after next."

His only response was a raised brow and a motion from his hand, ushering her to continue.

"I am asking for the day, so I can visit with her. I know I will have to be granted permission from Mrs. Kennelworth, but as I will be gone for the entire day and the children will still be here, and since you are technically my employer, I wished to have your permission before I move forward."

"You may go," he briskly replied. "No need to speak with my sister. I will have a word with her and will have Miss Bowden care for the children that day. You have been a loyal governess, Miss Faraday, just know that personal days at Arrington are few and far between for such fresh workers." He finished his sentiment with a tired sigh but could not help but notice the bright smile that the governess was trying to hide under her poised posture.

"Thank you, sir," she breathed a sigh of relief as the words slipped through her lips. She could not wait for the day she could see her dear Emma once more. Mr. Worthington enjoyed the sight of her joy, but then remembered how far his estate was from the village. He sat a little straighter, preparing himself for the oncoming war he was about to have with the woman.

"You may also take a carriage," Mr. Worthington began, only to be cut off by the woman, now standing, in front of him.

"No, sir," her voice cut through the air, firm and precise. "I do not even require a horse. I am just asking for a day to visit the market to see a friend. I will be back at Arrington before nightfall."

"Give me some piece of mind, Miss Faraday," he returned with a sigh, slumping further into his seat. "It is a tremendously long journey, especially tiring, even on horseback. Please take the carriage so I may know that you will be safe. I cannot trust the passing carriages and men on horseback to assist you, should anything happen, or not to harm you. The children would not be pleased if something should indeed happen."

"Sir, really, I will be quite alright," Annabelle insisted.

"Miss Faraday," leaning forward in his seat, Mr. Worthington's voice was now firm. It was the voice he used when discussing business and chastising workers who do not handle themselves in a respectable manner. "I am not a man to compromise and should something occur that I could have prevented, I will be especially aggravated when I must return to Auburn to enlist the services of yet another governess."

"Well I am pleased to hear that your concern for my safety comes from an attempt to ease your aggravations, sir," frustrated now Annabelle was well aware that she needed to succumb to his wishes to be able to visit Emma. "I will indeed take the carriage if it means this conversation could see an end."

"Very good, Miss Faraday," the man had to fight a smile as this was the first time Annabelle had willingly stepped down from one of their disagreements. "It will be ready for you the morning of your journey. Be sure to tell the stable manager Mr. Collins of your intentions and the date so he can prepare the horses."

"Very well," she curtly threw back as she turned and trekked away mumbling under her breath, "insufferable man."

"Stubborn woman," he whispered to himself with a smile as his back fell into the chair, all while pinching the bridge of his nose in frustration after the door to his study closed, following her exit.

****

"Why was he so persistent, Grandmother?"

"What do you mean child?"

Turning towards her grandmother, the young girl continued her questioning. "Why did he need her to take a carriage so badly? She walked to Arrington after leaving Auburn, did she not?"

"Ah, but he did not know her then, did he child?" The grandmother responded with a small smirk, and expression that the little girl rarely saw cross her grandmother's features. "He cares for her now and wishes for her to be alright. He was hoping to ensure her safety when he sent her in the carriage. It would also make her journey easier as she would not be so tired. He used frivolous excuses because he did not see that he truly cared for her well-being. Not necessarily in a romantic way, but as one person hopes that another has a safe journey, wherever they may be going."

****

The next days passed fairly quickly for Annabelle as she readied herself for her short journey to the village to see Emma. The morning of her trip she awoke with the sun and the birds, her excitement barely containable. Too nervous to hold anything in, she only had a quick drink and a piece of bread before she ventured out to find the coachman in charge of her journey. Before long, she was sorted in the carriage and began venturing to the market.

She took the carriage to the village, as requested. While the ride was shorter by hours compared to what her walk would have been, she could not help but to think that she had sent the wrong message to the man by allowing him to care for her so. She did not want him to believe he was making progress with her, because she could not let him become any closer to her than he already was.

Regardless, it was a good day for a trip to the market. The sun was bright in the sky, and while the air had a distinct chill that would nip at her skin, Annabelle was more than comfortable in the back of the closed carriage with her blanket draped around her. She only moved to glance out the window at the trees flying passed. She had been given her earnings earlier in the week and could not contain the shiver of excitement that passed her bones as she thought of seeing her good friend after so long. She only hoped the carriage driver would be kind enough to allow her as many hours as possible before taking her back to Arrington. The man had strict instructions to deliver her back to the estate by nightfall, and life could be very unpleasant when you are the recipient of Mr. Worthington's ire.

Once they pulled up to the market, the coachman dismounted and opened the door for Annabelle, while she tried her hardest not to fall from the steps. It had been years since she had spent time in a proper coach, and when she was younger she always had her father's hands on her waist to gently lift her down safely. She felt akin to a newborn attempting to walk for the first time as she looked for stable footing and adjusted to the jostling carriage as she climbed down.

Once safely on the ground she curtsied to the man and said a simple, but sweet "thank you" with a gentle smile. The man could not help but smile in return and ask her to meet him back at the carriage at 4:00.

After the short conversation, the coachman left to tend to the horses and Annabelle began the short walk through the village, into the market, looking for a familiar friend that she had not seen in far too long.

Just as she thought she would, Annabelle spotted her lovely friend looking over the vegetables that were for sale. Emma had always loved peppers, and Annabelle could see this clearly in the way she scrutinized the vegetable in her hand. They were about to go out of season, so it was no surprise that Emma was looking for the very best in the batch. Annabelle saw this vulnerable moment of distraction as a perfect opportunity to surprise the girl who had become like a stranger.

Biting her lips shut to suppress her giggles, Annabelle crept up behind Emma and with lightning movements, she pinched her sides softly, just hard enough to gain a noticeable jump as Emma squealed in surprise. Annabelle was quick to grab the pepper that went tumbling to the ground in her friend's moment of fright, and held in her hand proudly, a bright look on her face as her flustered friend wore a shocked expression as she turned around. With a grunt and a shove, she promptly pushed Annabelle backwards a step, before gripping her shoulders tightly and pulling her back for a suffocating embrace, one Annabelle enjoyed and returned tremendously.

"Oh, my sweet Anna," Emma began, throwing her arms tightly around Annabelle. "How I have missed you!"

"I have missed you as well, my dear," Annabelle responded with a stifle laugh. "How has your lovely husband been treating you?"

Pulling away from the tight embrace, Emma's smile grew as happiness etched into her features deeply. "Would it be cruel to say that I have never felt such bliss. He adores me and I, him. I could not imagine still being cooped up in that awful place. He saved me Anna, and I will be forever grateful."

Annabelle smiled a bright smile at her friend's happiness.

"And the masters of his estate? Have they treated you well?"

"Yes, they have!" She squealed with fervor. "I have even begun working as a handmaiden for the lady of the house. It is no governess position, but it keeps me busy while my love does his work, and now we are both protected under the household."

Annabelle could not be more pleased to hear of her friend's fortune in life.

"I am so happy for you, my sweet Emma."

"And how have you faired, Annabelle. What news of Arrington? Have you found your happiness?"

Annabelle stiffened at the thought.

"I do not know if true happiness is the correct term. I liken it more to contentment of my surroundings. The children are lovely, and the staff has been very kind. The mother of the children is very rough around the edges, but that cannot be helped I suppose."

Her voice sounded sullen as she answered her friend's questions.

"And the master of the house?" Emma inquired. "A handsome man he is. How has he treated you, Anna?"

Annabelle took quick offense to the comment.

"I fail to see what you mean, Emma," she responded with a sharpness she had never spoken to her friend in before.

"I meant no offense, Anna." Emma quickly attempted to right the situation. "I only meant to ask if he was similar to his sister. He is devilishly handsome, and I only wondered if his personality also embodies the beast."

Unable to understand why, Annabelle took fiery offense to that comment. Mr. Worthington may have been rough around the edges, but a devil, he was not.

"Anna, let us not talk about the master of the house anymore," Emma cautiously began. "I have missed you so and have so much more to tell you!"

The girls spent the afternoon talking and laughing and browsing the market. Annabelle did not purchase anything but enjoyed the scenery and witnessing all the townsfolk commune together. Moments like this reminded her that she was never alone in the great expanse of the world. After assisting Emma in purchasing ribbons for the lady of the house she was employed at for an upcoming ball, the girls walked down the dirt covered road to the small white church Annabelle had spent so much time in while she was at Auburn. She simply wanted to see the building to be assured that it was still there and still healthy as ever. It was a safe place in her world of confusion, and she could never have been more grateful for such a place.

"I have had a most joyous day, Anna," Emma whispered in her ear as they embrace, preparing themselves for another unpleasant goodbye. "I shall write you again soon, my dear. I shall miss you far too much to not set up another meeting before the weather grows too frigid for it."

Annabelle smiled through the embrace at her friend's words. A lovely afternoon spent with a very special friend was just the medicine she needed for the frustrations plaguing her life currently. She did not have a care in the world this afternoon causing a mix of dread and anticipation to pool deep into her being as she thought about her return to Arrington. She was unsure which emotions were the strongest, but confusion and fear were two prominent ones at the thought of returning to the estate. Some days she had been more content than she had been in years, especially when she was spending time with the children, but other days she was on edge, especially when she dealt with the man of the house.

After bidding Emma a loving farewell, Annabelle ventured back to the carriage for the long ride back to Arrington. Clouds had drape over the sky, and night was drawing upon the countryside quickly. She knew she had spent too much time with her friend, but she would gladly face any reprimands, for she had the loveliest time with Emma and could not think of a better way to have spent her day.

Smiling at the coachman as he held the door open for her, offering his hand to assist her while she ambled into the carriage, Annabelle relaxed against the velvet cushions that graced the seats of the covered carriage and prepared herself for the journey. The sound of hooves beating against the road and the vision of the trees passing by the carriage at amazing speeds lulled Annabelle into almost a comatose trance as she thought about all that had occurred since she arrived at Arrington. Replaying every moment since she first walked onto the grounds had transfixed her, causing her to not notice the carriage come to a stop. It was the darkest of nights as she was pulled from her thoughts by the latch of the carriage door, notifying her of their arrival at the estate.

Bidding a sleepy goodnight to the coachman as he moved the carriage towards the carriage house, Annabelle slowly staggered up the step of the grand building. An "architectural masterpiece" her father would call it, with beautifully smooth stones creating the outside walls and intricate details etched around every window and beautiful vines of ivy clinging to the walls akin to a lifeline.

"Such a place is frivolous, but magnificent," she tiredly muttered under her breath with a huff as she strenuously climbed the last few steps and knocked on the door, praying to be let in quickly, as she was on the verge of slumber, and would much rather spend her night in her bed as opposed to the stones that lined the front of the home.

A moment later Mr. Rubin Longfellow, the longtime butler for the Worthington family, opened the door for Annabelle. The long journey from the village had left her body tired and her heart weary. The only thoughts that passed through her mind at this moment were those that concerned her bed and the idea of slumber. Her feet resembled slugs as they carried her through the doorway. Extensive effort on her part was used to send a small smile Mr. Longfellow's way as he nodded his head in response.

Through the dim hallways of the estate, Annabelle leaned heavily on the walls for support as her exhaustion grew. Every chaise lounge she passed looked undeniably comfortable. She only wished it were appropriate to curl up as a cat would and spend the night there, willing to do anything to avoid the stairs that awaited her through the kitchen. Annabelle jolted with a fright as she rounded a corner in the maze of hallways only to walk straight into another human. She squeaked out a yelp and jumped backward before looking up. Her deliriously tired state cleared for a moment as she took in the sight of her brooding boss while she rubbed her forehead where she had bumped into the man.

"My sincerest apologies, Mr. Worthington," Annabelle stated to the man half hidden by shadows. She was much to worn out to put a fight with the man about creeping around corners. She supposed someone could very well do as they wished in their own home.

"Are you alright, Miss Faraday?" He questioned. As tiredness continued to consume Annabelle she could not help but let out a small giggle at his clouded form, wrapped in shadows. He simply cocked an eyebrow at her outburst, to which she responded by simply walking around the man mumbling a quick "goodnight, sir," over her shoulder before tripping over her own feet and tumbling to the floor. Laying on her back, the blonde governess erupted into multiple fits of laughter melded with egregious yawns, letting out a small squeak at the end of each one.

After multiple minutes of Mr. Worthington attempting to persuade Annabelle to rise from the floor, and her not possessing nearly enough energy for such an act, the frustrated man bent to her level, only to lift her into his arms after she began twisting on the rug as if she were about to fall asleep there, in the middle of his hallway.

Annabelle only hummed in acknowledgment and laid her head on his shoulder.

"I am so very tired, sir," she whispered. Mr. Worthington felt as if the statement went much deeper than her current physical state, but as she burrowed into his arms as he carried her to her quarters, he chose to let his suspicions go for the time being.

The following morning Annabelle woke to the birds outside her window chirping happily as she laid in her own bed, still clothed in her garments from the day before. It only took a moment for the memories of the previous day to flood her mind and she swiftly buried her flushed face into her hands and groaned. She had made a fool of herself in front of Mr. Worthington and could not think of how she would ever be able to face the man again. Mortified, she contemplated staying locked in her quarters for the remainder of the day, but the sheer thought of Mrs. Kennelworth's ire directed towards her caused her to rip the covers from her body and rise with a shock.

Taking slightly longer than usual to ready herself, Annabelle was hoping that Mr. Worthington would be barricaded in his office with business dealings by the time she collected the children and ventured to the kitchen for breakfast. Luck, however, was never quite fond of Annabelle, as the first thing she saw when she descended the staircase into the kitchen was Mr. Worthington discussing the upcoming ball with Mrs. Nettles as she put her finishing touches on the day's first meal. Over a month was left until the event, but Mr. Worthington and family were leaving for France for the holidays in the coming days and would not return to Arrington until just days before the event. The entire staff was in a bit of a tizzy over the preparations that still needed to be finalized before the family's departure.

The children skipped to a stop at the bottom of the stairs and cheered their good mornings to the kitchen staff, causing all eyes to turn to the group of three. She would not meet his eyes, though she was sure he was looking her way. Instead, she met Mrs. Nettles gaze head on and sent her a bright smile, ushering the children to the dining room while doing so.

A quick prayer of thanks was sent to the Heavens when Mr. Worthington did not follow her, but she could not help but wonder if he would confront her about the day prior and tease her about her actions. It would not be a very gentlemanly thing to do, but considering their past ribbings of each other, Annabelle was almost expecting a comment or two.

Noontime found Annabelle happily seated with Mrs. Nettles in the kitchen, enjoying her lunch as Mrs. Kennelworth handled the fittings for the outfits the children would wear to the ball. A woman without a care in the world at the moment, she happily retold the events of the previous day to the curious cook.

"Mrs. Nettles, it was beyond lovely seeing my friend after so many weeks," Annabelle spoke with joy running through her voice. "It is true you do not realize how much you rely on another human until you are removed from them. I simply do not know how I have gotten on without my dear Emma."

It was during this simple retelling that Mr. Worthington strode into the room, ready for his own lunch.

"I heard you were quite a sight to see last night," Mrs. Nettles teased with a wink causing a vibrant pink to coat Annabelle's already rosy cheeks.

"I am not as in control of my actions as I wish I could be when sleep comes upon me so heavily," Annabelle mumbled back, suddenly very interested in her plate.

"Well," Mr. Worthington spoke, making his presence known. "I am just pleased that she calmed down before the walls began to shake with the sheer volume of her laughter. I am surprised you could not hear it in your cottage, Nettie."

Annabelle flushed deeper as Mrs. Nettles let out a light chuckle at the conversation. Their teases went on for only a few more moments before the conversation suddenly turned serious. As Mrs. Nettles prepared his lunch, Mr. Worthington turned towards Annabelle.

"Truthfully speaking, Miss Faraday," He began in a serious tone. "I can only hope we will not have a repeat of such actions as those of last night anytime soon. We have the ball coming up, and I certainly cannot have giggling governesses lining my halls as English nobles are dancing."

Clearing her throat, Annabelle nodding before delivering a genuine apology.

"I am truly sorry for my actions last night, sir," she tentatively began. "I will be sure to control myself better from here on out. I shall not stay away from Arrington for so long should I be allowed leave to visit Emma again."

His only acknowledgement of her apology was a stiff nod before he diverted the conversation to the upcoming ball.

"Only a little time stands between Arrington and its annual ball, Miss Faraday."

"I am aware, sir," she replied, looking up at him, acknowledging the strict matter of this conversation.

"I do hope you understand that your presence at the event is expected and required as my sister cannot care enough to pay attention to her own children, and I cannot have them running amuck at such an event."

Annabelle could only nod as dread flooded her. She did not wish to attend the ball. She had selected a book from Arrington's library specifically for that night. She was to hide away in her quarters and not be heard from until the next morning. She was certainly not pleased with the prospect of attending such an event. It was a long while away, but with the holidays looming, Annabelle knew it would sneak up on her quickly.

"Yes, sir," she simply replied, turning back to her food as he collected his from Mrs. Nettles and made his way out of the kitchen.

"I guess I am attending a ball," she whispered to herself, suddenly at a loss for her appetite.

CHAPTER 6

The stars glittered against the sky, dark as ink, as droplets of pure light. Yellow flames were littered against the shadows that clouded the roads and entryways of Arrington. The estate has not seen so much excitement in months as countless carriages rolled up the road to the estate that sat proudly, cleaned to Miss Bowden's standards and ready for the onslaught of the best England had to offer. The annual ball was larger this year than it had been since Mr. Worthington took over the estate. The family had returned two weeks before the event after spending four weeks in France to finalize the preparations as the ball did indeed creep up quickly.

Annabelle stood by her window watching the commotion below, twirling her fingers together and knitting them tightly. Her nerves were haywire, and her heart was racing. The last time she had attended a proper private ball was with her parents. She wore the most beautiful dress that looked as if it had been bathed in moonlight with her blonde curls wrapped in her head and a pearled tiara that sat on the crown of her hair. Her smile was bright and her heart full of glee as she danced with her father while her mother looked on with pride. Admiration covered her father's features as the small girl lightly climbed onto his feet for the waltz. All their practice had not been in vain and they left all the attendees awestruck and jealous at the scene before them. It was truly one of the happiest nights of her life.

Tears threatened the brim of her eyes as she tilted her head up to attempt to thwart their efforts to fall, an action that she did in vain. As the minutes went on, Annabelle heard the orchestra begin as more and more carriages ventured to her neck of the woods. All she could hope for was that the night went by quickly, and she passed through the party unnoticed, which would be easy considering the simple dress she was wearing.

A knock at the door interrupted Annabelle's thoughts and she peeled herself away from the window to answer. Opening the door a crack, Annabelle was greeted with the sight of Miss Bowden looking better than she had ever been in a beautiful emerald ball gown made of satin and adorned with lace at the hems.

In her arms she held a large garment box that made Annabelle curious. She chastised herself for a moment for wondering how the woman could afford such a garment with employment as a housekeeper.

"My dear," Miss Bowden began. "Tonight is the night of the ball and I thought it best if I came to you to assist you in preparing yourself."

A puzzled Annabelle quickly replied, "that is very kind of you ma'am, but will not be necessary. For as you can see, I am already prepared for the night." She gestured to her simple green dress that had small daisies imprinted into the fabric. It was the only dress given to her by Mrs. Kennelworth with strict instructions to be worn whenever she would be seen with the children by anyone who was not on staff, as she was a depiction of the family she was a governess for.

"Oh, my dear," Miss Bowden scoffed. "You cannot attend this type a ball in such a dress. It may have served you well in country gatherings, but we represent Mr. Worthington and his family. He is so kind to allow us to attend the event, even though some of us continue to work throughout the night. He even purchases all of his employees' dress wear for such an event."

At her conclusion she held up the box to Annabelle's shocked face.

"I cannot accept such a gift," Annabelle began, only to be cut off by Miss Bowden once again.

"He insists. And seeing how you will be caring for the children while they attend the event, Mrs. Kennelworth insists that those who are seen with her children only wear the best. I am sorry Miss, but you do not have much of a choice."

This caused Annabelle to huff and stew for a moment before taking the box from Miss Bowden and opening her door to allow her in.

Once she peeled the lid from the box, Annabelle was awestruck at what awaited her inside. A beautiful eggshell colored dress waited to drape her skin. A lace bodice adorned in pearls would lay over the expensive corset and would give way to a beautiful layered chiffon skirt that had a thin coat of lace draped over it. A low neckline, but nowhere indecent, travelled up into long lace sleeves that would hug her arms and give small peeks of her skin underneath. Tears brimmed her eyes at the beauty before her and all she could think about was how her mother would have adored this dress. Annabelle even took notice of the full back of the gown, knowing that it would cover her scar on her shoulder blade, and could not help but feel the corners of her mouth rise as warmth flooded her body at the gesture.

****

By the time Annabelle had put herself together in the new dress, the ball was in full swing on the main level of Arrington.

Miss Bowden had left Annabelle after buttoning her dress earlier to begin readying the children until Annabelle was ready. It was while Annabelle was venturing to the children's quarters to pick them up and escort them to the ball when she saw a silhouette in the window at the end of the hallway, knowing immediately who it was.

"I see someone is ignoring their host duties," Annabelle chastised as she saw Mr. Worthington leaning against a windowsill at the end of the hall.

"I only put on these events to pacify my sister," he replied, not breaking his gaze away from the expensive spectacle he paid for that took place outside the window. "This ball is an annual event that my family has put on for decades, but it has been many years since we have put this much effort into it. This is also the first time in a long while that I am forced to stay for the duration. Typically, I sneak into the kitchen with Nettie or run away on horseback for the entirety of the ball."

"Is that so?" Annabelle smiled at the thought of him pestering Nettie all night long, hiding from society's finest.

"Yes," he replied curtly, before spinning to look at Annabelle and continuing. "But seeing as I now must make an appearance, would you mind accompanying me downstairs, Miss Faraday?"

Her eyes widened with the proposal. No self-respecting society man would allow himself to be accompanied to a ball by a servant.

"I regret to inform you, sir, that I cannot," she responded formally, meeting his eye in a gentle stare. "I must tend to the children and escort them downstairs to their mother after they are finished preparing themselves."

"Do you need assistance?"

"Anything to avoid a ball, sir?" Annabelle inquired with a sly smirk gracing her face.

"Yes indeed," he replied with a small boyish grin of his own as he ducked his head to the floor, before raising his eyes to hers in a hopeful gesture.

"I suppose Lucas could use some assistance," Annabelle thought out loud as she cocked her hip to the side and leant against the wall. "Miss Bowden is with them, but I must relieve her. I am sure the children are making her crazy right about now."

He simply chuckled in response and motioned his hand down the hall, as they began moving towards the children's quarters.

The pair reached the children's quarters to an incredible sight. Lucas was atop a sofa jumping as high as his little legs could take him, while tears filled Isabelle's eyes as a frazzled Miss Bowden attempted to tie the ribbon that laid around her waist. As Mr. Worthington let out a mix between a snort and a chuckle, Annabelle thrust her elbow into his side before entering the room to help the poor woman attempting to take charge of the children.

"Let me, Miss Bowden," Annabelle gestured to Isabelle's ribbons. "Please take your leave. I will happily care for the children from this point forward."

Relief washed over the face of the aging woman as she happily handed over the responsibility of the crazed children for the remainder of the night. She was surely too old for such a task. Annabelle quickly leaned down to look Isabelle in the eyes and dried her tears quietly.

"Do you think you may be able to convince Lucas to cease his abuse of the furniture?" Annabelle question, raising her eyes to the brooding man in the corner. His response was swift as he strode over to the couch and grasped Lucas by the waist, ignoring his startled squeals, and lifted him over his shoulder, so his head was dangling down Mr. Worthington's back. Striding to Annabelle, he quickly deposited the boy to ground and looked at her startled expression with a smirk.

"That is not at all what I meant, but I suppose it will do," she stated with a low chuckle. Isabelle had calmed down at this point, and even released at few giggles at watching her brother be thrown over her uncle's shoulders. Annabelle did not speak a word as she sent a sharp look to Lucas, clearly telling him to behave as she tied the ribbon around Isabelle's waist in a perfect bow.

Mr. Worthington watched on with awe as the children picked up on all her silent cues and behaved marvelously for her. Their faces lit up when she smiled, and their nerves grated when she was frustrated. They truly adored the little governess and were giving the respect she had spent months earning with them. He was so busy looking upon Annabelle in adoration, he did not notice Lucas struggling to re-secure his necktie as Annabelle helped clasp pearls around Isabelle's neck. He knew nothing about children, and against his better judgement, he leant down to Lucas' height and moved his hands away from his neck.

"Allow me, Lucas," Mr. Worthington cautiously began, taking hold of the fabric and adjusting his collar. "There is no shame in asking for help when needed."

He looked the young boy in the eye when he spoke these words, hoping to convey the message properly.

"Yes, uncle," he replied in a small voice, unsure of what would happen next. His uncle never spent much time with him or Isabelle, so any form of interaction was always unusual.

Annabelle gazed at the pair after Isabelle's necklace was secured properly around her neck. She could not remove her eyes from the scene before her where Mr. Worthington carefully and with gentle hands taught his nephew how to properly fasten his tie. She heard him murmuring instructions along the lines of, "be sure no wrinkles crease the fabric" and "every man should know how to properly tie their own tie."

The sight almost brought tears to her eyes as she watched the determination grace little Lucas' face as he attempted to remember every word his uncles was speaking.

"Very well," Mr. Worthington broke the comfortable silence as he rose from the floor and adjusted his jacket. "Shall we enter the ball?"

Annabelle and the children took the staff stairs to the bottom floor where the ball was being held, despite protests from a moody master of the house, as he wished for her to enter with him from the balcony of the ballroom. She was quick to reject him, thinking he only craved her presence as a reason to ignore his party goers. Her father had always told her that a host has an obligation to their guests that cannot be ignored. They could do as they please during their party, but only after they have thanked the guests for their presence and would not let the man skirt his duties because he was not in the mood to be around people.

****

"Now, my dear," the grandmother began. "Just from the expression on your young face I can see that you have a question. Do not be bashful. Ask."

The young girl let out a large breath, relieved she could ask. She was worried she had interrupted her grandmother's story too many times and was desperate to hear the end, even if it meant biting the inside of her lips to hold them shut.

"Grandmother, why did Mr. Worthington hate balls so much?" She inquired with a raised brow. "I find parties and events great fun, especially when you let me eat chocolate without Father's knowledge."

Her daughter never minded, but the man she had wed would be furious when the children were too excited to go to bed after the festivities. A smile crept upon the elderly woman's face at the memories of sneaking chocolate behind her son-in-law's back with his children. Memories were lovely, the good and the bad ones. They all marked a moment in her story, but she could not deny that the good ones were her favorites.

"It was just his personality, my dear," she simply stated. "He did not believe in wasting time on frivolous things, and to him, balls, while enjoyable for some, were very frivolous. He also did not do well in large crowds and had a reputation that preceded him. As you will soon see, not many people took time to know him personally, they only chose to listen to the rumors that floated around him."

****

Entering the ball, Annabelle was astonished at the sheer beauty of the ballroom. Candles and pure white tablecloths were spread around the outskirts of the room, while a band played the most beautiful music, it was like a lullaby that could transport her in time to when she would dance with her father. She was so lost in the beauty of the ball that she did not even notice the balcony doors opening as the music ceased to play. It was not until the children began pulling on her hands that she noticed the change in atmosphere.

Mr. Worthington stood proud at the top of the balcony as he looked out over the guests of the ball he thought was rather wasteful. He saw his parents looking at him from the bottom of the staircase, but as his gaze swept over the crowd below, his eyes only looked for one head of blond hair in a lace dress adorned with pearls. He chose not to speak any words to the people below as he slowly descended the stairs in search of Annabelle. He felt an undeniable pull to the lady and knew a sarcastic comment from her would surely be the best part of his night.

Annabelle watched the man walk down the steps carefully, eyes like a hawk searching fervently for something. Her gaze broke from him at the sound of the children's complaints of hunger. Happiness grew in her chest at the thought of escaping the ball for some time to see Mrs. Nettles and feed the children. She used to adore the party atmosphere and the gaiety that flowed through the rooms at such events, but a ball this elegant only brought back memories of her parents she was not sure she was prepared to deal with as of late.

"Come children," Annabelle whispered to the two young ones clutching her hands. "Let us go and fill your bellies. I am sure Mrs. Nettles has something special made just for you."

Bright smiles overtook the faces of the young ones as they began pulling Annabelle out of the room to the kitchen. The ball's host took note, having finally found the woman in the crowd and almost let out a smile at the now perfect opportunity to escape the hell draped in satin he was currently standing in the midst of.

Arriving in the kitchen, Annabelle immediately noticed a frazzled Mrs. Nettles, dancing around the room threatening anyone who may be in her way with her cooking utensils. She had to clamp down on her lips with her teeth to prevent the smile fighting to break through. The children were not so vigilant, as they released a mountain of giggles at the image of the woman in front of them, causing said woman to turn to the little ones with fierce eyes.

Before she even had a moment to condemn the children's actions, Mr. Worthington sneaked into the room and wrapped his arms tightly around the woman who was turning red with rage and stress. Everything that could have gone wrong, went, and she would not send out less than perfection for those attending this ball.

"My dear Nettie," Mr. Worthington soothed the woman. "What ails you so? All I hear is the best from those enjoying your meals."

Dissolving into the comfort of the man she helped raise from a boy, Mrs. Nettles let out a tiresome sigh.

"I am truly too old for this, Sheri," She began in a tired voice. "Next year you shall acquire a new cook for this event, as I will be in the ballroom with my dear husband, dancing and enjoying the fruits of someone else's labors."

"Very well, my dear Nettie," he replied, resting the side of his face upon the crown of her head.

Staying like that for a moment, Annabelle and the children could feel the calm drape over the entire corridor as Mrs. Nettles breathed deeply. Annabelle almost felt as if she were intruding on a moment far too special for her eyes, but quickly tucked that thought away as the pair began to pull apart from one another.

"Come children," Mrs. Nettles beckoned. "I suppose you are in search of food. Have the adults strayed you from the serving tables in the ballroom?"

At the nods of their heads, Mrs. Nettles began to whisper harsh words concerning the English elite as she prepared plates for the children, as well as a plate for Annabelle. At his raised eyebrow, resembling a begging boy, Mrs. Nettles simply scoffed at Mr. Worthington.

"Get your behind back out to that party, Sheri," Mrs. Nettles chastised. "You are the host and must make your rounds. Your parents did not throw this party, so you cannot simply run away this time. Food is available to you in the ballroom, and that is precisely where you shall eat it."

Surprise littered across his face, Mr. Worthington simply bowed at the women and without a word, strode back out to the ballroom all while scratching the back of his neck in confusion.

Annabelle stifled giggles as she watched the man mumble about his cook, each step slowing as he neared the ballroom. Mrs.

Nettles simply laughed at the governess' reaction with a breathy chuckle before she placed food in front of the three.

The food slowly disappeared from the plate as Annabelle delayed returning to the party as long as possible, hoping to tire the children out quickly so she could retire to her quarters.

"Mrs. Nettles, that was lovely," Annabelle exclaimed to the cook as she cleared the plates.

Seeing right through her bright eyes and hopeful expression, Mrs. Nettles replied, "you can compliment and flatter me all you want dear, but the young ones have to make at least one more appearance at the ball and I am meant to stay in the kitchen until all the food has been served."

With a frown marring her features Annabelle gathered the children, who happily waved to the cook on their way out and returned to the hell Annabelle had only shortly escaped from. Upon reentry into the party, the children quickly dispersed from Annabelle, weaving through the waves of guests until Annabelle could no longer hear their laughs or see Isabelle's hair whispering through the candlelit air behind her dress. Annabelle could only hope they would behave themselves as she walked the perimeter of the room, searching for the slightest inclination that the children were even still present at the event. It was not until many moments later that Annabelle witnessed the toes of formal shoes peeking out from underneath the dessert table. She rounded the back of the table as the candlelight dimmed, and whispered through the fabric of the tablecloth.

"Come little ones," she began. "It is time from sleep and peaceful dreams away from all of this ruckus."

The pair crawled out of under the table with sleepy yawns, tired eyes, and sluggish movements, following Annabelle to their rooms, into their night clothes, and off to a dreaming sleep.

She did not wish to return to the ball, but the social standards that had been instilled in her by her loving parents prevented her from sneaking off to her own bed for the night. Instead, she descended the staircase to the main level only to pause for a moment at the door to the event. She slipped in quickly and searched for the man of house, only to say goodnight and then take her leave for night. She found the man looking particularly miserable, sipping his wine slowly in a darkened corner, looking almost haunting as dim flames cast soft shadows across his features.

"Hiding in the shadows, are we?" Mr. Worthington did not even flinch with surprise at her voice as she neared him.

"I find it the only way to cling to what is left of my sanity, Miss Faraday," he spoke in a dark voice, clearly not pleased at being cast out to the ball.

"There is more than one way to shelter your sanity in these moments, sir," Annabelle confidently stated as the man in front of her simply quirked an eyebrow in her direction.

"How so, Miss Faraday?"

"You could join the madness, sir," she smiled, remembering how her father would whisper to her during their dances, reminding her that existing in the essence of other madness is acceptable, but one must never allow themselves to be maddened. "Just do not let their madness rub onto you and you will surely survive the night."

"Do you have any suggestions for joining the madness?" Mr. Worthington began, searing Annabelle under his watchful gaze. "Dancing, perhaps?"

"Ah, but in order to dance, sir, you would have to find a lovely young lady who was willing," she began with slyness lacing her voice. "Unless, of course, a young lady is not your type, but I do not see you as the type of man to cause such a stir in society."

She did not know where her brass words had formed in her mind, but before she could stop them they found their way through her lips. The only evidence she had ever spoken them was the abashed look that contorted onto Mr. Worthington's features. She could only snap her mouth shut and wait for him to respond. His deep laughter that flowed through her ears with reverence, however, was the last reaction she expected. It was raw, feral, and almost felt uncontrollable as the man of stone bent his head in hopes of reigning in his gaiety. He had never met such a woman, but his life had become insurmountably more interesting since she entered it.

"I can assure you, Miss Faraday," he responded in a hoarse voice as he leaned towards her. "I am most certainly interested in the more feminine sex."

Red painted Annabelle's face as she twisted away from him and bent her head, hoping to hide her reaction, but from the proud smirk lacing Mr. Worthington's face, she knew she had failed and could not muster an intelligent response. She could only turn back to him and meet his eyes after her face had calmed its flames. She did not even notice him hold a hand out to her, too lost in his eyes.

"May I have this dance, Miss Faraday?"

Shock covered her features as she contemplated her answer. Surely dancing with this man would fill the gossip mill, but she could not tame her tongue quickly enough as she found herself muttering a whispered "yes."

His face gave nothing away as she placed her dainty hand into his and allowed him to lead her to the dance floor and pull her into a waltz. Dancing in silence, not meeting the other's eyes, Mr. Worthington chose to focus on the dance. Annabelle moved across the floor gracefully, following his every movement swiftly. She had been taught this. He was sure of it. They were almost halfway complete with the last dance of the night when Annabelle broke the silence, from inside Mr. Worthington's arms.

"I do not believe I ever had a chance to thank you for this beautiful dress, sir," she spoke with such confidence, finally meeting his eyes as they moved across the floor, ignoring the stares that followed. "It is truly lovely."

"Yes, I believe the children were extensively distracting."

"Have you seen your parents this night, sir?" Annabelle asked, hoping to change the subject quickly.

"Yes, Miss Faraday. They spent the day with my sister and left the ball shortly after it began. I believe they only wished to see that I would follow through on my word, knowing my discontent for such events. They are journeying to London as we speak, before venturing back to France."

"So soon?" Annabelle questioned. The elder Worthington couple had hardly spent 24 hours in the home. "Do you not miss them?"

"I do," Mr. Worthington began, thinking of the long conversation he held with his father about business, among other things, in his study last night, and waking up to his mother laughing with Mrs. Nettles in the kitchen. "They enjoy their life in France, and I leave for extended visits with them twice a year. They visit here multiple times a year, but close friends of theirs are having a large ball similar to this one in the coming weeks, so they must return. I do miss them while they are gone, but I find that being home, even in their absence, is no longer as unbearable as it used to be."

She felt as if his eyes were burning her with the intensity in which he was gazing at her face. He unconsciously clutched her tighter to him as they continued their stares, only to be disrupted a few short moments later, not nearly long enough for Mr. Worthington.

"Worthington!" A voice that sounded distantly familiar to Annabelle cut through the crowd. An astute man twisted through the crowd with relentless grace, dressed in the finest silk suit money could buy, holding the hand of an equally endearing woman who strode effortlessly beside him. The pair walked with purpose as they continued towards where Mr. Worthington stood, still holding Annabelle close.

"Worthington, my dear boy," the man began. "I did not think I would see the day when I witnessed you throwing a ball in this estate. What wager did you lose to cause such an event?"

Annabelle watched, bewildered, as laughs escaped Mr. Worthington and he took the hand of the man who Annabelle finally made eye contact with. He quickly disregarded her employer and stared intently at the young governess. Such scrutiny caused Annabelle to twist away from the scene and duck her head, hoping she could hide in the dim lights of the ball forever. Mr. Worthington noticed her discomfort almost immediately, and with an arm still wrapped around her waist, pulled her even closer than before while clearing his throat to gain the attention of the aged man in front of them.

As if realizing his mistake, the man and his bewildered wife quick broke out of their reverie and sought forgiveness for making the young woman so uncomfortable.

"I'm sorry, young lady," the man began apologetically. "It is just, you look so much like a woman I used to know. She was married to my dear friend. It is like you are a mirror image of her. Prey tell, what is your name?"

Annabelle recognized her Uncle Monty immediately and could not think of a way out of this situation. She was overcome with emotion after seeing the man and woman who spent so much of her childhood by her parents' side that she could not even think to answer, only stare at the couple.

The man did not take his eyes off her, analyzing her and her features that so closely resembled friends he lost long ago. Maybe he was just missing them, as he was told years ago that their Annabelle had perished from tuberculosis. This could not be the little girl who would skip through the gardens ahead of him whenever he and his wife would take a walk on her family's property. The resemblance, however, was uncanny.

The tension that now surrounded the group did not go unnoticed by the ball's host. He could see Annabelle's discomfort clearly and felt his curiosity pique even more than before but decided to assist the young maiden in this situation.

"I'm sorry, Mr. Griffith," Mr. Worthington began. "But I must usher my governess back to the children. It is far past their time for slumber and I know my sister would skin me alive if she found out I kept her governess for such a time."

The puzzled man quickly bowed to Mr. Worthington muttering his apologies. All the while, Annabelle looked on in confusion, knowing the children were already tucked away and fast asleep. She could only come to the conclusion that Mr. Worthington had decided to assist her in her time of discomfort. She felt a flush creep up her cheeks at the situation she had found herself in. She had not been so startled in a long time, never expecting to see her dear Uncle Monty once again after all these years, let alone in the presence of the insufferable man she was employed by.

The couple in question quickly scurried away after speaking with Mr. Worthington for a moment. They sent nods in Annabelle's direction, but she was far too lost in thought to even acknowledge them. Mr. Worthington took the moment to inspect her whist she lost herself in thoughts. Her brows were creased with worry as she glared hard at the ballroom floor. Her breaths came out in hard pants as if she were distressed, and her eyes held vision, but saw nothing. He could tell that she either knew Mr. Montpellier and his wife or was disturbed by the thought of being recognized. Both scenarios piqued his interest greatly, but as his feet protested the continual standing motion, he decided this mystery could wait one more day before being solved.

"Miss Faraday," he began, gently grazing her arm in hopes of acquiring her attention. "Shall I escort you upstairs?"

At her widened eyes and frightened stance as she whipped her head up to meet his, he immediately felt the need to clarify his suggestion.

"I mean only to ensure you arrive to your room safely," his tone gentle, hoping to ease her worries. "There are far too many drunken blokes lurking about my estate searching for a coach to carry them home, and I only wish to confirm none of them give you grief on your journey to your quarters."

Annabelle let out a heavy sigh at his clarification. Her body protested any movement after the long night and she could only nod slightly before shuffling out of the ballroom that now only held a few scarce stragglers. Mr. Worthington carried himself next to her as they wound through the halls of Arrington and up the stairs. The only light that could be seen was the golden aura of the candelabras that lined the stairwell. Silence surrounded the pair as they neared her room. Faint crashes and drunken laughter could be heard echoing through the halls, and with a glance out the window, Annabelle's eyes grew as she watched a man stumble down the steps into a carriage that lay in wait.

Mr. Worthington winced on multiple occasions as he was sure he would have to deal with broken items in the morn. He could only praise Miss Bowden for putting away anything of real worth that would have found itself in danger this night.

As they reached her door, and Annabelle grasped the handle, Mr. Worthington chose to break the deafening silence.

"Do you see why, Miss faraday, I prefer to run the other direction when a ball is mentioned?" He questioned the young woman walking next to him. "The sheer thought of the gaiety of such an occasion has my skin crawling."

"The evening was not too horrible at the beginning, was it, sir?" She questioned him right back, not realizing that her words implied the time they spent together before entering the event. "But I do agree, being shackled to the building entertaining such an event is tiresome, especially when those attending do not leave at a reasonable hour."

She tilted her head to the window, where guest floundered down the steps as more laughter was heard trailing up the corridors.

"Yes," was his simple reply. "I must go and make certain that they all leave. I will entertain such madness for the duration of the ball, however, the second the music ceases, such behavior is no longer acceptable on my grounds."

Replying with a nod, Annabelle began to open her door as she replied.

"I hope your work is not too tiresome, sir," she began. "Even the man of the house deserves his rest."

Her eyes met his at the end of the sentence as he stared deeply through her. He studied her. Growing weary under his gaze, Annabelle whispered a soft "goodnight" as she entered her room.

"Sleep well, Miss Faraday," his deep timber replied just as she closed her door for the night. Silence would have shrouded her if it weren't for the click of his boots as he trailed away from her door, the sound being the only reminder that the events of the night had indeed occurred and were not a dream.

CHAPTER 7

It was morning when a knock sounded through the halls of Arrington. Mr. Worthington, who was in his study at the time, rose when Mr. Longfellow, one of the head butlers, entered. A month had gone by since the ball and Arrington had returned to its normal atmosphere. Mr. Worthington found himself surrounded by work and Annabelle spent her time taking charge of the children.

"Sir," the aging man began. "Mr. Kennelworth has arrived from London and is asking to be let in."

Ire welled in Mr. Worthington as he responded.

"I did not send for the man, Longfellow. How has he ended up on my doorstep if he was not welcome? Has my sister sent him an invitation?"

"I am not aware of any invitations being sent for him, sir," Mr. Longfellow responded. "He is at the door and is requesting entrance and an audience with yourself."

"I will be there in a moment, thank you."

Pinching the bridge of his nose in an attempt to alleviate his frustration, Mr. Worthington contemplated how to handle the arrival of his brother-in-law. He never liked the man, a sneaky fellow who always had his eyes on the family's silver. He did not attempt to mask his discontent either.

Annabelle heard the commotion from the downstairs as she readied the children for the day, but ignored it seeing as it was no business of hers and continued prepping the children for their morning meal.

****

"Grandmother, why did Mr. Worthington not like his brother-in-law so much?" The young girl questioned. "Are we not supposed to love family?"

"Yes, my dear, we are to love our family," The grandmother began responding the tricky question. "However, I can promise you, Mr. Worthington had reasons for disliking his sister's husband. We are not always happy with everyone, are we not?"

"I guess not."

"Just listen closely to the story, my dear, and I am sure you will see his reasons."

✳✳

Mr. Worthington strode through the halls of Arrington breathlessly, bathed in grace. He held his head high and mentally readied himself for the tiresome conversation he knew was to come from dealing with the man. The cause of his frustrations became visible as he reached the door.

"Rufus, what on Earth has brought you to my doorstep?" Mr. Worthington laced every word that fell from his lips with a thick coat of exasperation to ensure the man knew the frustration his disturbance caused.

"I have come to bring my family home, Sheridan," Mr. Kennelworth took a step closer to the man as he entered the home without permission, attempting to intimidate him. "They have been gone from me for long enough, and I am sure you cannot be bothered to continue to house them here."

"You do not think that in a house so large I actually notice them, Rufus," Mr. Worthington shot back. "They may leave when your wife sees fit, not a second before."

"Do not think I have not heard about you extending their stay here. What could possibly possess you to keep them? Usually you cannot stand the sight of your sister, and I know my children drive you near madness, so what, Sheridan, had caused you to strip my family from me?"

Mr. Worthington cocked an eyebrow as he stared the rat down. "Do not be misled Rufus and think I actually believe you are a loving husband and father to your family. I know many of your little indiscretions you wish to keep hidden. My sister may be trying but she is certainly not the fool you make her out to be. As for their extended visit, maybe your little family has grown on me, or maybe I do not wish them to return with you. Either way, they are here, and they are staying. My reasons are none of your concern."

It was then that Mr. Kennelworth saw Annabelle walking down the hall with the children. The three of them entered the dining hall and he turned back to Mr. Worthington, only to catch him staring at the maiden.

"Are you sure it has nothing to do with a little governess that would have to come home with me, should I bring my family back to London?"

At his question, Mr. Worthington took a step forward and cornered Mr. Kennelworth between himself and the wall. "You really think I would let her walk out the door with you, let alone leave my grounds? You mistake me. I do not toy with women and use them as playthings like yourself."

"Are you sure?" Mr. Kennelworth sneered at the man, his discontent showing loudly. "Since when do you care about the feelings of a woman?"

"Just because I do not pay mind to every woman that crosses my path, does not mean my heart is so cold that I am uncaring. Be warned Rufus, I may seem reasonable at the moment, but take one step near the girl and I will gladly become the snake society sees me to be."

Without letting the rodent of a man speak one more word, Mr. Worthington spun on his heel and took off towards the dining hall. He knew his sister's miserable husband had not touched her, but he had to be sure she was alright. His feelings were his weakness, but as long as she did not leave Arrington, he did not see a problem with allowing himself to have a weak moment or two. If he knew where she was, he would have peace of mind.

Mr. Kennelworth's threat was the very reason Mr. Worthington had extended his sister's stay more than once. With the ball completed, however, he was running out of reasons to keep the brood at Arrington, not that his sister wished to return herself and her children to the man. She had been more than willing to stay right where she was when Mr. Worthington had spoken to her, but society would soon ask questions, and he knew his sister could never ruin her reputation, even if she did have to return to such a man.

Much to his relief, Annabelle was helping the children to get seated when Mr. Worthington entered the hall. He did nothing except stand in the entryway and stare at her. Uncomfortable at the attention, she turned her entire body to face him, hoping for the eye contact to cease or ease the tension between the two.

It did only after Mr. Worthington sent a nod in her direction and proceeded to his spot at the head of the table, to be followed shortly after by Mr. Kennelworth, a ratty man, who looked Annabelle up and down shamelessly. She knew who he was, having heard him being greeted by Mr. Longfellow as he entered the home, but she scurried up the steps before he could see her. She only caught a short glimpse of the man but knew instantly of her dislike for him.

Now extremely uncomfortable, she quickly wrapped her arms around herself, caving into any security she could provide in the moment and looked down at the ground, hoping the fact she could not see his eyes roaming her would make it stop, but she burned under his continued gaze.

It was not until Mr. Worthington threw both of his palms to the table, slapping loudly over the wooden surface, that Mr. Kennelworth jumped and scurried to his seat like the rodent Annabelle knew him to be. She had only known the man a few moments and could already tell he was the type of man that did not treat women well. It was no surprise to her that Mrs. Kennelworth kept extending her stay at Arrington. She did not mind the fact either, for the longer the Kennelworth's stayed at the estate, the longer she did as well, and after so many months away from the only place she had ever known since losing her parents, Annabelle found herself wishing she never had to return to such a place.

"Annie," Lucas cheered from his seat at the table. "Please come sit next to me!"

There was a space left between Lucas and Mr. Worthington, that Annabelle presumed was for Mrs. Kennelworth, seeing as it was directly across from her husband's position. Annabelle was ready to decline when Mr. Worthington's head rose from his plate and his gaze burned through her, igniting every fire in her she never knew existed.

"Yes, Miss Faraday," he began, his voice deep and earthly as the morning. "Please be seated with us. No sense in making the children upset."

She had no choice but to meander to the seat next to Lucas. Lowering onto it, she handled herself with her usual poise and grace. Shoulders back, head up, fingers laid gently in her lap. She remembered practicing this pose every day during her childhood. Her mother had told her she had to be able to sit like a lady to join the family dinner parties. The stubborn part of her did not give up until she sat perfectly, sometimes sitting still for over an hour a day until she had her form faultless. She adored the pride that graced her parents eyes each time one of their guests would complement her posture and demeanor. All she ever wanted was to make them proud.

She was, once again, broken out of her reverie by a noise. Annabelle was startled for a moment and quickly earned a questioning glance from Mr. Worthington as everyone in the room turned to the entry to watch Mrs. Kennelworth enter the room. The woman was visibly shaken when she caught sight of her husband seated at the table, and even more so when she saw the governess seated across from him.

As Annabelle waited for the woman to take her seat, she mentally scolded herself for her day dreams. She had not gotten lost in her thoughts nearly this much when she attended Auburn. The memories were always too hard to bare in such a cold place, but here, they haunted her, invading her mind at every opportunity.

"Ah-hem," Annabelle looked up to see the scalding glare of Mrs. Kennelworth. "Brother dear, the governess is in my seat."

She did not address Annabelle directly, but also did not take her eyes off her. The deathly look sent her way had chills running across Annabelle's skin as the room suddenly felt at least twenty degrees cooler.

"Calm the dramatics, sister," Mr. Worthington began in an exasperated voice. The antics of this woman were increasingly tiresome to him. "Miss Faraday is perfectly fine where she is currently seated."

"She most certainly is not!" Her voice cracked through the air as she raised her hand to point at the woman. "Where shall I sit then, brother? It is not proper for a wife to sit next to her husband."

"Goodness me, this is not a dinner party. He is your husband, is he not? Are you so repulsed by the man that you cannot stand to sit next to him for a simple family meal?"

He was cut off in the middle of his thought by the shrill voice of the woman he calls family. "But she is not family!" Mrs. Kennelworth accused, pointing at Annabelle.

"And your husband is not family to me, yet I still allow the man a seat at my table. Sit down and allow yourself to be served or I will send your food to your quarters and have you eat in there. I do not have patience for such trivial drama this day."

With his sharp words the conversation was over, and Mrs. Kennelworth threw herself onto the seat next to her husband, who paid her no attention, as his eyes were set on Annabelle.

The meal drug on excruciatingly slow for Annabelle with Mrs. Kennelworth pouting worse than her children through the majority of the meal and Mr. Kennelworth's uncomfortable stares that lasted longer than necessary, and only ceased when Mr. Worthington cleared his throat or conversed with the man. It seemed he would do anything to draw the man's attention away from Annabelle.

By the time the meal ceased the children were already on their way up the stairs to the study and the Kennelworth's had left to the misses' study. It was only after everyone had gone that Annabelle realized she would be alone with Mr. Worthington again. Her nerves spiked, and her heartbeat sped as she busied herself stacking the plates to be taken into the kitchen.

"They are quite the pair are they not?" At Annabelle's confused glance, Mr. Worthington further clarified, "my sister and her dear Rufus."

Annabelle giggled, not only at the man's name, but the way Mr. Worthington scrunched his nose as if saying the man's name left a poor taste on his tongue. He smiled at her as she reigned in her laughter. If it were up to him, she would always laugh. It was one of the most pleasant sounds he thought he had ever heard.

"Yes, I do believe they are," Annabelle responded through her sniggers.

She continued to collect the plates from the meal, as Mr. Worthington looked on. He had given up long ago attempting to make her leave them for one of the wait staff. She always insisted on making another's life easier by making hers a little more difficult. It was then that, in Annabelle's opinion, Mr. Worthington did the most remarkable thing. He began picking up the plates and silverware along with her. Stacking them in his hands, he followed her into the kitchen and laid them out upon the countertops.

Annabelle was dumbstruck. The only other man of his standing she had seen do such a thing was her father. He never wanted a large staff; therefore, he and Annabelle's mother assisted the small staff at hand in taking care of her home. She had no words for the man as she watched him lay the plates down and tip toe behind Mrs. Nettles. She was further dumbstruck when he whipped his head around to her and wink, the actions tinging her face the shade of a rose.

The heat gracing her cheeks was no longer one her mind when she watched Mr. Worthington, filled with glee like a child, silently wrap his arms around Mrs. Nettles, holding her tight in a hug. It was a sweet notion, until Mrs. Nettles screamed. It was then Annabelle realized that the man wished to scare the aging woman.

Mrs. Nettles screamed and wrenched herself away from Mr. Worthington, spinning around to give him the coldest of glares.

"Hello Nettie," Mr. Worthington said with a smile. He was not a child but was barely 27 years of age.

Annabelle realized that even men with the world on their shoulders need to find reasons to smile.

His smile was quickly wiped away when Mrs. Nettles grabbed a rag from the table next to her and began whipping Mr. Worthington with it. Annabelle chewed on her nails in the corner to muffle her laughs as Mr. Worthington cowered away from the woman who helped raise him.

"What is wrong with you, boy?" Mrs. Nettles screeched. "Scaring a woman of my age, you could have killed me!"

Through his own deep laughs that Annabelle became entranced by, the man, who looked like a boy when being scolded, spoke. "Nettie, you are made of the finest materials. There is no way your body is ready to give up just yet."

He clearly thought his charm would wear her down, but the woman was fervent in her whips as she followed the man around the kitchen. She was nowhere near his height but made him run away nonetheless.

"You should be lucky that I am not telling my husband about this, Sheridan Worthington, for he would have you mucking stalls for giving me such a freight," Mrs. Nettles huffed before hitting him in the face with the rag and going back to her duties.

Annabelle was far too busy watching Mrs. Nettles work that she forgot all about Mr. Worthington; that is until he crept up behind her and whispered in her ear.

"I think I may have pushed her a little too far this time," Annabelle slightly jumped at his deep whisper and the heat emanating from his body into her back. "Thoughts?"

"Maybe just a tad," Annabelle responded with a small smile. "Viewing you run around like a scolded child was well worth it though."

Again, Mr. Worthington heard her giggles fill his ears and smiled himself.

Turning to face Mr. Worthington, Annabelle was taken aback by their proximity. As she spun, her face almost collided with his shoulder, and his breath grazed her face as she met his eyes.

"Excuse me sir," she began in a small whisper. "But I really must go. The children are waiting for me."

"Very well Miss Faraday," he responded with a bow as she curtsied and scurried out of the room. He caught Nettie's eye and just smiled a boyish grin at her as he backed out of the kitchen and down through the halls of his home.

Annabelle could hear his boot's heels echoing through the corridors, and the sound that used to make her nerves rise in apprehension, now only made her heart beat a little faster and a smile grace her face.

The exchange, while not understood fully by the two participants or the other present kitchen staff that had scattered while the aging woman attacked their employer with a cloth, was clear to Mrs. Nettles, who wore her own smile at her Sherri's joy.

****

"Child, it is time for a break," the grandmother tiredly began. "My voice is rough and my throat dry. Chamomile tea is necessary at this moment."

"Grandmother, can we not continue for just a little longer?" The small girl pleaded, twisting her fingers together and widening her eyes as far as they could go. "What did they not understand, Grandmother? I am confused?"

The woman raised her hand to one of the staff members, signaling to them to bring her some tea and crackers.

"Dear child, let me soothe my throat and I will joyfully continue," the grandmother reasoned. "These two stubborn people could not see that they were allowing themselves to care for the other. Mr. Worthington caught on soon enough, but poor Annabelle stayed her sinfully naïve self for far too long."

The grandmother happily continued the story once she finished her cup of tea, taking an extra few minutes than necessary, amusing herself with the small girl twitching on the sofa, attempting to mind her manners, but wishing for the story all the same.

****

The winds continued to freeze the brave creatures that ventured outdoors as the days continued. It was days like these that reminded Annabelle to enjoy as much nature as possible even as it all was frozen away for winter. Most of her days were spent locked up by the warmth of the fireplaces inside of Arrington, but this day was warmer than most, so Annabelle ushered the children outdoors for some fresh air, whether they enjoyed themselves or not.

"Annie, I do not wish to kick the ball any longer," Lucas whined after having lost to his sister more than once. "Please do not make me!"

The boy had her heart as he poked out his lower lip and squinted his eyes, making it look as if he were about to cry.

"My dear Lucas," Annabelle sighed, clearly affected by the young boy's display. "Please just try once more, for me."

She spoke the last words lowly as she knelt to his height and looked him right in the eyes. Just as her heart was melted by him, his was enthralled by her. Wishing to please her, he nodded quickly and ran to retrieve the ball from him sister, who held it just a tad too high for him to reach. The girl feigned innocence once Annabelle looked at her but broke into giggles once Lucas tackled her to the ground. Annabelle could not help but to join in Isabelle's laughs as she watched the scene in front of her.

It was days like these that made her miss her girls at Auburn. She spoke many prayers for them throughout the day, and almost cried the day when Lucas and Isabelle asked if they could pray with her as well. She dearly missed Emma on these days, remembering how they would curl up to conserve warmth and speak for hours about every bout of nonsense they could recall. Some days Jennifer would join the pair in their giggles, others, it was just the two of them braving the cold.

Having not seen her dear friend since December, Annabelle had been writing to her vigorously, and was always thrilled to receive a letter in return. In their last correspondence, Annabelle had been invited to spend Easter weekend with her friend as the Worthington's were travelling to France and Annabelle was told she would not be needed over the weekend. Mr. Worthington's exact words something akin to "my sister birthed the children, surely she can keep them alive for the extended weekend. And if not, the children adore my mother."

She had yet to ask for permission to leave the estate though.

Annabelle remembered letting out a laugh at his words. She had not told anyone of the invitation, as she was not sure if she would take her friend up on the offer, but the opportunity weighed heavy on her mind constantly.

Pulled from her thoughts by the sound of Isabelle's shrill scream, as she ran from her brother, Lucas had finally retrieved the ball and was ready to try once more for his governess.

"Annie, are you watching?" The small boy hopefully questioned.

"Of course, dear Lucas," she replied from her place on the grass with a smile.

It took a moment, but Lucas rose and set the ball down on the ground before taking many steps back and running towards the ball at full speed. A smile lit up Annabelle's face as she watched the determined boy race towards the ball. The ball became airborne the second his foot grazed the worn material of the toy, pushing it through the air until it found an unhappy home, stuck in a tree.

"Bugger," Lucas mumbled.

"Lucas!" Annabelle gasped at the word that filtered out of the young boy's mouth.

Knowing he had made a mistake, the boy quickly looked down and started kicking the dirt. "I am sorry Miss Faraday," he began, using Annabelle's formal name for his apology. "Father says that word every time something makes him upset. Is it an adult word?"

Annabelle quickly walked to the boy in hopes of rectifying the situation.

"Yes, Lucas, it is," she spoke in a stern voice, one the children rarely were on the receiving end of. She made sure to look at

Isabelle as well to make certain that she understood. "You are not to use it again. Are we understood?"

Both children nodded towards their governess. Seemingly satisfied with their reaction, Annabelle began striding towards the tree. Gripping a low branch, she looked back to the children with a smile.

"Now, stay right there a moment while I retrieve our ball, are we clear?"

Both children looked at her with a mix of shock and excitement written across their young faces as they nodded and saw their governess begin to climb the tree, easily maneuvering each branch until she reached the one that held their ball. They were so entranced that they did not even notice their uncle, who was strolling through the grounds checking up with his staff.

"Isabelle, Lucas," he began in a fierce tone, frustrated that the children were without supervision. "Why are you alone in the fields? Where is your governess?"

Fear paralyzed both children as they whipped towards their uncle's cross looking figure. He stood stiff and intimidating as he awaited an answer.

"Your frustrations would be validated, sir, if they were alone," Annabelle began from her place in the large tree. She sat atop one of the sprawling branches as she spoke to the man who was twisting his head looking for her. She held back a laugh as she continued. "But, as you can see, they are not alone. It was simply too marvelous of a day to stay inside so we ventured here. Poor Lucas got a ball caught in the tree, but not to worry, for we have rectified that situation. Have we not, Lucas?"

He had a bright smile as he looked up at her and replied, "yes we have, Annie."

Finally noticing the governess in the tree, Mr. Worthington moved his hard gaze to hers.

"Miss Faraday, while I am sure the children have enjoyed their fresh air, even in this winter chill, could you please remove yourself from the tree, so you can closely watch after them?"

She merely nodded in response.

"Sir, if you would please," Annabelle began, motioning to him.

"If I could please what, Miss Faraday?" He responded, clearly confused, as his eyebrows have scrunched together, an action Annabelle notices every time he is taken by the emotion. "Do you wish for help to get down? You should have not climbed such a tree if you could not climb down from it." His voice took on a teasing tone as he moved closer to the tree.

"No, sir," she threw back firmly, unappreciative of his lack of faith in her abilities. "I can get myself down quite easily. I do, however, need you to turn your back as I cannot guarantee that my skirt will stay at my ankles as I lower myself."

Fighting with himself to stop the flush he feels through his body from rising to his cheeks, Mr. Worthington quickly spun himself around and stalked towards the children to have them do the same. He also kept an eye in the distance, ready to force any worker to avert their eyes, should they see the lady in such a position.

Annabelle dropped the ball to the ground with a thump and braced herself on the branch by her arms, swinging her legs down so they dangle beneath her, she breathed a quick prayer and let go, hoping to land on her feet. Her feet find the ground quickly and soon after, as did her rear. Confused for a moment on how she went from looking down towards the ground to now gazing at the sky, she can only let out a giggle, which caused all three to turn back to her, watching on as she lay upon the grass in the sun, laughing as a toddler would.

Isabelle and Lucas were quick to join her on the ground, laughing with her and thanking her for retrieving their toy, while also congratulating her on not hurting herself from the fall. Mr. Worthington witnessed the awe come upon the children's faces as they retold the tale of their governess climbing a tree to the woman herself. With a smile, he ventured over to the group and took a seat on Lucas' right, who was next to Annabelle. Isabelle was seated on the other side of the woman.

"I always loved this tree as a child," Mr. Worthington began after the children had calmed down and began to play with their ball again. "Nettie would have to come out here and bribe me with sweets or threaten me with her spoon to get me to come down for a meal. I could be anything as I hid in the branches."

Annabelle watched as the man spoke of his childhood wistfully, almost as if he were wishing to go back.

She knew that feeling very well but was broken out of her thoughts by his voice.

"Where in the world did you learn to climb a tree like that, Miss Faraday?"

Annabelle found herself excited at his question, for now she could go back for a moment as she remembered her parents and her safe haven.

"My father would lift me up into the branches," she began softly, her head upturned towards the tree. "My mother would sing along with the birds every morning and my father would have me sprinkle seeds and such onto the branches to feed the birds. They all had built nests into the trees around our home, but he knew how much my mother loved the birds so every day that he was home with us, he would collect seeds and would lift me up into the trees closest to our home and would have me sprinkle them onto the branches, to ensure the birds never grew hungry, that way they would never leave. They would always leave for a time in the winter, but every spring they came home and sang to my mother again. I would occasionally fall from the lower branches, but he would always catch me before I hit the ground."

Mr. Worthington was in awe of the smile that graced her face as she spoke of her father. It was as if she were taken back to that exact moment and were reliving it continuously. He had never seen her so happy but was almost addicted to the sight and was already thinking of ways to bring this happiness back.

"Feel free, Miss Faraday, to spread seeds on any tree you like along the grounds," Mr. Worthington began nervously, hoping the woman would enjoy his offer. "I quite like the birds, and I know Lucas would love to climb the trees along the grounds."

"Sir, that is a very kind offer, and I would gladly take you up on it if I thought your sister would support such an act, but I know steam would surely erupt from her should I put her son in a tree," Annabelle replied, grateful for the offer and saddened that she could not act on it.

Mr. Worthington began to chuckle at the thought of his sister coming upon her son in such a situation. "Ah, but Miss Faraday, witnessing steam bellow from my sister's ears is part of the fun."

Annabelle smiled at the thought.

"Besides, I shall take care of my sister. This is my home and I quite like the company of the birds. I would suggest beginning soon so they can begin to create their nests; their homes for the upcoming season."

Mr. Worthington then abruptly rose from the ground and looked down at Annabelle.

"Excuse me for a moment, Miss Faraday."

Annabelle was left confused, gaping at the now empty space that Mr. Worthington had filled not a moment before. She went over their conversation continually attempting to take note of what forced him to venture off so abruptly but was soon given his answer as he journeyed back a few moments later with a small pouch filled with seeds, stolen from Mrs. Nettles, Annabelle was sure. He was grinning as a child would when they had accomplished a great feat as he held his hand for her to take and pulled her up from the ground.

Annabelle took notice of how he did not immediately let her hand go as he called for the children but attempted to ignore the buzz that flowed through her blood at the action.

"Hold these, would you please?" Mr. Worthington was looking towards Annabelle, still clutching her hand, as he held the pouch towards her in his other. She moved both hands towards the pouch, freeing hers from his grip as she took it with a nod.

"Mrs. Nettles will not be pleased," she whispered with a smile. He merely looked over his shoulder and winked at her with a smile of his own that made her heart beat a few paces faster.

"She will surely forgive me once I explain the situation," he spoke with self-assurance and distinct confidence.

"Ah, yes," Annabelle replied with a small smirk. "But she will not let you explain until she has struck you with her spoon at least once or twice."

A small wince crept up Mr. Worthington's face at the thought, but as Annabelle's laugh filled his ears, it was all worth it, he was sure.

"Lucas," Mr. Worthington called to the child, who quickly looked up in awe at his uncle addressing him. "Come here please."

Lucas almost tripped over himself as he ran from Isabelle to his uncle's waiting arms. Mr. Worthington swiftly lifted the child into his arms, so he could explain the situation.

"I have a project for you," he began, noting the boy's excitement and quick nods. "We have to feed the birds, so they come home after the winter. Would you like to help?"

Lucas was so excited he could only nod quicker than before.

"Alright then. I am going to lift you into this tree and you will sprinkle the seeds we give you along the branches. You must be careful though. I do not wish you to fall."

Mr. Worthington spoke in a stern voice to the child to make sure he understood.

"Yes, Uncle," Lucas responded, attempting to quiet his nerves. His uncle had never paid him much mind before, and he did not wish to make him irate by doing his job wrong.

"Sweet Lucas," Annabelle began noticing the boys nervous state. "My father used to do this with me as a child, and it is meant to be fun." As she stated the word "fun" with extra annunciation, she sent a sharp look to Mr. Worthington, who averted his eyes noticing her frustrations. "Please do enjoy yourself, and know that if you fall, we will catch you."

She ended her words with a warm smile that had Lucas quickly mirroring her actions as he replied with a quick, "yes, Annie."

At his understanding, Mr. Worthington quickly lifted the boy into the tree and placed him on the branch. They gave him a moment to steady himself on the wide branch, which the young boy straddled, before they passed the seeds. It was decided he would not walk on the branch, but rather, scoot across it, to lessen his risk of falling. An amused Isabelle came over to watch her brother as he meticulously completed his task, looking down every so often to make sure he was completing it correctly, only to be met with a nod from his uncle and a smile and wave from Annabelle.

Only once did he slip off the branch, but was quickly caught by his uncle, who could not help but smile when Lucas giggles filled his ears as the child lay in his arms. He found out the boy's skin was very sensitive, and spent a few moments tickling him with his own smile on his face before he lifted him into the tree once again. Annabelle could not be happier to watch the children get on so well with their uncle who hardly acknowledged their presence months earlier. The action brought a bright smile to her face as she watched Lucas catch his breath from all the laughter that passed his lips as Isabelle laughed at the tired expression her brother wore. Mr. Worthington, naturally, noticed Annabelle's smile as the one on his face grew.

The group continued to sprinkle seeds until the pouch was empty. Isabelle even got a turn of her own after Annabelle took the back of her dress, brought it through her legs, and tied it to the belt on the front, to make an illusion of pants, so the girl could scoot along her own tree branches spreading food for the birds.

The children had laughed and chased each other as they all ventured back towards Arrington, Annabelle and Mr. Worthington behind the children.

As they entered the home, Miss Bowden quickly scooped the children up, preparing to feed them, as Annabelle and Mr. Worthington sat down for food as well. Nettie silently prepared the plates but gave Mr. Worthington a few swats on his back with her spoon and he feverishly attempted to have her cease her attack long enough to explain. Annabelle and the children could not hold in their laughs at the scene, and even Miss Bowden let out a chuckle or two at the sight.

"While that is a lovely reason to steal my seeds," Mrs. Nettles began, still waving her weapon of choice in the air. "I expect more from you Sherri. I taught you how to ask for things and say please, did I not?"

"Yes, Nettie," he monotonously replied, pouting worse than Lucas would when he would find himself in trouble.

"Well, now you know better for next time," the woman proudly stated before declaring she was venturing home for the night to her husband. Mr. Worthington stood up and gave her a large hug and laid a kiss on top of her hair before she walked out the door to begin the short walk to her cottage on the grounds.

From then on, it was a silent meal, with Miss Bowden sending curious glances in-between the man and woman whenever she was not berating the children for making a mess with their food. Annabelle rose after she finished, about to take the children upstairs, when Miss Bowden cut in.

"I will put the children to bed tonight, dear," she stated sweetly while ushering the tired children out the door. "Take a night for yourself. You all seem to have had a long day."

Annabelle responded with a smile as she collected both hers and Mr. Worthington's plates to be washed, as he had just finished while Miss Bowden was collecting the children. She felt the man's eyes on her as she cleaned the plates and dried her hands but did not say a word until her task was completed. She then turned to the man, preparing to bid him goodnight.

"Sir, thank you for a lovely afternoon." Annabelle looked up at Mr. Worthington with bright eyes and a large smile on her face. She was content and relaxed. She could live a thousand afternoons like this one and be just as gratified each time.

He had no words for the sight before him as he felt twists in his stomach and the air in his lungs leave him. Breathless. That was what she made him. He could not even think, and it was as if control was taken from his mind and given to his heart, as he began to move closer towards her. She did not make a move towards him but did not move away either. She only regarded him with a nervous curiousness. It was not until his body touched hers that her breaths deepened, and her eyes began to close. She was uncertain, that was until she felt his fingertips brushing her hair out of her face.

Once she realized what she was doing, she spun away from him quickly and began walking towards the steps. Mr. Worthington had caught on to her movements and gently clasped her wrist in his hold as she reached the fourth step, while he stood at the bottom. She had almost let him kiss her. He heard the breath in her lungs grow heavy and labored. Just as it had in his. Moving her hand into both of his, he decided it was time to make a confession.

"Miss Faraday, I feel that I must make my intentions known to you," Mr. Worthington began as Annabelle grew more and more nervous about the coming conversation. "I seem to not be able to help what I am feeling towards you."

"I am sorry, sir," Annabelle said in a questioning voice as she could feel her heart beat wildly deep within her chest. "I do not understand."

"Miss Faraday, I have affections towards you," Mr. Worthington ushered the words out of his nervous lips with false confidence he could only hope she did not see through. "When I am alone all I wish for is to be near you, and when I find myself near you all I wish for is to be the reason you smile. I do not know the extent of these emotions that plague me, but I would very much like an opportunity to court you to see where this may lead."

"To court me?" Annabelle was baffled by the man's confession. "What should happen to me if it should not be compatible, sir? Will I be sent back to Auburn? Will I be left here to rot away in the discomfort of being in your presence? Sir, courting is nothing I wish to bother myself with. Love is not something I am searching for."

Her eyes were desperate, as if pleading with the man to end the conversation so she could continue her life and pretend that it never happened. She did not have the time nor will to decipher her own emotions towards the man and wished he had not taken the time to look into his.

"How can you not be looking for someone to care for?" He took a subtle step closer to her as he watched layers of her mask start to slip away from her. "Someone to care for you?"

"I cannot allow myself love, for it always leads to heartbreak." The only people she had ever loved so deeply were stolen from her. She could not let this man break into her heart. She kept those around her at arm's length for a reason.

"Why not let yourself be loved," he said as he rose the next step.

She backed away from him and with a shutter in her voice and tears in her eyes, she pleaded, "sir, please."

Before she could finish her thought, he swept her face into his hands and pressed his lips against hers. Shocked at first, she eventually allowed herself to be kissed. He kissed her fiercely at first, pushing every emotion he felt into her through their lips, but after a moment, the kiss broke, and he gazed upon her. Her flushed cheeks and red lips. Her bright eyes stared at him in shock, but she made no move away from him. Taking a chance, he placed his hand on her cheek and kissed her gently once more. She moved her hands from his chest to wrap them around his neck for a moment, allowing the kiss to wash over her, and then, as if day had turned to night in an instant, she placed her hands back on his chest, opened her eyes, and pushed against him, breaking his hold of her.

Tears once gain welled up in her eyes as she berated him. With her heart racing and her lungs unable to hold a breath, she looked upon the confusion in his face.

Her voice cracked as she said, "I cannot do this" and turned around. She ran up the stairs as fast as she could. She heard nothing except for the sound of his boots trailing her and a faint "wait" echoing up the corridor. She reached her room and locked the door as she crumbled to the floor and cried. She allowed herself to feel something, and she would never forgive herself for it.

CHAPTER 8

Annabelle stayed on the floor for what felt like days but had only been hours. More tears had fallen from her eyes since she arrived at Arrington than had fallen in all the time she had been at Auburn. Her head and heart were awash with emotions and memories. She could no longer lock them away like she once had, and she was furious at herself for it. He had broken her. She was fine until she had met this stubborn man who said all the wrong things. Every day he infuriated her, and today was no different.

"How dare he do that to me," she whispered to herself, rising from the floor, determined not to let another tear fall at his expense. "Who does he think he is? I am not that kind of governess."

She paced the worn floors of her room as she wondered if he had done the same thing to Catherine. Had he done this to all his female workers? Anger filled her at the very thought of letting herself be tricked by this man, and at the thought that Catherine could have given him her heart as well.

The troublesome feelings forced her to sit on her bed to catch her breath. She had received an invitation from Emma and was going to accept it. Now, she just had to be granted permission to leave for a few days to visit her friend. She was undecided as to whether she would return but was certain that she would leave over the Easter holiday. She went to bed, forming a plan, and after the most restless night of sleep she had ever had, she was ready to put it into action.

Rising to her feet and readying herself for the day, and with a turn of the knob on her door, she headed out into the corridor. Sure that Mr. Worthington would find her as soon as he was aware that she had emerged from her quarters, she made her presence known. Speaking to every servant she passed, she allowed her voice to echo through the halls. She walked through the kitchen fighting back the blush that emerged on her cheeks when she passed the steps where Mr. Worthington had cornered her the day before. She then took a stroll to the gardens, and while watching the buds begin to grow on a rose bush, she heard the familiar click of a certain pair of boots that spent a great deal of time in her presence.

Her steps ceased just before the greenhouse, a marvelous structure made of iron and glass that held the sun's warmth. The sunlight danced along the grooves and waves of the thick glass that made up the walls, as Annabelle busied herself watching the gardeners care for the plants that call the building home, listening to the click grow nearer, increasing in sound. His steps slowed and almost faded into the breeze as he came to a stop next to her. Unsure of what to say, he stood motionless, waiting for her to speak.

"Good morning, sir," Annabelle began with her arms crossed tightly atop her chest twisted into each other in a vice or a grip, encasing her nervousness and stress. "It is a beautiful day, is it not?"

It was in this moment that Annabelle noticed a few birds dancing along the branches that were decorated with seeds only yesterday. They would surely call Arrington home now. Her emotions on the matter were unclear, but her heart twisted at the sight before her and the memory of the day before.

"That it is, Miss Faraday," he tentatively responded.

"That it is," she whispered, not paying the man any attention, but watching the birds in the distance.

"Miss Faraday—"

"No," she snapped.

"I am sorry," he ignored her protests and continued to speak.

"Sorry?" Her curls whipped in her face as she turned to the man, beginning a ruthless stare down. "What exactly for, Mr. Worthington? Sorry for manipulating your role as my employer? Sorry for pretending to care? Sorry that I did not fall for your act? Tell me, what are you mournful over?"

"Act?" He was now confused. "Miss Faraday, I can assure you my actions are genuine."

"Did my poor Catherine suffer at your hand as well, sir?" She questioned, an undeniable accusatory tone lacing her voice.

"Suffer?" His brow furrowed, and his lips turned into an intense frown. "Is that what Arrington is to you? A place to suffer?"

"I am not this type of governess, sir," her hands flew out to her sides as she struggled to find the correct words to speak. "You cannot cure your loneliness with my presence. Was my lovely Catherine tricked by your charms as well?"

"Miss Faraday, I met your Catherine on a total of three occasions, having spent most of the time she lived at Arrington out of the country," his terse voice replied to her accusations. "Is that really all you think of me? A man looking to take advantage of his position over you?"

Her body was angled away from him, but she was easily able to pin him with a rueful glare.

"I do not know, sir," she began with a fierce, but tired voice. "I know little about you. How should I be able to understand your actions? You treated me as the dirt under your shoe when I first arrived, and then just yesterday corner me in your kitchen. What is a woman to think?"

"I thought the moments in between would have been enough to answer your questions, Miss Faraday," he began in a gentle voice. He did not handle any part of this situation correctly, and now he would surely pay. "I only wish for an opportunity to know more about you. See if love, or at least friendship could be found in our future."

She bristled at the use of "we" when describing the future. She had not seen herself being a half of a "we" at all in her lifetime. Everything about this man and his actions was foreign to her, but she knew what he could offer was not something she could ever accept.

"I cannot, sir."

She did not meet his eyes, only looked down so intently she could see the ants walking along the grass.

"Prey tell, why?" He forced his voice to be steady, like stone. That was what the world expected of him, so it was what he would give. "Do you not believe fate has brought you here?"

To be honest, he had never put much stock in fate, but having this woman with the perfect manners and mysterious past stumble into his life with such a fire inside of her he could only be drawn to her warmth, he found himself willing to believe in miracles.

"To be loved is not my fate," she snapped back at him with a fearsome tone, whipping her eyes up to meet his. So certain of the fact.

"How can you possibly know your fate?"

"I know my fate better than you do, I'm sure," the ire in her voice did not go unnoticed by Mr.

Worthington.

"And you get to decide your fate?" He knew she would not be pleased with his next words, but he was grasping for anything that could assist him in understanding this woman. "What about God's hand? Where is he in your fate."

"I have just as much say as my Lord does in where my life will lead."

"So, you would doom yourself for the sake of choosing your fate?" Using her words against her, he spoke determinedly. "How is your will greater than God's?"

"For a man who says he does not believe, you are quick to throw my faith back at me for your own selfish measures," she let out a chuckle as she spoke the words with venom in her tone. He had chastised her for her faith and questioned it at every turn, but now would use it as a nail in her coffin.

"You are letting your fear cloud your judgment," he reasoned. "What are you afraid of? Let me slay your demons for you. You cannot possibly stomach all of it alone."

"So now you call me weak?" Her disbelieving tone reached his ears as surprise took over her features. "How will insults get you what you wish, sir?"

His frustration grew, and he took a moment to inhale a large breath before he spoke his next words.

"I do not wish to insult, and I do not wish to use your problems selfishly," caution covered his tone as he hoped she could understand him. "I only wish for your happiness."

"And if my happiness does not lie here?"

"I do not believe that," his reply was short and the certainty behind his words concerned her. "You could be happy here. We could be happy here. You need only give me a chance."

"I have given more chances than I can count and every one of them has let me down," she could not continue to stand here with him. He made her question what she knew to be true and his very presence tortured her heart. Memories were flooding her mind behind her eyelids and all she could think about was finding a quiet corner to be alone. "I could not survive the fall from another chance."

"Not even one more?"

"Not even one more."

Stares were shared as the pair looked at each other, catching their breaths from the heightened emotions flowing through their veins. Mr. Worthington broke the calming silence first.

"I do not understand…"

"Never mind, sir," she snapped. The spell had been broken and she remembered her intentions of finding the man in the first place. "That is not what I came here to discuss…"

****

"Did she receive permission to visit her friend, Grandmother?"

"Yes, my dear," the grandmother responded. "That she did."

"Why did she not wish for love," the girl spoke, not to anyone in particular, but out of confusion.

"My dear, she lived a hollow life for so many years," the aging woman explained in a thick voice. "A desperate soul can convince themselves of anything, and guilt is a fierce motivator for such thoughts."

"But, Grandmother," the girl replied, forgetting her manners as her large eyes gazed up at the woman. "What was she guilty of?"

"We are not at that point in the story yet, Darling," the grandmother replied with a smile, knowing that while she could never answer all of the young girl's questions, she could give her a story.

****

Her request had been granted, and the kiss was not spoken of again. His permission held stipulations, as always. A carriage would take her to the estate, and return her once her visit had concluded, and she would not leave even a second before the family took off for France. These conditions, however trying, were not unreasonable. Mr. Worthington had her best interests at heart in providing her with a carriage, but that was what worried her most. She did not wish for his emotions to be directed towards her, nor would she acknowledge any emotions she may or may not possess for him. She simply wanted to care for the children and tutor them.

She spent her days following their last encounter avoiding Mr. Worthington and shuddering under the uncomfortable stare of Mr. Kennelworth. He slunk around the estate hiding in the shadows. Annabelle always had an extra eye out for the man who made her increasingly more uncomfortable with every glance. He had been wandering the grounds more often than when he first arrived, and the increase in frequency of his visits had both Annabelle and the children on edge. They clearly had conflicting opinions about their father. Isabelle scared of him, and Lucas, desperate for some form of male approval. It broke her heart when she remembered her lovely father and acknowledged the fact these children would never feel such deep love from theirs.

Mrs. Kennelworth was clearly not pleased by her husband's surprise visit as well. Annabelle often heard the arguments that plagued the marriage of the Kennelworths' as she walked back to her quarters for the night after putting the children to bed. She never stayed long enough to eavesdrop, but their thundering voices echoed through the corridors following her on her journey to the wing the staff called home.

"You putrid man!" Mrs. Kennelworth shrieked. "You think I do not know what they say of me back in London. You have made a mockery of myself and our family."

"My dear, please," he tiredly replied. "Maybe if you begin by telling me what I have done wrong, I will be able to forge an appropriate excuse for my actions. You have no choice but to move past whatever issue this may be. You cannot hide away in Arrington forever."

"You cannot believe that I support your actions, Rufus," she began at a slightly lower volume. "What kind of man pays a woman for silence?"

"The kind that has too much to lose," he replied sharply. "I remember you once appreciated that quality about me years ago."

"That was before I knew you as a man," she scoffed in reply. "I was blinded by the gold you hung in front of my face, but my brother has more wealth than you tenfold, and he has happily kept the children and I under his roof, so I do not understand why you even come here. He will not let you leave with us."

"You think you are the reason he keeps you here?" Mr. Kennelworth questioned. "I have never seen him even look at our children, but suddenly he is happy to disrupt his life for their sakes. No, my dear. I believe it has something to do with the blonde lass that follows the children throughout the day. She surely is a sight. Even I would put up with you for the promise of the young governess."

"Whatever his reason, he shall not drop her into your clutches," she seethed.

"Ah, but he will not have a choice," Mr. Kennelworth conspired. "Spring is upon us, and there is a party every other night we are expected to attend. The man cannot keep you all from me forever. You are mine."

****

"Grandmother?"

"Yes, Dear."

"Why were Mr. and Mrs. Kennelworth so unhappy?" The little girl questioned with a thoughtful face that looked just a tad amusing to her grandmother. "Are you not supposed to love the one you marry?"

"My Darling," the grandmother began to respond. "I believe they had love for each other once they were first married, but after years of worrying more about the garments they wore and the opinions of others, their love faded, and they became people even they did not recognize."

"But you are always you, Grandmother," the girl was exceptionally confused. "You do not stop being you, do you?"

The grandmother could only chuckle at the struggle her granddaughter faced attempting to understand something you needed to learn.

"Yes, my dear," she began. "But after you spend years caring about things that do not matter, the hollowness in your heart grows and you change. You become a different type of person when you deprive yourself of the things in life you need most. The things that cannot be bought by money. My love for you is free, as is your parents. When you do not allow yourself to cherish those important things, and instead hold tight to the things that money buys, you are not the same. Unfortunately, many characters in this story learn this lesson the hard way."

"Oh," the little girl simply replied, still far too confused, but wishing to move on with the story.

****

"Good morning, Miss Faraday."

Annabelle jumped in the hall as she spun to come face to face with Mr. Kennelworth. She was on her way to the children's study to begin her tutoring for the afternoon. Lunch was just completed, and Annabelle had eaten hers in the kitchen with Mrs. Nettles. She tried to limit her interactions with the Kennelworth parents as much as possible, thus leading to her spending more and more time in the presence of the kitchen staff, not that Annabelle was complaining. She quite liked their company and adored their stories they would share of their many years spent within the walls of Arrington.

"Mr. Kennelworth," Annabelle cautiously responded as she curtsied for the man. "What can I help you with?"

He began a predatory stride towards her, which caused a panic in Annabelle as she backed up quickly until she found herself against a wall with nowhere to go, as Mr. Kennelworth arrived in front of her.

"There is so much you can do for me, my lady," he responded in a terrifyingly deep and rough voice as he leaned even closer to the governess in front of him.

Annabelle only held her breath, wishing for the moment to end as she could not find a way to respond, nor an avenue to escape. Mr. Kennelworth, however, took that silence as an invitation to bring his face closer to her, but before he could fully invade her personal space, he was stopped in his tracks.

"That will be all, Rufus," Mr. Worthington's sharp voice cut through the deathly still silence of the main hall. Annabelle stood paralyzed, hoping if she did not move, she would eventually disappear. "Your wife waits for you."

The rat-like man who had Annabelle cornered only scoffed at the suggestion his wife wished to see him.

"We both know my wife does not wait for me, Sheridan," his breath was quickly becoming suffocating to Annabelle and he felt her face twisting, hoping to escape the stench. "I am amazed she has not taken up a lover whilst she has been here, hidden away from the prying eyes of society. In London, unfortunately I am not so lucky."

His eyes shifted back to Annabelle as he spoke those last words. "The country is very lovely though. A man could quickly learn to love it."

Frozen in fear, Annabelle only diverted her eyes to the floor, shutting them tighter than the safe of the Bank of England. Mr. Worthington was quick to pick up on the uncomfortable stance Annabelle held and walked over to the pair. His mind was raging, and he was certain he would resort to force if his brother-in-law would not leave of his own accord.

"Miss Faraday is a member of my staff, Rufus," Mr. Worthington spoke his name as if it pained him. "And I do not take kindly to guests exerting power over them. I would suggest you step away and retreat to your quarters. If it is required, I will gladly have someone assist you. We would hate to see you tumble down the steps because you cannot function."

Mr. Kennelworth scowled harshly but understood he would not win this battle today. He did enjoy riling his brother-in-law up though and took a step closer to Annabelle. He clearly saw Mr. Worthington tense rigidly from the corner of his eye, more so when he lifted his hand and stroked Annabelle's cheek one last time before stepping away and stumbling out the door in search of his bed. His ears rung as Mr. Worthington promised this was not the last he would hear of this incident on his way out the door.

Once Mr. Kennelworth had gone, Annabelle slackened against the wall with harsh tears burning her eyes. Mr. Worthington was at her side in a snap, catching her before she fell to the stone ground. No words were spoken, and Annabelle was able to steady her breathing with Mr. Worthington's gentle hand rubbing her back, consoling her. Able to stand, she did not waste a moment before rising from her slackened state.

"Thank you, sir," she began in a hoarse voice. "I am not sure how I ended up in such a situation, but I am grateful to you for helping me out of it."

Mr. Worthington could still sense a discomfort radiating off her at the memory of what had taken place just a few moments earlier but could not deny the sincerity in which she spoke. Looking her in the eye, he only nodded as she curtsied and strode out of the room and down the hall to the staircase that would take her to her bed. On her way up the steps, she heard the faint click of boots, so soft he must have been walking on his toes. A miniscule grin took residence upon her face at the thought of him walking her to her room, just to make sure she was alright, and his devious brother-in-law did not make a reappearance.

She reached her door, entered, and locked the door tight once she knew it was safe. Her bed was welcoming, and as she prepared herself for night, she only hoped her nightmares would not make a return.

A little over a week had passed since the incident with Mr. Kennelworth and Annabelle finally began to feel peace once more. His eyes no longer followed her, and conversations were scarce and always related to the children. Whatever Mr. Worthington spoke to the man, it had done the trick as safety in this large estate was finally becoming a reality once again.

It was in the past week, though, that Annabelle had hidden away with her dear friend Catherine. It was the only place she could hide from both men in peace and still be able to speak the words from her heart that troubled her so.

"Catherine, I hope you can hear me up in Heaven," Annabelle began as she found a place one the grass that would suite her for her visit. "It is quite lonely here at Arrington. I love listening to Mrs. Nettles tell her lovely stories and Ms. Bowden is always a pleasure, and of course the children, but since I have been hiding from the men in the house, I find that I also avoid those in the house they speak to the most. Now I spend much of my days alone in my quarters when not caring for the children."

Tears welled in Annabelle's eyes as she took a deep breath and lifted her face to look at the trees. The sun, as always, poked through the branches and danced along the grass. She cherished the warmth brought on by the light. Every time she came here, she was more grateful to Mr. O'Connor for choosing such a resting place for her friend. Where roses lay only feet away during spring and summer and the birds sang constant songs. It was a beautiful little piece of the world.

"Enough about me, my dear," Annabelle continued, drying her tears. "How are you? I wish the angels treat you well and that you sing glorious songs to the Lord every morn. I remember how sweet and soft your voice was. I hope you can hear me, and my words do not die in the distance that now separates us. I know you never knew about my life, but if you happen to find my parents in Heaven, please tell them I say hello and I love them. It is a foolish notion, really. Heaven must be a very large place, and you do not even know what their appearance is, but if you come past them, please give them my message."

Annabelle spoke for a few more minutes to Catherine before she said a prayer and carried on with her day. Mr. and Mrs. Kennelworth had taken the children to the village for the day, bringing along Ms. Bowden in case the children became restless, so Annabelle had a day to herself, and lunch waiting back at Arrington.

Back at Arrington, Mr. Worthington waited for the governess to return. He knew where she ventured to each day and had a gift for her he could only hope would brighten her day. He did not know how to navigate this situation or his feelings, but he knew he could not push her, so he had given her space the past weeks. His fierce conversation with his brother-in-law last week caused him stress, so he kept a close eye on the governess, but he would wait for her to be ready before initiating another deep conversation.

He did, however, plan on telling her of his surprise when she arrived back from her journey.

****

"Miss Faraday –"

Annabelle froze in her tracks as she passed the entryway of the estate at hearing the sound of his voice. She had successfully avoided him for days and could not force down the fear that rose in her at the very thought of this oncoming confrontation.

"Mr. Kennelworth," she spoke cautiously as she turned to face the man. "Good afternoon."

"Good day, m'lady," he began with a strange smile on his face. "Do not worry, Miss Faraday, I am only here to let you know that Isabelle received a flute today while we were in town. She spoke so much of how lovely you play the piano for her and her brother and begged us for it. I only wished to ask you to work with her as she learns to play the awful thing. She attempted such in the carriage, and I almost threw it out the door with how miserable she sounded."

"Yes, sir," Annabelle stated, unsure how to answer him, but frustrated with his hateful words towards his precious daughter. "Is that all?"

"Yes, Miss Faraday," he spoke as he strode away, never letting his gaze on her drop until he was out of sight.

Annabelle could only shake off the encounter as she strode towards the kitchen. Her walk had taken significantly longer than she thought it would and she lost track of time during her time with Catherine. Night had almost fallen when she arrived back to Arrington, and her stomach was screaming for nourishment.

She had just completed her meal and putting her plate up to be cleaned when she jumped as her name was called from one of the entryways of the kitchen.

"Miss Faraday," Mr. Worthington spoke.

She had avoided two men for so long, and they both had found her today. She turned to him, a mustered as much of a smile she could while panicking from inside.

"Mr. Worthington," she began. "How are you today?"

"I am well," he responded shortly. Nothing fierce in his voice, but businesslike, as if this conversation had a very specific point. "There is something I wish to speak with you about, Miss Faraday."

With growing nerves, Annabelle could only nod as he strode across the kitchen. She tensed, worried he was venturing in her direction, but instead, he walked to the corner by the door leading to the gardens. There was a large object wrapped in paper, waiting to be revealed.

"Please, Miss Faraday," he extended his arm to her, wishing her near. She took a deep breath and walked across the stone floors until she came to a stop only a few feet away from him. Mr. Worthington motioned to the large package situated on the floor as he spoke. "Open it, please. I commissioned it for your benefit."

Deeply confused, Annabelle could only kneel to the floor and begin to peel the paper away from what she now saw was a large slab of stone. It was not the ornate stone that caused tears to fill her eyes, rather, the words written upon it.

Catherine Strout
Beloved Governess and Dear Friend

Annabelle could only cover her mouth with her hands to muffle her sobs as she gazed upon the sweetest gift she had been given in years.

"I do not possess words to display my gratitude, sir," Annabelle began, rising to her feet once again to face the man. "Thank you so much. Catherine would adore this beautiful gift you have bestowed to her."

"Let me be clear, Miss Faraday," he spoke clearly, piercing her with his gaze and sincerity. "I did this for you, and you alone. My cares for Catherine are no match for the onslaught of emotion for you."

"I do not understand…"

"You spend your days with your friend in that meadow," he explained. "Do not think I did not know you sneak off for your visits after your lessons with the children are complete. She should be remembered by those who live upon these grounds years from now, and a simple cross, while a lovely thought, will not carry her memory as much as a stone that bears her name. She was important to you, therefore preserving her memory has become important to me."

And just like that, her body betrayed her. She took a step forward and fell into him. Her lips cascaded onto his as her fingertips grazed the line of his chin. Within moments, a tender encounter turned into a moment of heart between the two. His arms encircled her waist as the kiss grew. Annabelle felt her back meet the stone walls of the kitchen as Mr. Worthington's free hand held her cheek, his thumb gently grazing her face. In an instant, just as quickly as she let her guard down with this man, Annabelle remembered herself. She opened her eyes and snaked out of his reach. Leaning against the frame of the stairway, trying to catch her breath, a few words slipped through her panting lips.

"Sir, I am your governess."

Her eyes never lifted from the floor as her beratement began. Cutting off her thought, it took Mr. Worthington only two strides to cover the same distance that had taken her many more. He rested his hands on the walls on each side of her, closing her off to anyone but him as his eyes turned cold staring at her. Catching his breath well before Annabelle, his return was less than cordial.

"I have made my intentions clear, Miss Faraday." His voice deep and clear. "It is you, who is confusing the matter."

"Me?" She responded with a sharp tongue. "I have done nothing of the sort, sir. I have tried to keep my distance from you…"

"Is what just happened what you call distance?" He whispered heavily, moving closer towards her.

Her eyes lifted to meet his, only to find them fiercely demolishing her resolve. The only way she could win this argument was to stand her ground, and with his eyes sinking into hers, she would never be able to.

"I am your governess, sir," she struggled out of tightened lips.

"Would it be better if I released you from your duties?" he replied. "Is that your only excuse?"

Anger filled her at the very thought. She was fighting for a better life, and he would rip it away from her just to prove a point.

"I deserve more than just someone's body, sir," she threw back shortly. "I deserve their heart, and that is something you are incapable of giving, and something I do not wish from you."

"My heart is mine to give."

"And my heart is mine to keep," Annabelle said as she turned to weave her way around his arms.

Refusing to let her go, Mr. Worthington met her eyes once again. "If you do not want my heart, what is it you wish for?"

"Freedom, sir. Freedom and happiness. Fortunately enough, they are mutually exclusive."

"So, you will be a governess for the rest of your life?" He questioned throwing his arms and taking a step back from her while frustration rose in him. "Where is your freedom? I do not see happiness either."

"It is a better option than allowing my fate to rely on the actions of others. If I am to be miserable for the entirety of my life, it shall be on my terms."

"Your argument makes little sense. Where is the misery in a life with me?"

"You would ruin me, sir," Annabelle's voice now determined and rising. "I am not deserving of what you have to offer, and once you realize this, you would shatter me, and I would surely not survive it."

She took a step back and her back fell against the wall, supporting her as her knees began to give up her weight.

"That is not your decision to make. You cannot possibly know my actions," he said, taking a step closer to her, only to be met with cold eyes that had replaced her soft and warm ones.

"But it is one I have already made," she replied in a faint whisper. Mr. Worthington let out a deep sigh, and Annabelle took this moment of distraction to twist away from him and up the stairs, fighting tears. Not even attempting to follow, Mr. Worthington only pressed his forehead against the wall and clenched his fists in exhausted frustration. Her heart had not been shattered yet, but every day with her, he felt his own twist and crack a little more.

Fumbling up the stairs, Annabelle hid away in her room for the remainder of the night. She chose not to eat her dinner in fear that she may run into Mr. Worthington. She did not know how she would behave around him. Her body had already betrayed her once today and she could not give her heart the chance to do the same.

It was as she was sliding herself into bed in nothing but her nightgown that a knock rang out from her door. Her heart raced from the thought of Mr. Worthington on the other side of the wood. She did not know what he could want this late at night but was decidedly furious that he would call on her at such a scandalous hour. She could not and would not have her work and relations disrupted by this man. Rising from her bed, she was determined to give him a piece of her mind.

Much to her surprise, however, Mr. Worthington was not waiting for her on the other side of the door. It was another, looking as pale as the moon in the candlelit corridor and nervously rocking from side to side. He looked up at Annabelle with cold eyes as she eased the door open only a few inches, sure that all he could see was her face.

"Mr. Kennelworth, what, may I ask, are you doing here?" Before she could even collect her thoughts, he pounced.

CHAPTER 9

He threw the door open while simultaneously grabbing Annabelle in a vice-like grip. She tried to scream, but with the force of his arm pinning her to the wall, her voice was lost to her. The air escaped her lungs, fleeing from the ensuing violence; something she envied, as she could not twist her way out of his grasp. Clasping her mouth shut with his free hand, he kicked her door closed, and Annabelle's last hope of freedom disappeared with the light behind the door.

Panic flooded her body as she tried to pull any and all air into her lungs to scream, but Mr. Kennelworth's grip was too fierce. Keeping one hand on her mouth, he released her chest from his arm, only to replace it with his torso as he snaked his now free arm around her waist and pulled her closer to him. Thrashing in his arms, she threw her hands at his chest and face, attempting to force him to loosen his hold, even for a second, but this only fueled his fury. Releasing her waist, he grabbed her wrists and pinned them above her head and used his weight to throw the rest of her against the wall so hard, her head began to spin. Pinning her thighs to the wall with his knees, his cold stare turned ravenous as he leaned in close to her ear.

"I knew you would let me in," he husked. "I knew you wanted me as badly as I wanted you."

Tears flooded her eyes and ran down her face as she attempted once more to loosen his fingers clamped around her wrists. Breathing became more tried from the lack of air filling her lungs and lightheadedness began to set in. Her mind was screaming, but her body could not find a voice. With her rebellions slowing, Mr. Kennelworth let go of her mouth and began moving his hands over her body. As soon as his hand reached her thigh and grabbed onto her nightgown, it was as if her body had woken up and decided to fight once more. As oxygen refilled her lungs and her head stopped spinning, Annabelle realized that Mr. Kennelworth's lips were kissing her face, and his hand was half way up her skirt. She twisted her face from his and screamed as loud and as long as she could.

"No!"

Her shouts did not last long because within seconds Mr. Kennelworth struck her head and sent her spinning once more. She could not focus, and darkness set in. The room was only lit by the dim moonlight, and as Annabelle tried to lift her head once more to fight, she felt the night surrounding her once again; encasing her in a pain she knew she could not recover from.

That was, until Mr. Kennelworth released her, and she fell to the ground. Her vision, blurred from tears and confusion, did not immediately notice the light return. Her door was open, and boots filled the foyer of her room. Grunts and shouts filled the air, but Annabelle did not notice any of it right away, she only wanted to regain her breath and take inventory. Neither happened though, as tears more violent than ever poured from her eyes like cascading rapids.

It was Mr. Worthington who ripped Mr. Kennelworth from her. He threw him against the stone wall in the stairway as Annabelle crumbled to pieces on her bedroom floor. Her tears could not be calmed, and her cries could not be silenced as she held her stomach, crossed her legs, and dropped her head to the cold floor. Miss Bowden stood frozen in the doorway in a state of pure shock until her senses returned and she rushed in the room to hold Annabelle, grabbing a blanket from the bed and wrapping her up in it.

"What has happened?" Mrs. Kennelworth said as she rounded the spiral stone staircase leading to the staff quarters. As soon as she saw Mr. Worthington with his right forearm pressed firmly against her husband's neck, she knew something had occurred, and once she looked upon Annabelle on the floor, she knew exactly what had happened, for it had happened once before.

"You pitiful excuse for a man!" Berated Mr. Worthington. Rage overtook his eyes as he was ready to throw his brother-in-law down the stairs and right out the door, if he did not kill him first. He refused to listen to his sister's pleas to release her husband as he pressed his arm further against the rat's neck, making it difficult for him to breath. Gasping for air, Mr. Kennelworth tried, and failed, to pull Mr. Worthington's hand from his neck. His cold eyes grew dim and his gasps slowed, his relents almost coming to a complete stop. The only noises left in the corridor were those of Mrs. Kennelworth crying for her brother's mercy, and the sobs that escaped Annabelle's lips. There was only one noise that Mr.

Worthington listened to.

Annabelle looked up from her agony for a moment and felt no remorse for what she saw was about to happen to this man. The man who had stolen her safety, and almost ran off with her virtue. She would not attempt to stop Mr. Worthington. None of the other staff would dare cross him in this state of vehemence, and stood by, waiting to see what would happen next. Miss Bowden, the kind and caring soul she was however, saw a need to intervene.

Rising from the floor next to Annabelle, Miss Bowden hurried over to Mr. Worthington and placed her hand on his left arm and squeezed. "Please sir, there has been enough evil and heartbreak in this wing for the night."

Mr. Worthington then turned his head and caught sight of Annabelle, still lying on the floor, covered in sweat and tears. Her face had turned bright red from her screams, and stress caused her veins to become prominent on her face and neck. She was in distress. As she shifted her weight to lean against her bed, her eyes met his, only for a second, and he immediately released Mr. Kennelworth from his grip.

Mrs. Kennelworth caught her husband who immediately fell to the floor, attempting to catch his lost breaths. Miss Bowden walked back into Annabelle's room, and shut the door behind her while Mr. Worthington hung his head, running his fingers through his hair aggressively, she was closed off from her. This pain she had been caused happened in his home. Her safety was destroyed at the hand of family.

No longer able to see her, the anger he felt began to build again as he turned to his brother-in-law. Ripping him out of his sister's grasp, he hurled him down the steps. He ignored his sister's screams as he told two of his servants to lock him in his room for the night, and to let him out for no reason. He would deal with him in the morning, for if he did it tonight, it would likely end in his death. Looking at his sister's face, he knew this was not the first time her husband had assaulted a woman, and he was sure the last time he was successful.

"Please brother…" She began grabbing at his feet, pleading for forgiveness.

"No!" He thundered, spinning around and looking down on her. "You brought this wretched man into my house. You brought his evil and his demons, and now they will have me to contend with." He kicked his feet to release her grasp and walked down the steps and through the house to his study. Mrs. Kennelworth laid on the steps in tears. Tears for Annabelle, and for herself. Her reputation, all she cared about, would never recover from such an event. She did not know what would come of her husband, but the more she thought about the events of the night, the less she cared. She had loved him once, and therefore wished no death upon him, but after that, her compassion ran thin.

Annabelle had spent most of the night lying in bed crying with Miss Bowden at her side. Her blanket was soaked with sweat and tears as she felt the bruises begin to form on her skin. Her wrists had begun to turn a blue hue and she could feel sharp pains on her thigh where Mr. Kennelworth had pinned her against the wall with his knee. Every time a memory rose about the event, she shut her eyes as tight as possible, hoping to squeeze away the pain, but it only made the tears flow faster. Eventually, as Miss Bowden stroked her hair with her fingertips, Annabelle fell into slumber from sheer exhaustion, and stayed this way all night and into the morning.

"I must speak to her!" Mr. Worthington said at her door as the sun began rising into the sky. He clearly had gotten no sleep and was vexed from not knowing what state Annabelle was in.

"Sir, I would strongly caution against it. She is not ready for interaction of any kind, especially that of a male. Not in her condition."

Rubbing his face and looking upon Miss Bowden with tired and shallow eyes, he pleaded. Hanging his head and mumbling in a soft voice, "please?"

"No sir," Miss Bowden demanded. "I will not allow it. She needs to be left in peace to heal from the events of the night. Women have been scarred from much less. She needs time, and if we truly care for her, we will gift it to her."

Miss Bowden then reentered the room, and after determining Annabelle was okay, went downstairs to take charge of the children, closing her door tightly behind her. Mr. Worthington was not going to leave her unguarded but swore to Miss Bowden he would not enter the room.

Light made its way through the glass of her window and settled on her face, waking her. Her eyes eased open with the light of morning. For a moment, she had forgotten what had occurred the night before, and much to her dismay, the memories were worse the second time around. Shifting in the bed, the weight of her body collapsed as pain infused her head. She let out a sharp gasp at the headache that was consuming her. Even the sweet songs of the birds outside her window felt like broken glass to her ears. Writhing in pain and breathing heavily, to Annabelle's amazement, she still had more tears to shed.

****

"Grandmother?"

"Yes, dear?"

"Did she ever get out of bed that day?"

"Yes, she did," the woman responded, staring intently at the cup of tea in her hands. "She boxed away her pain, for if she dwelt on it any longer, she would have drowned in it or crumbled beneath it."

"But pain is not real, Grandmother," the little girl responded. "How can you crumble underneath it? It is not like water. You cannot drown in it."

"Child," she began in a slow and heavy voice. "We cannot see pain the same way we see other things, but it makes it no less real. Annabelle was covered in bruises and every time she closed her eyes, she remembered what had happened to her the night before. We do not drown in pain the same way we drown in water, for pain is much worst. It is a slow death brought on by horrible memories. Sadness can make us sick, and that is what it was doing to Annabelle."

"So, the sadness was what was hurting her? It was making her sick?"

"Yes, darling."

"Why did she not just see a doctor?" the little girl questioned.

"For there is no cure for a broken heart, my dear."

****

Annabelle slowly rose from her bed and walked over to the mirror hanging next to her fireplace. Staring at her reflection, she saw the damage that had been done the night before. Lifting her hem to examine her bruises, she shuddered at the sight of blues and greens covering her skin. The bruises that covered her neck and collar bone were especially dark, and the shape of Mr. Kennelworth's fingers plagued the back of her thigh in a purple hue. These marks could be hidden under a dress, but the bruise on her jawline from where her attacker struck her face was not so easily tucked away. Draping her hair over her face could not even hide the memory of the previous night.

She wrapped herself in her dainty chemise and then draped a faded green dress over her body. With long sleeves and a collar that reached all the way up her neck, this old dress was the best garment she had to hide her pain. Her hair was braided and pinned up as Annabelle willed her reflection to only be a dream. Letting a deep breath fill her lungs, she stared at her face in the mirror, certain that she would not let this event ruin her. She would move on. She would survive.

"You can do this," she whispered to herself, fighting back the warm tears that began to pool in her eyes. The birds had stopped singing and thick clouds hid the sun as Annabelle walked over to her door, flinching with every step. She took in one last deep breath before gripping the handle and pulling the door open, only to see the astonished look of a certain gentleman as she emerged from her cave.

She did not smile and the light from the sun no longer shone upon her face. Her dark eyes rose to his, and she could see the quizzical look marring his face. Before he even had an opportunity to ask her, she stated, "the children need me." The only explanation she could give as to her presence. She came down from her room to do her job and had since locked away the memories of the night to be dealt with at a later time.

Annabelle turned and raced down the stairs before he even had a chance to respond. Realizing she could not be talked out of her decision, Mr. Worthington headed towards the wing that housed his sister and her despicable husband. If Annabelle would not nurse her wounds today, he would not let them grow any larger at the sight of his brother-in-law.

Barreling through the door to his study, where he had summoned his rascal of a relative, Mr. Worthington had lost his sense since the night before and was sure he should have to be restrained should his brother loosen his tongue while in his sight.

As the doors flew open, beckoning his arrival, Mr. Kennelworth jumped in his seat. The man's face, looking worst for the wear, turned a deathly sheet of pale at the sight of Mr. Worthington's face. He noticeably gulped, his nervous wife at his side, as his mind searched for words to convince the man of Arrington to let him leave the gates of the estate with his head still on his shoulders and his reputation intact. He should have known better than to approach the governess last night, but indeed, alcohol had not agreed with his sense.

"I only need one reason, Rufus, to let you leave here with your face still intact," Mr. Worthington seethed as he stomped towards the impish man seated in the corner of the room. "Please, attempt to make it a good one, for I do not accept simple excuses."

"Sheridan," Mr. Kennelworth croaked, his windpipe still sore from the night. "I promise you, I am not so dense when I am in my right mind. Intoxication plagued me. I would never harass a woman in such a way…"

"Lies!" Mr. Worthington's voice cut through his excuses like a blade. "Do not act as if this is the first time, for the recognition in my sister's eyes as she looked upon the governess in the middle of that chaos tells me she has seen such actions from you before. Intoxication cannot be blamed, for drunk or sober, your actions are your own."

"So what will you do, Sheridan?" Mr. Kennelworth taunted. "I have power in London! Would you ruin me, ruin my family? Your family? That is all that could be done should this event reach the light of day. Let it die in the shadows."

"I have not decided what I will do, Rufus," Mr. Worthington heatedly replied. "I will have to consult my father before my choice is made, but you will be off of my property by the end of day, not to return under any circumstances. My family stays here."

"You cannot do that!"

"I can, and I will," he promised. "I suggest you behave yourself when you arrive back in town, for I will have people keeping a close eye on you and all of your actions. Another maiden shall not suffer from your illicit affairs. I will make sure of it."

The remainder of the conversation consisted of bickering between the master of the house and the rat that scurried along his halls. Mrs. Kennelworth did not speak a word during the duration. As long as her brother did not make society aware of the incident, she could continue to live her life. She was under his roof and protection and no longer questioned his actions when he insisted they stay. He had grown to care for her children as well as the maiden who cared for them.

She could never legally separate herself from her husband, but she could hide away in Arrington most of the year for as long as her brother would allow. No matter what, she would not return to her home in London, not that Mr. Kennelworth would miss her and the children much anyway.

Mr. Worthington found himself especially agitated after the confrontation with his brother-in-law. The rodent had not been fond of the demand to leave his family under the care of Arrington, but a stern look and a few threats from Mr. Worthington had changed his mind on the subject quickly. Having not yet spoken to his father about the incident, Mr. Worthington could only make sure the snake never laid another aggressive hand on a woman as long as his family could stop it.

If Mr. Kennelworth feared Sheridan Worthington, he positively dreaded any interaction with the senior Worthington. His wife's father had made it clear that he possessed enough connections to make the man disappear without a trace before Mr. Kennelworth wed his daughter. While it was true, he would never actually commit such an act, but the terror present in his soon to be son-in-law's eyes at the time made it clear his message was received. The younger Worthington considered passing the duty of dealing with the man to his father, who was taking a trip to London later in the month. One meeting with him could easily scare Mr. Kennelworth celibate. Mr. Worthington had the job of picking up the pieces at Arrington to worry about, and there was a young lady who deserved more of his attention at the moment.

****

"What happened to Mr. Kennelworth, Grandmother," the little girl question, her expression quickly changing from inquisitive to a scowl. "He truly is an awful man, is he not?"

"Yes, my dear," the grandmother replied with a heavy sigh. "That he is."

At the prolonged stare of her granddaughter, the woman realized she would not let the story move forward until her question was answered.

"He returned to London, my dear," she began. "He was given a frightful meeting with his father-in-law and was no longer allowed contact with his children alone. His father-in-law was always to be present, but this only continued for a few years as Mr. Kennelworth died an early and painful death from consumption. He did not take care of himself and enjoyed one too many London parties, thus leaving his children without a father and with a bitter mother."

"Oh."

At the solemn tone of the young girl's voice, the grandmother took that as a cue to continue with the story.

****

"Nettie," desperately Mr. Worthington pleaded with the woman as he paced the kitchen. "What should I do? What can I do? Her eyes hold such sorrow and her voice is laced with fear. How can Arrington become her home?"

Mrs. Nettles looked upon the boy she had known for so many years and she felt her heart crack. He had been so frigid for so long and just as his heart warmed, the object of his affections is speared away from him like a lowly deer in the woods. His heart was pierced just as hers was, and he still looked for a way to piece herself back together, for she was the only glue that could reassemble him.

"Please, Sheri," Mrs. Nettles cautiously responded. "You only need to make sure she knows you are there for her. That she has your support. Her mind will be her enemy, but only she can win this battle. You cannot fight it for her."

With a stiff nod and a displeased grunt, Mr. Worthington stalked out of the room, lost in his thoughts, furious that he could not do more for the governess. He would give her what she needed, but only after he heard the words pass from her lips. He hid away from the world in his study for the rest of the day, while Annabelle found her own hiding spot for the day.

The children were not aware of the events of the night before, much to Annabelle's relief. No child should know such demons dwelling in their parents. As much as she loathed the man who stole her safety, she could not let the children pay for his sins. If they had known, their hearts would break, and they would never treat Annabelle the same, and she would not be able to regain the lovely trust and love they shared. She knew the kind of destruction evil and guilt could wrack upon one's soul. It would be worst for the children, as the sins they would suffer from were of their father, not their own.

She found solace in the laughs and smiles that graced Isabelle's and Lucas' faces as she taught them about the world's geography. Lucas enjoyed this subject in particular because he would always turn the globe when Annabelle's back was turned and loved the confused stare she held when she noticed. He knew not to push her too far, as her smiles were not as bright today, but he enjoyed testing her limits as well.

Teaching the children about the world just made Annabelle wish she had seen more of it. She was reminded of promises her father made to take her with him on trips when she was old enough to accompany him. She was promised ballrooms in Paris and tea in London. He even conceded that she may be able to see the fireworks of China, should he ever have to travel to the country. He made sure she had a thorough education, so her mind would not negatively affect her life, and had dreamed a large life for his child. She knew he would be disappointed with her life in a cage.

Shaking her head, wishing the negative thoughts away, Annabelle continued on with her day. Lunch was served to the trio in the children's study and by the time supper came around, Annabelle was tired and at war with her mind. The children had been summoned after to lunch to bid their father goodbye as he left to return to London, and Annabelle had to field inquiries from the children as to why their father had marks on his face and neck, and why his departure was so abrupt. So much time spent with such inquisitive children had been heavy on her heart. She had been using the children as a distraction, but now she felt the previous night clawing its way out of mind in the form of memories.

Feeling her resolve break, Annabelle sent the children away to eat while she stayed in the study endeavoring to reign in her emotions.

****

While the man of the estate brooded in his displeasure floors below, Annabelle found herself still in the children's study hours later, gently tapping the piano keys, not making any particular music, but allowing the fingers of her right hand to graze the keys and make noise to drown the silence that slowly suffocated her. It was not pretty, nor ugly. Nothing like the usual compositions she poured out of the instrument. It was simply noise, and it was exactly what Annabelle needed in this moment.

No candles were lit and the only curtains that remained pulled were the ones she stood in front of. Shadows danced across the room, looming around her like vines suffocating a tree. The noise did not keep her monsters at bay, but kept them at arm's length, which was far enough away for Annabelle.

Having just walked from his study into the kitchen for a meal, Mr. Worthington heard this noise bouncing off the stone walls of the estate, as if it were calling to him. He knew it was her, so he let the sound lead him through the halls to the room where she stood.

He walked into the children's study as softly as his feet could take him, but his boots had a sound that always gave him away. Annabelle lifted her hand from the piano and stood next to the window, reveling at the sunset that leaked through the glass planes, cracking between the darkness. She had not accompanied the children to dinner, and stood frozen in place, looking at the artwork God had brushed across the sky. She had not intended for him to find her, only wished for the silence to stop, but she was not surprised. He always appeared when she least wished him to, and here he was.

"No need to hide, Mr. Worthington," she spoke softly. She had not called him by his surname in a long time, settling for "sir." He did not like it. Mr. Worthington sounded too formal for what he felt for the maiden. "Your boots told me of your entrance. Will you not state your business?"

He hated the way she spoke, especially to him. He wished for the fire that burned beneath her to make an appearance, but she was cold. He could see her mind at war, her heart shattering, and he felt utterly helpless. He did not know how to rectify the situation any further. His brother-in-law had been taken care of, but that was clearly not enough.

Determined to assist her, he strode slowly to her side and stood stock still, gazing at the beauty that lay before them. He did not see how it compared to the beauty beside him, but he could appreciate the view. He had seen many sunsets at Arrington in his life, but sharing the view, even without words, with another human, just made the experience a small bit brighter. The sun was dipping lower in the sky when he turned to her to speak.

"How can I help you heal from these wounds?" he asked softly, placing his thumb on her chin.

"I need time," she replied in a shuttered voice as she pulled her face from his grasp and turned away from the window, letting the shadows surround her. "I will be alright. I always am with a little time." Her head hung low and her eyes never lifted to meet his. She simply turned and walked away from him, holding back tears that were about to burst from her eyelids as a cloud bursts at the start of a storm.

He did not chase her. He only watched her walk away.

CHAPTER 10

Weeks went by as Mr. Worthington continued to roam his estate, keeping a watchful eye on his surroundings. He would not have another event such as the one that marred the memories of Annabelle plague the halls of Arrington. The governess, however, avoided the man at all costs. Even with the hasty departure of the subject of her ire, Mr. Kennelworth, Annabelle still could not find it in her to confront Mr. Worthington. She held no ill will towards the man, but his very existence twisted her mind and her heart wretchedly. She only wished for relief from the grievances her life had cast towards her but could not seem to find them within Arrington's walls.

Annabelle did not visit Catherine for Easter and the Worthington family did not venture to France for Easter. Too much had happened in the previous weeks and leaving would only cause more chaos.

It was not until the man of the estate had to depart across country for business that Annabelle felt as if she could breathe again. The air was warmer, and the sun shone brighter. Fickle as it may seem, it had taken her weeks to speak her daily prayers and read her Bible once again after the attack. Her heart felt gruesome pain and her faith became woefully conflicted. She could not decipher her God's purpose for such an event, but soon realized that we never truly understand God's reasons. She strayed from her faith for exactly 17 days until little Lucas asked in his soft voice if she could pray with him before he fell into slumber.

The peace that blanketed her soul after the short minute reminded her of why she clung to her faith so fervently in the first place. She would never understand everything in the world, as it was not her job, but she could continue to believe in the good of the one far greater than her. The one who currently held her beloved parents in his hands.

Slowly she found her way back to herself. Her brightness had not fully returned, and the world was not as agreeable as it once was in her eyes, but she surmised that all humans were not wicked, and all stories are not always joyful. Mr. Worthington would cross her mind every now and again, but she was quick to discard the thoughts. The less she thought about him the better, for he only brought with him confusion and doubt, two things she could happily live without. But, as it would seem, she could not hide behind Arrington's walls forever, for his business soon ended and he returned, bringing with him a new determination to convince the young governess to see reason.

She had successfully avoided the man for a total of 6 hours and 54 minutes since his return from business. Now that the air was bringing on the first signs of Spring, the children had begged to be allowed to spend their afternoons in the gardens. Mr. Worthington had arrived on horseback and immediately asked Mrs.

Nettles to prepare him a meal which he ate in his quarters and then, according to the gossip of the maids, had bathed and taken a moment to catch up on sleep, before emerging to address the heads of staff about his absence. After the meeting, word quickly spread that he had locked himself away in his study, not to be disturbed. Annabelle simply hoped the gardens could hide her from an encounter with the man that frazzled her mind and caused uncomfortable flutterings in her heart.

She had ushered the children outside to the north lawn of Arrington after being shooed from the gardens by Mr. O'Connor and his son after Isabelle picked one too many flowers and Lucas got stung by a bee. He was brave though, telling Annabelle that he would not shed a tear, for big boys could handle small amounts of pain without such frivolities. A saying she was sure he had learned from his father.

After relocating to the North lawn of the estate, Annabelle had borrowed a ladder from the nearby gardening apprentice. It was there Mr. Worthington found the group. He had returned from business only hours earlier but was met with stacks of odious letters for business that had nearly drowned him until he put them aside for the rest of the day and moved on. He much preferred when such things fell to his father's lot, but now the responsibility was his.

Annabelle stood on the bottom rung of the ladder while Lucas sat atop a branch on the tree, spreading birdseed, as they had done months prior, inviting all the birds to form new nests on the grounds of the estate. Stopping for a moment to gaze upon the scene before him, Mr. Worthington decided this was what he wished for. This simple life surrounded by birds and flowers and a lovely woman. He was entranced by her as she smiled at Lucas and helped him down from the tree, only to bring Isabelle up next and allow her a turn. The giggles of the children broke him from his reverie, as he had been spotted by Lucas, who cautiously treaded over to him.

"Welcome home, Uncle Sheridan," Lucas said in a small voice, gazing up to his uncle. He was nervous about the encounter, but hoped their relationship grew enough to where he could approach him without repercussions. Annabelle turned from Isabelle at this moment to regard the man. The look she wore on her face was stern, warning Mr. Worthington to behave as best he could. She was not sure Lucas could take another heartbreak of being rejected by a man he idolized. First his father, even though he was a wretched man, had not answered a single correspondence the young boy sent to him. She would not have his uncle treat him the same. An unconventional move for a governess, as they normally only did what they were told, and hid in the shadows of the home, not interacting with anyone, but Annabelle had proven more than once she was anything but conventional.

"Good afternoon, Lucas," Mr. Worthington, noticing the sharp glare the young governess was impaling him with, lowered to ground to be at eyesight level with the boy. "I trust you have behaved well in my absence?"

Lucas brightened immediately at being answered by his uncle. "Yes, sir. I have been on my best behavior. You can ask Annie and she will surely tell you the same."

Mr. Worthington could not help but smile at the child, something he had been doing more and more as he rose to his full height, before lifting Lucas into his arms and walking towards the girls. "I believe I shall do just that."

Lucas met his smile with one of his own, equally as bright. The pride he felt at the attention of his uncle rolled off him as he waved to Annabelle. Her heart warmed at the sight as she assisted Isabelle off the branch and lowered herself from the ladder.

Once the pair reached Annabelle and Isabelle, Mr. Worthington bowed in respect with Lucas still in his arms. The young boy was quick to follow his uncle's lead and bow his head as well, causing a small grin to creep on Annabelle's face as she curtsied back.

"Welcome, Uncle Sheridan," Isabelle's voice rang out as she acknowledged her uncle while curtsying. "I hope you are well from your journey."

"Yes, sweet Isabelle," the young girl smiled shyly, a faint warmth coating her cheeks at the endearment her uncle used. "My journey was pleasant indeed. Have you behaved yourself in my absence?"

"Yes, sir," she replied in a quiet voice, gazing up at him only slightly. Conversations with her uncle were always very short and usually ended with a long sigh from him and the sound of his footsteps walking away. He had been different in recent months, and she could only hope the changes would soon find themselves permanent.

"And you, Miss Faraday?" Mr. Worthington lifted his eyes to meet hers. "How have you faired in my absence?"

Annabelle was taken aback by the bluntness of his inquiry, her shock written clear on her face.

"Well, sir," she replied with narrowed eyes, silently scolding him for such an interaction in front of the children, both of whom found the encounter amusing. It was no secret between the two that they wished for Annabelle to become family. "I have been well in your absence."

"Not very well?"

She could not help but succumb to his musings. "No sir, not very well, nor poorly. Simply well."

The serious nature of her statement and her level voice did not go unnoticed by Mr. Worthington as his eyes gazed deeply into hers, looking for a key to unlock her heart.

"Very well, Miss Faraday."

"I trust your business went well, sir," Annabelle said in hopes of sparking a conversation to end the terse silence. They looked on as Lucas and Isabelle employed themselves with a ball in the neighboring field, giving the pair time for a conversation that felt significantly overdue.

"Indeed it did, Miss Faraday," his cool reply slipped from his lips effortlessly.

"Not very well?" She was quick the quip back at the man, surprised when her words elicited a full smile from him.

"No, Miss Faraday, only well."

He was not pleased with nature of the conversation but had come to acknowledge that pressuring the governess to speak about subjects she did not care for had hardly ever worked in his favor. Still, he knew he had to skew the conversation at some point, and only wished to do it seamlessly. "Thank you for taking such interest."

"Do not misunderstand me, sir," Annabelle began, still not wishing to glance at the man. "I have no interest in your business goings at all. I only endeavor to make pleasant conversation in an effort to follow the rules set out by society for daily interactions. I have no understanding of such business, so why should your work interest me?"

She knew her reply was terse and would elicit a response from the master of such a large estate, but within herself, she knew this was what she wished for. Their relations had begun with terse interactions and heated discussions. She enjoyed such interactions. Matters of the heart were far too complex for her and she wished to be taken back to a simpler time, when her employer drove her mind into a frenzy with such stubbornness, and she strove to surprise him with little notes of her upbringing she would share now and again. Her emotions locked away inside her now were too much for her to handle at the moment, and she could only hope he would humor her, if only for a short time.

His lips twitched in amusement as he caught one. She was baiting him.

"I am terribly sorry, Miss Faraday," he replied, readying himself for the blow that was sure to accompany his next comment. "It indeed is too much to expect a governess to understand the complexities of business ventures. I apologize, I will be sure to only speak of simpler subjects in your presence."

He knew she understood much more than she let on, and he was certain that her intelligence rivaled some of the most educated in London's elite society. It was with bated breath that he awaited her reply.

Annabelle, however, was dumbfounded. He had shocked her to silence. How could she reply to such a statement when she had spoken of not understanding business matters just a moment ago. She wished for a rise out of the man, not for him to turn her words against her in an attack on her intelligence. A clever man indeed, she surmised.

"Sir, please do not misconstrue my words," she tentatively began, now turning to face him. "I am sure if there was anything remotely interesting about your business encounters, I could find the energy to learn about them, but such tedious and loathsome work could even bore the most intelligent man in England. No worries though, if you should not be able to locate a maiden to tolerate such long hours, you will always have your money to keep you company."

Such words were a low blow that hit Mr. Worthington hard. He knew the troubles his business caused him. It did not matter how respectable and honest his work was, the money that accompanied such a living would never cease to haunt his interactions. He had not shared such feelings with Annabelle, so he could not count her remarks as cruel, only simple ribbing in hopes of riling him up, but internally he felt a twist of pain at the reminder that he should only ever be known by his hard exterior and the number of pounds in his pockets.

"Do not worry, Miss Faraday," he began, brushing off deep seeded feelings of hatred towards gold and embracing the opportunity to steer the conversation elsewhere. "For I have found a young maiden whom I fancy greatly. She has seemed to tolerate me thus far, and I can only hope she continues to do so."

The very conversation she had been avoiding had been thrust in her lap. Had she thought that this man could have met and courted another in his time away, she may have even felt an awful green monster arise in her gut, but she knew him. He was too kind to thrust another in her face, and far too intelligent to pass up such an opportunity to corner her. She had to stay in the field to care for the children, and as master of the estate, he did not need a reason to join her.

"Sir, you should not desire me," she whispered, turning her head back to the two young children kicking their ball mere feet away. Lost in laughter and smiles, they did not even acknowledge their uncle or their governess, rather chose to focus on their sibling bond that had grown so much closer since arriving at Arrington.

"Prey tell, why?" His eyes urged her to turn back to him, but her stubbornness stood firm and she did not remove her own from the children.

"I would only live to disappoint, sir," she began. "My demons are far to great for me to conquer. I fear I shall be forced to wage war with them for the entirety of my life, slowly drowning in darkness. Surely you believe you deserve better."

"Annabelle," he whispered her name, forcing the air travelling to her lungs to stop in her throat. She could not think of the tenderness that laced his tone, or the perfect way his lips formed her name. She could not think of any of it and attempted to reason with her heart not to be impacted by such a simple action. "Do we all not have demons we must overcome?"

"Sir, I am sure yours are far easier to fight than mine," she spoke after gaining her breath once again. "But mine will only assist yours in causing you suffering. I will drag you into my darkness, and for that I would not forgive myself."

"You are wrong," such a simple declaration spoken in a firm tone told her that this man believed his words, but she would not give up so easily.

"No, sir, I do not think I am."

"My demons are threatened by your light," he said in a strangled voice, as if his words were causing him indescribable pain. "My pure sense of being is threatened by your life. They cower at your brightness and lose energy with your smiles. You are slaying them slowly, simply by existing."

"What do you wish from me with these words, sir?" Annabelle threw back, lifting her determined eyes to his. "I have nothing to offer you. No money, no connections, no family. Nothing."

"I want the purest form of you that was sent to me from Heaven," he began, raising his stare to hers, getting lost in her silver eyes. "I want to know all of you. Every single part. To heal your hurts and kiss away your tears. I wish for you and nothing more. I will keep you safe."

"Sir, I cannot afford to give myself to another," Annabelle replied, growing teary. "I belong to myself, and myself only."

With two large steps, closing the distance between their bodies, Mr. Worthington stared into her soul as he whispered, "woman, you have enraptured me. How can I go on without you?"

"I will be here, sir," Annabelle began as a tear betrayed her and slipped down her cheek. "But I will not be yours. You must find another. I cannot love you correctly and I am not deserving of such an emotion being directed towards me."

"What has caused you to believe such madness?"

"My life," the words slip out of her lips in a most determined tone. "You know nothing of what I have been through…"

"Then tell me so I may understand why you feel so," he interrupted, ignoring the possible repercussions of such an action.

"Has the man of stone cracked?" Annabelle let out a cynical laugh as she belted the words from her lips, a look of insincere disbelief marred her face. "Where is your foundation, sir?"

"You shatter me more each day," the sincerest tone he could muster laced his words. His heart was in front of her and he could only hope she did not grind the remnants into dust under her heel. "I cannot control my heart, no matter how I may try, the wretched muscle always turns back to you."

"Is that an insult, sir?" Her brows furrowed as, with a quick tone, her words snapped through the air like a crack of thunder.

"No, it is the truth," he almost pleaded with her to understand. "Do you think it is easy watching you from afar like this? But still my body tortures me by wishing to be close rather than let you stray far away. I need you here in any capacity for my sanity."

"Love is a weakness, sir," Annabelle looked away once these words leave her lips. The shame she felts fogged around her like the thickest clouds in her storm of emotions. "One I cannot afford in this lifetime, not that my God would allow it in any right."

"That may be true, but I have never felt as alive as I do near you, so I would take a weak man's life, if only I could be happy," Mr. Worthington murmured as his lifts her face closer to his, forcing her gaze to rise from the floor. "I have had a heart of stone, and it is indeed a cold existence. Now, do not think you have strayed my mind from your past, Miss Faraday. You can tell me, or the I can find out another way. Any information can be bought at the right price."

"Do not waste a shilling, sir," the words slipped out as soft as a breath. "It would surely be a waste on such a sorry tale. You will not hear the truth slip through my lips, nor will you find the information you are looking for. My past has been forgotten by everyone and everything, except me."

And with that she turned away from the brooding man and went back to the children, who stood across the field, unmindful of the heated confrontation taking place mere feet away from their joy. A distraction of laughter and smiles for Annabelle would certainly do the trick today.

****

"Grandmother, why did you stop?"

"My dear," the grandmother began, her voice hoarse from speaking for so long. "It is time for lunch, and I am in desperate need of a cup of tea to soothe my aching throat. I did not think clearly when I agreed to give you the entire story in only one day. My vocal chords are quite upset with me."

The little girl only giggled at her grandmother's description but nodded. She, as well, was in need of nourishment, a fact made blatantly obvious by the loud rumble that erupted out of her small belly and echoing across the room. The grandmother gave a horse laugh and bright smile at the action as pink tinged the young girl's cheeks.

"Come child, let us eat," the grandmother spoke as she slowly rose from her seat. She then extended her hand to the young girl as they ventured out of the study and into the dining hall for lunch. "We must feed you, and fast, before that monster in your belly takes matters into its own hands."

The girl let out another giggle as she skipped down the hall next to her grandmother.

"We will continue the story once lunch is over, will we not, Grandmother?"

"Of course, child," the grandmother spoke down to the girl while looking at her with fondness in her eyes. "Of course we will."

****

The tension from her last encounter with Mr. Worthington had been plaguing her body for days, and she could not wish time to go any faster as another visit with her dear friend was to take place in a few days. It had been far too long since the pair had seen each other as Annabelle's visit with Emma had been delayed by weeks, as the Worthington's did not leave the estate for Easter, forced to stay at Arrington and rectify the mess Mr. Worthington left.

Luckily, the conversation about her new visit did not take place with him. Annabelle approached Mrs. Kennelworth about the day first, only to be given almost immediate permission and transportation needs. She suspected the woman still felt horrid at the actions of her husband, but Annabelle would never bring the event up with her in conversation, so her musings were her own and not based on fact.

Once the flowers bloomed and the animals rose from their slumbers, however, Emma and her lovely husband Peter, had to take a last-minute trip to London. A wedding was in order for his cousin, and the pair was expected to attend, forcing Annabelle to wait two more weeks for her friend to return. Finally, the first Wednesday in May, she found herself in a carriage on the way to the Trowsdale Estate, where Emma lived and worked. She had wished to visit in the market again, only to be insisted upon by Emma through her letters that Annabelle had no choice but to visit her humble dwelling space. She was quite proud of it and Annabelle did not have the heart to deny her such a joy of walking her through her very own home.

Annabelle had to leave before the sun awoke to begin her journey. The 18-mile journey to the Trowsdale Estate would take most of the morn, and she was sure to not return by nightfall after spending the day with her friend. Mr. Worthington knew Mr. Trowsdale and had spoken to the man, but had insisted Annabelle return to Arrington, even after he offered Emma the next morning off to allow Annabelle to stay the night. The excuse for her return was that the children needed her, but even Annabelle knew he was worried of the world almost as much as she was since her dreadful encounter with Mr. Kennelworth more than a month before.

Awoken by the sunlight peering through the window of the enclosed carriage, Annabelle rubbed her eyes and sat up on the bench in hopes of composing herself before she arrived at the Trowsdale Estate. She peeled back the curtain to gaze outside and was struck by the beauty that surrounded her. They were travelling along the drive of the estate, not as long as Arrington's, but still grand. Annabelle was comforted with the knowledge that such an estate could support her friend with work for many years to come. She was sure this family would not lose their fortune any time soon.

While only able to catch a glimpse of the main house on the estate before the road divided to lead to the staff quarters, just the small glimpse had Annabelle in awe. It was a grand home, slightly smaller than Arrington, but warmer. She could tell more people cycled through the halls of this house than the one she had been assigned to, likely an active choice made by the family of the estate. Mr. Worthington disliked people far too much to open his doors more than absolutely necessary, but Annabelle found that she enjoyed the solitude Arrington had to offer. The children were not restricted to one wing of the home most days as there were few who came to visit, and even fewer who stayed the night. This led to Annabelle having almost complete access to the property, away from the prying eyes of society where the help was not treated with such luxuries.

Another ten minutes passed on this road before the carriage came to a stop in front of a small and worn stone cottage. It was sweet and perfect for her dear friend, Annabelle thought. Such thoughts were interrupted by the slam of a door and the distinctive squeal Annabelle knew well. Peeking out the window once more, Annabelle witnessed her dear friend hopping and waving to her as she skipped down her steps towards the carriage. Her body did not consult her mind when a bright smile grew on her face in response. She was just as overjoyed as Emma at their visit.

"My sweet Emma," Annabelle gushed as her friend met her at her carriage. They embraced in a hug so tight it would exhaust their lungs, but neither would let go until their bodies were screaming for air.

"Oh Anna, how I have missed you!" Emma gleefully replied.

The pair walked inside the small cottage arm in arm, reveling in the presence of the other.

After a quick tour of the lovely cottage Emma now called home, the women took comfort in Emma's parlor for a cup of tea in hopes of catching up. They had not seen each other in months and had much to share.

Annabelle listened as her friend spoke to her of her trip to London for the wedding, and her daily duties to the lady of the estate. She also listened to her speak with a sparkle in her eyes about her husband. All she saw on her friend's face was the purest form of love and gratefulness. This wonderful man had rescued her friend from a life of loneliness, and no matter how quick the courtship and wedding had taken place, Annabelle could clearly see the love they shared.

Peter popped his head into the room once he arrived home from work and greeted the ladies with a smile.

"Good afternoon, Annabelle," Peter greeted. "It truly is a pleasure having you visit with us for the day. Emma has been excited for your visit and spent all night last night fussing around the house preparing for your arrival. I was not even allowed breakfast this morning in fear that you would see unclean dishes on the counter..."

He was cut off swiftly by Emma slapping his arm with a gasp. The man merely responded with a sly smirk and a kiss to his wife's head. She quickly caught on to his ribbings and turned a bright shade of pink, but Annabelle could only softly giggle at the encounter.

"Sorry for the interruption, ladies," Peter began to bow out of the room. "I only wanted to make you aware of my arrival."

Turning to Emma, "my dear, I will prepare the meal for tonight. Are you joining us, Annabelle?"

Annabelle met his eyes with her own as she thought through the invitation, but the long journey back to Arrington loomed over her head, so she declined the offer. With that, Peter left the room and the ladies continued their hours long conversation. Annabelle listened intently to Emma's stories, and Emma giggled softly as Annabelle told the tales of the children she spent her days caring for. She also told her friend of the lovely staff of the house and of their dear friend Catherine.

"Emma, he made her a headstone," Annabelle began softly, emotion lacing her tone. "He gifted her a place to lay and ensured she would be remembered."

Emma was taken aback by the generosity the man had shown. From the stories she heard of the man, and of England's high society, she did not think any employer would do such a thing for a simple governess.

"Goodness Anna," Emma began. "I wonder why he did such a thing. Lovely as it is, I have never heard of an employer taking such an interest in the resting place of an employee, especially since you have told me he hardly knew our Catherine."

Annabelle studied her quizzical expression and wondered if she should inform her friend of the other encounters she had with Mr. Worthington. If anyone could assist her in deciphering his true actions, it was most likely Emma. She knew true love here with her husband, and just maybe she could help Annabelle understand how it felt.

"Emma," Annabelle began, continuing when her friend rose her eyes to meet hers. "How did you know you were in love with Peter?"

Emma jumped in her seat a little at the question. The sun was setting fast, and the room, now lit by candlelight and the embers from the fireplace, held a calming tone as the woman thought over her answer.

"I do not really know how to explain it, Anna," Emma began, smiling at the thought of her husband. "He just treated me so well. We could go on long walks and talk about everything and nothing for hours and I just never wanted the time to cease. He would always walk me right back to Auburn's door to ensure my safety and paid for everything when we would stroll through the market. He cared about me and wished a better life for me. But not only a better life, but a life with him. He worked so hard after we knew each other only days to ensure he could provide a life for me. Within weeks of knowing me, he had informed his employer, Mr. Trowsdale that he was going to be wed, and agreed to work harder and longer hours to be given this cottage for us."

Emma started to tear up while speaking about her husband as Annabelle wiped her own in happiness for her friend finding such a man.

"He just loved me, Anna. I do not know how else to explain it. I did not know how to love romantically, having been trapped in Auburn for so long, but he showed me. We sit in this room on this couch for hours each night speaking of our day and he helps me with the housework. We cook our dinner together when we choose to eat here, and he always wishes for my opinion when making decisions. Not many men care about their wives as he does. He does not need to care for my opinions, but he does. I have never felt so important to someone as I do him. I really do not know if this answers your question Anna, but I know in my heart that this love for him is true."

Annabelle did not know if such an explanation answered her question either, but she far too filled with happiness for her friend to think much on the fact.

After Emma composed herself, she suddenly broke the peaceful silence to ask a question.

"Why do you ask such a thing, Anna?" Emma began. "Have you met someone?"

Her voice was laced with excitement for she could not think of anything better for her friend than to find a man to love her as his own.

Annabelle did not immediately respond, causing a bright smile to light up Emma's face.

"You have, haven't you!" She accused.

"No, maybe, I do not know, Emma," Annabelle spoke, quickly exasperated by her friend's excitement. At her friend's urging, Annabelle continued to tell her all of the moments she had with Mr. Worthington. Shock was written across Emma's face when she found out just who this man was but kept her thoughts to herself as she listened intently. She smiled when Annabelle told her of their first meeting and her fierce words to the man, giggled when Annabelle described the afternoon spreading birdseed, and thanked the heavens when Annabelle told her of how Mr. Worthington saved her from the clutches of Mr. Kennelworth.

With a large hug and a few tears shed for her friend, she continued to listen as Annabelle described the afternoon spent in Catherine's meadow, and every instance of the man getting beat with a wooden spoon by a spritely cook. Through it all she listened, and held her tongue, attempting to figure out how to tell her friend what she had learned in London.

"Emma, I do not know what to make of this man," Annabelle spoke intently, wringing her fingers togethers as the very subject of Mr. Worthington caused her mind stress.

"My dear Annabelle," Emma hesitantly began to respond. "I feel as if there is something I should tell you."

Annabelle's inquisitive stare turned towards her friend as her eyes pleaded for her to continue.

"I asked about your Mr. Worthington whist I was in London with Peter," she spoke slowly, attempting to ease into the subject as much as possible. "And, as it would seem Anna, Sheridan Worthington has quite a prolific reputation. He is spoken about in every ball and at many teas of leading women on and tricking their hearts into love, only to flee back to Arrington and never speak of them again."

Annabelle attempted to absorb the information Emma was filling her head with as she continued to stare at her friend, waiting for her to continue.

"Do you understand what I am attempting to tell you, Anna?"

Furrowed eyebrows and a frown marred her features as she slowly shook her head. She was not pleased with the information given to her, but many men in society lead woman on, and she had expected as much of the man.

"Anna, he leaves once he is given what he wishes," Emma uncomfortably continued. "Once he has had their bodies, he leaves without a word."

"My dear Emma, I cannot believe that," Annabelle quickly responded. And she could not. The man who had nursed her wounds and smiled at his nephew and ran away from Mrs. Nettles in the kitchen surely could not be such a man. She had seen the fire behind his eyes once he saw the destruction his brother-in-law's actions caused her. While not the same, because Emma said the women were willing, she could not picture her Mr. Worthington behaving as such.

"Anna, it is true!" She urged. "It is spoken of at every instance. Should you bring up his name in conversation and suddenly the entire room is filled with broken hearts. He is one of the most eligible bachelors in England and uses his power as such. Giving young maidens hope for a future, only to leave without a word."

A sick feeling overtook Annabelle as she pondered the possibility of being deceived by the man. Were these really his true intentions? She had been surprised by those she thought she knew before, but these types of affairs seemed too far fetched for her to comprehend. With a nod, she allowed the conversation to move on, never fully re-engaging, as she found her mind racing until it was time for her journey back to Arrington.

"Goodbye, my lovely Anna," Emma spoke as she embraced her friend on her doorstep. The carriage idled only feet away, waiting for Annabelle, but she delayed as long as possible, hoping to hold onto this moment. "Thank you so much for your visit. I promise

I will write and arrange another. Maybe this time I can venture to where you lay your head."

Annabelle brightened at the idea, enjoying the thought of introducing her to Mrs. Nettles and Miss Bowden, and taking her to where Catherine lay.

"Yes, Emma," she replied through her smile. "I would like that very much."

With one more hug and a wave out the carriage window, Annabelle was off to Arrington. The long journey back drug on as the sun slipped below the horizon and the stars brightened in the sky. As much as she tried to stay awake, slumber soon found Annabelle, forcing her eyes shut and her mind to ease into a resting sleep, only to be awoken once the carriage pulled up in front of Arrington hours later.

The house was brightly lit on the inside, telling Annabelle that someone was awaiting her arrival. It did not take more than one guess for her to know who it was, but her conflicting emotions from Emma's earlier words caused Annabelle to walk around the building and enter from the kitchen, being let in by a tired Miss Bowden, and scurrying up the steps before the man of the house realized her actions. Inside her quarters she changed quickly and nestled into bed, hoping to fall back to sleep quickly, only to have a restless night full of conflicting emotions and confusing thoughts.

She did not wish to allow Mr. Worthington and his actions so much space in her mind, but it seemed as if he had wormed his way in and was intent on making himself comfortable.

CHAPTER 11

The next morn, Annabelle rose just as restless as the night before. Her thoughts waged war in her mind as she struggled to come to terms with the new information she had learned about her employer versus what she thought to be true from her own experiences. She simply could not imagine Mr. Worthington to be such a man, but she trusted Emma more than anyone in her life and did not see a reason for her to lie about such a thing. She hoped the words Emma heard in London were rumor, but her mind could not be completely sure.

Her distracted thoughts followed her through the day as she readied herself and escorted the children to the dining hall. Determined to avoid the man clouding her thoughts, she took her leave and ate in the kitchen with the company of a very lively cook.

"Child!" Annabelle was briskly pulled from her thoughts with the waving of an object in front her face. She jerked backward once she found it to be a spoon that she had come to avoid at every opportunity. She had seen it struck many and would not be its next victim.

"Yes, Mrs. Nettles," she carefully spoke, praying not to find herself on the bad side of the woman.

"Dearie," she began determinedly. "I have been attempting to speak to you for minutes. I slave over your breakfast, making your oats just the way you like and almost losing a finger preparing your fresh fruits and your ungrateful rear cannot even spend a moment in conversation with me. What is clouding your head, darlin'?"

The balls of Annabelle's cheeks tinged rose colored at the realization that she had once again been lost in her thoughts. Ducking her head hoping to hide the act from Mrs. Nettles,

Annabelle instead, chose to inquire about the rumors she had heard from her friend. She was sure the only other people who knew Mr. Worthington better than this woman were his parents.

"Mrs. Nettles," Annabelle cautiously began, choosing her words wisely. "What do you make of the rumor mill in London?"

A loud scoff echoed around the room as the woman began to formulate her reply.

"Dear child," she began with a sigh as she turned away from the counter she was wiping down, and back to Annabelle who was still poking at her fruit and oats, clearly in distress. "I do not pay any heed to such thoughtless words. Do these people who say such things know the heart of the person they are speaking of? If so, they would not be sharing such information with the public."

Annabelle rose her eyes to meet the woman, thinking over her words. The desperate look in her eyes told Mrs. Nettles who she had heard such things about, and she could see that the girl wished for none of them to be true.

"No one knows that boy better than I do, sweetie," Mrs. Nettles began, seeing the surprise light up Annabelle's eyes as she began speaking of Mr. Worthington. "And I can tell you that most of what they say about him is falsities. I have heard every rumor there is, but I raised that boy, so I know his heart. He is an easy target for he does not dispute what is spoken of him, but I know better than to believe such things, as should you."

"Mrs. Nettles," Annabelle began. "I do not know who you think I am inquiring about, but I can assure you, it was an innocent question not asked in relation to anyone in particular."

"Okay, Dearie," Mrs. Nettles spoke to pacify the young maiden. She could see in her eyes that she was correct, but the stubborn girl would never admit such a thing. Continuing before the governess could flee, Mrs. Nettles grasped Annabelle's hands away from her utensils and pleaded with her. "I can only advise you that if you should hear such rumors about someone you know and care for, you should speak to that person about it. There is nothing more accurate in revealing lies than looking into the eyes of the person you are inquiring about. The eyes will always tell you where the truth lies."

With a pat on the top of her hands and a warm smile, Mrs. Nettles turned back to cleaning her kitchen, leaving Annabelle to force herself to finish her meal and leave to tend to the children, only slightly less conflicted than before. She had more confidence in Mr. Worthington, but anxiety was rising in her at even the thought of speaking with him about such rumors. She had no right to throw accusations at him, but her heart needed to know the truth.

****

"Why do people say such things, Grandmother?" the young girl questioned about the rumors Annabelle heard about Mr. Worthington. The pair had concluded their lunch and walked together through the withering estate. She did not understand what the rumors were, but she could clearly tell they were bad.

"Sometimes, child, people say such things to ensure others will listen to their words," the grandmother began her response as the pair walked back to the study. Two cups of tea had done wonders for her voice, but truthfully, she was ready for her day, and this story, to be over. "When you wish more attention in society, and those you wish to be acquaintances with do not pay you any mind, people will say anything. I will not say more, for we are almost to this portion of the story. Be patient, young one."

With a few more steps, they found themselves once again in the study, settling back onto the couch by the window. As much as the grandmother wished for the story to cease, witnessing the profound interest her granddaughter held urged her to trudge on and finish it by days end. She would not let her leave tonight without the conclusion.

****

Annabelle had spent the remainder of her day in the children's study. They read Shakespeare, much to Lucas' dismay, for much of the afternoon. By mid-afternoon, Annabelle decided to turn the focus of the day to music. She had not spent as much time teaching Isabelle how to play her flute as she would have liked and found today the perfect day to do so. Reading did not distract her thoughts, nor did the children, but focusing on music, she hoped, may do the trick.

Annabelle had been teaching Isabelle simple nursey rhymes such as *Hot Crossed Buns* and hymns like *How Great Thou Art*, but Annabelle could clearly see that she would have to return to the market to purchase more difficult sheet music for the girl, as she was progressing at an alarming rate. Nevertheless,

Lucas sat on a chaise lounge across from the piano as the girls practiced their music, Isabelle on the flute following along to Annabelle's accompaniment on the piano.

"Isabelle, you are performing lovely at your instrument," a voice come from the doorway. Three heads quickly turned to the culprit to find Miss Bowden standing there with a smile on her face.

Isabelle, however, became as shy as she had ever been, only whispering a soft "thank you" as she hid behind her brown curls. Annabelle had tied a robin's egg blue ribbon in her hair this morning, so it would not longer hide her eyes, but the large curls still obstructed the girl's vision when she turned her head to the ground.

"Do not hide, Issy," Annabelle spoke intently as she lifted Isabelle's face in her hands. "Miss Bowden speaks the truth. You are progressing at a wonderful pace and you should be proud of such achievements. Do not shy away from such compliments. Not when they are deserved."

Isabelle nodded her head and turned to Miss Bowden to speak a louder and firmer thanks for the compliment with a smile.

Miss Bowden was sure Annabelle did not truly understand the impact she had on the children, but it was clear as day to the aging woman that this governess had transformed these children. Lucas behaved with manners he used to feign ignorance about knowing, and Isabelle no longer hid from attention, only becoming shy when she thought she was undeserving. Both children had never smiled so much in their lives, and their intelligence had risen by leaps and bounds. She knew they loved Catherine dearly while she was here, but Annabelle's firm tone and sweet smile seemed just the right balance for these two troublemakers.

As she walked out of the study and heard the music begin once again, she could not help but to think of the first day she had met the governess, flushed and out of breath after her long journey and completely in awe of everything that was Arrington Estate. She had fit in here and had become part of their family, whether she realized or not.

The three in the study bid a quick goodbye to Miss Bowden as she slipped out before returning to the music. The merry rhymes that were played brightened Annabelle's heart while the hymns brought peace to her soul. Even though she had pushed thoughts of the day before and the morning out of her head during her time with the children, Annabelle already knew she would speak to Mr. Worthington about what she had heard. Whether she had a right to the information or not, she needed to know the truth.

Dinner passed quickly with Annabelle once again eating in the kitchen, only this time she avoided the inquisitive gaze of Mrs. Nettles. She would never let the woman know she was correct about this issue, for she could not face her if the information she gained was not what she wished to hear.

It was only after supper that Annabelle had gathered enough courage to confront Mr. Worthington. While on her way to ready the children for sleep, she had heard two maids in the hall say that he was locked away in his study for the night taking care of business matters. It was as if God had created this opportunity just for her to confront him. She was almost sure this was the truth, for sometimes God puts his children in such positions where they have no choice but to follow through with His will.

After putting both Isabelle and Lucas to bed after a round of giggles and a nighttime prayer, Annabelle found herself in front Mr. Worthington's study, holding her breath. She knew she had to knock but wished to delay the encounter as long as possible. Fate was not on her side though, for right when she was about to turn around and abandon the entire encounter, the door in front of her was swept open and she came face to face with the object of most of her thoughts.

"Miss Faraday," surprise was clearly evident in his voice as he spoke to the young governess standing in front of him. She looked as if she had seen a ghost, causing his worries to immediately grow. "Is something wrong? Why have you come here at this time of night?"

It was when he questioned her that she moved her eyes to take in his state. His dark hair was a tousled mess and deep purple hues hung under his eyes. The man was clearly exhausted, made clear by his physical appearance, but Annabelle still found his presence endearing. Such thoughts confused her even more as she tried to come to terms with the knowledge that she had no choice but to have the conversation she had been avoiding since the morning.

Forcing herself out of her surprised state, Annabelle registered the questions directed to her and attempted to form articulate answers in her head. With a little shake and a couple of blinks, she began to speak.

"I am terribly sorry, sir," she began. "Nothing is wrong, I assure you. I only had a question to ask, but it can certainly wait until the morn…"

"Not at all, Miss Faraday," he rushed, stepping aside and holding the door for her. "Please come in."

She almost smiled at the invitation, remembering earlier encounters they had about the issue, but forced a stoic impression to cover her face as she nodded and began to step forward.

"What is it you had a question about, Miss Faraday?"

"Uhm," she began in an uncertain voice. She quickly cleared her throat hoping to gain a little more confidence before she began such inquisitions. "While visiting with Emma yesterday, a long conversation was shared between us."

"Ah, yes," he quipped while taking a seat next to the fire, the same place he had been the first time Annabelle entered this room. She followed suit, taking leave in the seat across from him. "I hope you enjoyed your visit."

"Yes, sir, I did very much," she spoke back, meeting his eyes with an uncertain smile.

"Is this what you wished to speak to me about?" He questioned. "I can assure you, your departure was no surprise. My sister informed me of every plan for the day."

"I am aware, sir," Annabelle replied, wringing her hands together. "Your sister was kind enough to inform me of such."

"Oh," confusion was evident on his face. She had been avoiding him like the plague and he could not fathom what had led her here tonight. "What is it I can help you with then?"

With a deep breath Annabelle bit the bullet and rushed out the words she had wished to speak since she had entered this room.

"Emma informed me of rumors that are spoken of you in London, sir," she rushed, gazing at his face to gauge his reaction. "Your relations with women were an apparent popular topic to discuss. I took note of them as simple rumors."

"Yes, Miss Faraday," his reply was deep and slow as he realized what had brought the governess here this night and was already thinking of what words to choose next.

"They are only rumors, sir, are they not," her whisper was so soft as her gaze had now found her fingers incredibly interesting. She would not raise her eyes to his and was not sure he had even heard her desperate plea, but nonetheless, waited for a reply.

"Have you never used something to ease your loneliness, Annabelle?"

"Sir, I must ask that you behave as a gentleman," she began in a steely tone, rising from her seat as she whipped her eyes up to meet his, outraged by his words. "Please address me as Miss Faraday."

As he nods, she continues. "To answer your question, yes, I have used the smiles and laughter of other to assist with my loneliness, but never once have I used the body of another to do such a thing."

"I do not use their bodies, Miss Faraday, I use their words," he strangled out, realizing how his London counterparts have made him look in the eyes of the young governess. He too stood up, ready to intervene should she run before he spoke his peace. "I look for conversation. That from someone who wishes nothing from me. Being from wealth is the goldest form of hell. Everyone wishes something from you and it forces you to question those who you can truly trust. I am seen as a man who breaks hearts and commits to empty promises only because once women realize who I am in society, they flock to me as dehydrated birds would to water. They wish one thing from me, and it wears on my soul each time. Then I come home to this vast estate to only be thought of as a merciless employer. I am not longer the young boy who used to wander these halls with laughter and smiles. I have been reduced to a lonely and stone-like man. It is only with Nettie and you that I feel less alone in this world. Even my own niece and nephew fear me, Annabelle."

He paused a moment to take in a large breath only to exhale a few moments later. "You wish nothing from me, and that causes me to wish to give you everything. You listen to me, no matter which words I choose to speak. Even now, you have stood here, listening to me when you are angered with me, and will give me an honest opinion once my words cease. You do not spit sentences that will appease me or allow my pride to swell. You give me honesty, and in this world, I could not ask for more."

Annabelle did not know how to respond. The man in front of her was not lonely of his own doing. He had shunned the world in the effort of self-preservation. Few were allowed inside of his head and even fewer in his heart, and somehow Annabelle found herself a home in both.

Conflicted, confused, and on the verge of what she assumed was insanity, Annabelle took two large steps up to the man and wound her wrists around his waist. Her ear above his heartbeat told her he was, in fact, real, and he was human. She had not allowed him such a luxury before, but as she listened to the blood pump through his body, and felt his arms slowly embrace her back, she had decided that he was only a mortal, like her, and mortals would always be allowed to make mistakes, just like she had decided this embrace was. She was falling fiercely but was doing nothing to soften the blow she would feel when she hit the ground.

The embrace lasted a few moments longer before Annabelle pulled away. She did not take note of the confusion that contorted Mr. Worthington's eyebrows, nor the way his hands tightened around her, as if it were a plea for her not to go. She simply twisted out of his grasp and made her escape, walking out the door somewhat relieved at the information she was given, but weighed down heavily by her heart.

Breaking out of his trance, Mr. Worthington had decided he would not lay down so easily this time. She would have not been so worried about the rumors that plagued his name had she not cared for him in a way similar to the way he cared for her. He felt it in the kisses they shared and the embrace they just experienced. He would never forgive himself if he let her get away this time.

"Do you really expect me to allow you to leave after such an embrace?" He questioned as he followed her down the hall. "I am certain now that I am not the only one who has such feelings for the other. Why do you run from them?"

It took him only seconds to catch up to her as she sped down the hall on the way to the stairwell. She was too lost in her thoughts to notice his boots clicking away but was more than aware of his presence when he grasped her elbow and spun her around to face him.

"Is it truly running if I am free to go?"

"Who said you are free to go, Miss Faraday," he shot back, frustrated at her unwillingness to acknowledge her feelings. "I happen to know you are still under my employ. I am sorry to say, Miss Faraday, but you are stuck with me."

"I will not be ruled by a man," she whipped around with blazing eyes to stare down Mr. Worthington. "I have spent most of my life alone and am quite certain I could spend the rest of it the same way."

"I do not want to rule you," he replied with an aggravated sigh. Sheridan Worthington has never had to fight such a battle before, but now had to fight for a woman. Much to his dismay, the battle was proving harder than he imagined. Worst off, he was losing miserably.

"No, but you wish me to defer my dreams for your sake, so you do not have to know life without me," taking a step forward, Annabelle squared her shoulders, preparing for the coming disagreement. "Is that not the same thing?"

"Defer your dreams?" Looking bewildered, Mr. Worthington simply tilted his head in confusion and continued. "Am I not your dream? Is love not a dream?"

"Sir, I have never cared much for the love of a man," she muttered. "They have always let me down, so you can be sure that I do not put much stock in the words of the male sex. I can count on myself and only myself. Love and happiness are things I have not known in a long time. They are things I am undeserving of. Do not waste your love on me, for I will not allow it to be reciprocated."

Taking a step towards the object of his affections, he replied.

"But why must you shelter yourself and cast yourself into the world's derision? Do not you deserve more out of life?"

"No sir, I do not," words spoken with such finality, Mr. Worthington did not know which words to choose to change her mind. She was clearly determined to believe such an idea. "And I will not be put in a cage by something as fleeting as love. It is not a virtue I possess, nor one I expect to deserve during this lifetime."

"What could possibly haunt you so?" He spoke gently, brushing a strand of hair off her face, only to reveal welling tears, ready to stain her cheeks. "Is not everyone deserving of even an ounce of love?"

"If you knew what I had done," she began as the tears broke free with vigor and flowed down her cheeks, falling to the floor. "you would not think me worthy of love either, sir."

"Let me make up my own mind on that fact," he replied lightly, reaching for her hands.

Quickly pulling away from him, she let out a wail and collapsed to the ground. "So much has happened to me in this life," she said sobbing into her sleeves. "Surely this is God's punishment. Taunting me with things I know to be forbidden to me."

Not knowing what else to do to heal her ails, Mr. Worthington fell to the ground next to Annabelle. He collected her in his arms and held her as close as he could while she stained his shirt with her tears. It was there that they sat, huddled together in their own corner of the world. Annabelle attempting to stop her tears while

Mr. Worthington would kiss her forehead and rub his hand up and down her back while she curled into his embrace like a child. She had not felt such comfort in years. An embrace such as this rivaled the ones her parents would give her when she would come crying to them with cuts and scrapes. Even once her tears ceased, Annabelle stayed, laying in between his legs with her back against his chest and her head resting against his shoulder, while he kept his arms closely around her, as if his embrace could ward away her demons for a few short moments.

She was confused, her heart ached, and every time she closed her eyes she saw the faces of her parents. Her guilt and the traitorous thoughts flying through her head were quick to tell her that such comforts were not made for her. They told her that her only comforts could be found after death, once she could finally apologize to those whom she had wronged. Her beloved parents, whom she had allowed to be broken.

It was selfish, really. To allow herself these last moments of comfort. She knew what she needed to do. She needed the hatred in her veins to cease and the voices in her head to stop. The guilt of being content in such a moment would not relent, and Annabelle was sure she was slowly going crazy. She could not continue to relive that night as she had been doing. No amount of comfort Sheridan Worthington could provide would ward off all her demons. She did not deserve love and he deserved better than a broken orphan.

She breathed in his scent one last time as she rose from his embrace without a word and walked away without glancing back.

One glance would cause her to turn and sprint into his embrace, and she could not risk that.

He did not say a word as he watched her walk away, but he knew he had not felt such peace as he did holding her in his arms. All the words of love his father had spoken to him finally made sense and for the first time in years, he felt his heart beat. He always knew it was there, keeping him alive, preventing him from being as cold and stoic as some accused him of, but with such a beauty in his arms, he felt the muscle twitch and throb. She had pieced him back together, but he almost knew that she would shatter him as well.

As he rose from the ground, Mr. Worthington thought over the situation multiple times in his head. He knew Annabelle would not come out for the night. She hid behind a mask of happiness, when she was truly broken inside. He always challenged her emotions and she could not process them all on her own. He felt needed. He felt as if he was put on Earth to ensure that this woman slayed her demons. She would need to do it herself, but he would gladly be there to pick her up when she stumbled, to sharpen her sword when her resilience dulled. She was strong enough, but she only needed to understand the difference between the angels and the demons, the difference between fact and opinion. She thought she did not deserve love, but she did. She thought Mr. Worthington could find someone else to make him happy, but he would never be able to give his heart to another, for he already gave it to her and was not strong enough to attempt to take it back.

He entered his study and paced the room, running his long fingers through his hair until he resembled a crazed man. How do you make someone see how truly worthy they are? The only way to understand her demons was to understand her, and if she could not utter the words of her past herself, Mr. Worthington had decided months ago that he would find someone who could inform him, and he had.

Louis Cuttle had arrived at Arrington hours earlier but requested a break and a meal before he would encounter Mr. Worthington. Detective Cuttle had worked in Scotland Yard in London for over 20 years, but as a personal favor to Mr. Worthington, had taken a leave of absence to inquire about the mysterious young governess. Mr. Worthington was compiling everything he already knew about Annabelle into a file for the investigator when Annabelle had shown up outside his door tonight. Her appearance had surprised him and momentarily deterred him from his original purpose, but now that he was once again left alone with his thoughts, he finished the file and began the trek upstairs to his guest's quarters.

"One moment," a deep voice husked from the other side of the door Mr. Worthington had just knocked on. Much longer than one moment later did it swing open to reveal a middle-aged man with a gut that showed his fondness for his wife's biscuits, which Mr. Worthington knew from experience were delightful. The wrinkles around the man's eyes became far deeper as he smiled, pushing his ash colored hair away from his forehead as he moved to embrace the much younger man in front of him.

"My, my Sheridan," he began, his voice thick from the sleep he was clearly enjoying moments ago. "They have taken care of you here, haven't they?"

"My father's staff has always been the best, sir," he replied, feeling like a child speaking to a superior. Louis Cuttle was one of the closest friends of the Worthington family, and the younger Worthington had known his father's friend for most of his life. He was one of the few people who could make him feel like a child again, but he would never complain. The people who knew him before he took over the business from his father treated him the best and were always welcome in his home.

"Ah, but they are your staff now, boy, as they have been for years," the stoutly man replied with a chuckle and a heavy hand on Mr. Worthington's shoulder. The younger man only responded with and uncomfortable shrug as he rubbed the back of his neck. Quickly picking up on his discomfort, the man moved away and invited the man, whom he still saw as a young boy, into his room knowing full well that an invitation was not needed. Mr. Worthington could enter any room without an invitation, but the manner-minded man would never do such a thing. "Now, what have you got for me?"

Mr. Worthington took a seat next to the fireplace while Detective Cuttle occupied the one across from him. Handing over the file, Mr. Worthington waited patiently as it was read by the inquisitive eyes in front of him. If anyone could find out about this girl, it was this man. Puzzles were favorites of his and a love of mysteries led him to the police force in the first place. Mr. Worthington had mammoth amounts of faith in this man and only hoped he would not let him down.

"You couldn't pick an easy one, could you Sheridan," the deep voice rumbled from across the room. A smile tugged at the lips of Mr. Worthington as he took in the words. He had chosen her, and he had not regretted his choice for a second, no matter how far she pushed him.

"No, sir," he slyly replied. "I guess I could not."

A boisterous laugh sounded around the room as Detective Cuttle rose from his seat with a smile. He had waited far too long for his Sheridan to find a girl to settle down with. In his last letter with the elder Worthington, he had been informed that Annabelle Faraday was a beautiful and kind girl. The Worthington patriarchs made it no secret to their friend that they wished for the pair to settle down. They had not yet met the young maiden in person but had observed her with their son at the annual ball and had decided right there that she was perfect. He would do all he could to find her story for this family, hoping it would help free her from her past and allow her to move on to a bright future.

"You know me, Sheridan," Detective Cuttle began. "I will do everything I can to find out about her. Are you sure this is all you have? It only speaks of an educated orphan left on the doorstep of Auburn years ago. The only Faraday family I have heard of claim to have no more living relatives outside their immediate family."

"That is all, sir," Mr. Worthington replied. "Any information you can find would be a great help."

The man only nodded in response. With a handshake and a goodnight, Mr. Worthington left the aging man to catch up on much needed rest. The journey he had taken from London was long and he would not be kept awake any longer than absolutely necessary. As Mr. Worthington ventured back down to his quarters to continue business dealings, he could not help but feel a storm on the way. The clouds earlier in the day had not looked kind, and he could feel the rain moving over the countryside as the air grew cold and thick, he only hoped it would pass quickly and with little damage. He was fairly certain Annabelle would not arise from her room during the night but could not bear the thought of her being tormented by another nightmare.

CHAPTER 12

Mr. Worthington was correct; Annabelle did not leave her quarters for the rest of the night, for she was preparing. As the dead of night approached, Annabelle feverishly packed all her belongings into her simple suitcase, falling apart at the seams. She could not spend one more moment in this household out of fear that she would lose herself. Having lost so much in life, she could not lose her identity to a man, let alone a man with a reputation. The tears on her cheeks were wiped away with her sleeve as she put out the fire in her room. Taking a moment to stare at the embers as they faded away, she could feel the darkness of uncertainty wrapping around her. The very thought of it was enough to suffocate someone.

Slipping out of her room, opening the door slowly enough that the creaks could not be heard, Annabelle tip-toed down the stairs. She should have expected to be caught, for nothing passed by Miss Bowden.

"Where are you going at this hour, child?" Miss Bowden inquired, wrapping her robe around her as she descended the stairs. Her hair was loosely held in a bun, falling on her face, and her clothes hung loosely on her body. She looked comfortable and at ease, for no one was watching her every move at this hour of the night. She looked as if she could laugh or smile or cry, or all three at the same time. She looked free. Annabelle was amazed how silence and darkness could shackle her, but the quiet and solitude relieved enough pressure to set Miss Bowden free.

"I am sorry, ma'am," Annabelle began, tears welling up in her eyes at the look of sadness that wiped across Miss Bowden's face in the dim candlelight. "I cannot stay here where I am prisoner to my mind. I must move on."

Miss Bowden uttered no words, she simply stepped down and wrapped Annabelle in a motherly hug and let her cry on her shoulders. Taking her hand, Miss Bowden then ushered her downstairs and walked her to the door.

"I never had a child," Miss Bowden said, cupping Annabelle's face in her hands. "But if I had, I imagine she would have been a lot like you." Tears flowed down her cheeks as she gave Annabelle one last embrace, understanding that she would not be enough to make her stay.

Annabelle tasted the salt of her tears as she wiped her face and let go of Miss Bowden's hand. "You are always welcome here." And with that, Annabelle disappeared down the steps and into the night, running away from love.

Within an hour of her departure, heavy rains descended upon her on her journey. The cool drops whipped through the air, biting away at her skin. Tightening her grip on her case, treaded along on the road, she decided she would take refuge for the night in the church in the town she had spent her whole life trying to flee. In the morning, she would continue her journey. She had no destination but was determined to run. Her shoes slipped into the mud, soaking her stockings and causing her feet to freeze. Possessing no glove, her hands felt the unforgiving elements at full force, as did her face. She kept her head down to ward off the wind, and moved as quickly as she could through the storm, hoping with every step that town would be within her reach.

Miss Bowden watched worriedly at the kitchen window as the lightning cracked across the sky, illuminating the violent and unforgiving storm clouds that she was sure lingered over Annabelle.

Roars of thunder rose Mr. Worthington from his bed as he recalled the first time a storm had enveloped the estate after Annabelle arrived. Every time he closed his eyes, he saw her from that night, pierced with sheer panic and layered with pain. Movement in the corridors caused him to open his door to find Miss Bowden walking the halls.

As Miss Bowden came closer into his vision he saw her wiping tears from her cheeks. A pit grew in his stomach as he feared the worst, for there were few things that Miss Bowden allowed herself to become attached to, but he knew Annabelle was one of them. He jumped down the stairs, narrowing the gap between the two of them.

"Why have you tears, Miss Bowden?" He asked in a soft and concerned voice, clearly searching for any other answer than the one she was about to give.

"The child," she began through soft sobs. "She has left us, Master." He closed the last steps between them and took her hands in his. He rarely showed any sort of affection for his workers, but he looked upon her with a pain in his eyes as he diverted his gaze toward the ground.

"Where has she gone?" He asked through a stutter and a choked voice, clearly in distress.

"She has left, sir, and has not told me where. We know very little about the girl. It truly was silly for me to become so attached, but there is something in her face that makes you wish for the world to be kinder. All I know of, is that she came from Auburn Academy, other than that, you would have to find something in her room, or someone who knew her better."

Thunder cracked through the sky, and Mr. Worthington suddenly grew fierce as his heart twisted inside of his chest at the very thought of Annabelle alone in such a vicious storm. His breathing grew stronger as he released his grasp of Miss Bowden and raced down the stairs towards Annabelle's room. Pushing the door open, he froze, unable to enter. With every glance, he saw something awful that had happened here. As he looked upon her bed, he remembered the night he had to rip his brother-in-law from her. The window held her nightmare, and the fireplace held her tears. There was nothing here that would help him find her. She left without a trace and was much too smart to leave a trail. He had to wait until morning to search for her and spent the whole night pacing in his study before the fire.

When his anxiety became especially violent he would sit in the chair she sat in the first time she was in this room. At one point, he even prayed. Putting aside the anger his eight-year-old self felt towards God when his beloved grandfather, who used to fish with him and taught him to hunt, was stolen from him, Mr. Worthington turned back to God and asked him to help her.

"I do believe in you, but my contempt runs deep," he said as he placed his stressed forehead atop his folded hands. "But she is out there tonight with no one, and your mother nature is a force to be reckoned with."

His prayer was slow and contemplative. Every word chosen well.

"I ask you put your muses for my demise aside and protect her. She loves you fiercely and passionately and believes in you like I never deemed possible. When she couldn't rise from her bed, she turned to you, and when her head could not rest at night, she spoke to you. I do not possess such faith, but would you punish those who do? She is alone, and she needs you. Please be with her."

Few tears streamed down his face as he turned to the one thing he had sworn off long ago for comfort. "Please, my Lord, do what I cannot. Save her."

Annabelle strode down the road in fierce determination as the rain pelted her from above. Her tears of frustration and heartbreak were mixed with the droplets of water falling from above, tainting them with salt and sorrow. She tried to ignore the howling pain in her heart and the hollowness that encroached on her mind with every step she took away from him. She had spent hours shivering from the night's cold, but now she could no longer feel. Her fingertips were ice and her feet felt as if they were trudging through a river. Mud dragged along her hem as the water wished to drown her. Little did the storm know she was already drowning in something much worse than mere liquid.

"Why?" She mumbled repeatedly. She pushed the word out harshly through shivering teeth and lips stained blue. "Why have you cursed me with this life?"

She knew she had come close to her destination as the road grew sturdier and buildings became more frequent. The little village that housed her torments was close, as was the church that held her peace the years she spent at Auburn.

Stumbling through the church doors in the dark of night, the sun was only mere hours from rising by the time she arrived. Annabelle's clothes were heavy and dripping from the cold rain that she had been walking in all night. Peeling off her coat and her hat, she sat shivering in a pew. Her face had gone pale and her hands grew colder by the minute as she knelt down to pray. Warm tears trailed down her cheeks, challenging the ice-cold raindrops that laid stagnant on her skin.

"Who is this man, and what has he done to me?" She questioned through her sobs and deep breaths. Her eyes were glued shut as she agonized over her heart and the pain she felt from her feelings for him, leaving him, and her long walk here. She clawed at her chest as if it would ease the distress she felt. Nothing had ever hurt her so much or been so difficult. The only event that rivaled this emotion was the loss of her parents, but even that was no match for the agony she felt, for this agony was entirely her own choice.

"God, save me. Save me from this man," she breathed.

His face flickered behind her eyelids as she remembered their first meeting and the arrogance that surrounded him. She then remembered sitting in his study with him, and in the children's study, berating him for his words about Catherine, and then her mind trailed to the kiss in the kitchen. For the first time in years, she felt completely safe in that moment, safe in his embrace.

Snapping out of her memories, Annabelle assured herself she made the right decision.

"I am not worthy of such emotions," she whispered. "Why be cruel and tempt me with happiness, Father? He has a reputation.

Surely, I would be wounded once again. I would not be gifted such a love in this lifetime. He cannot be real."

Her cold hands reached for a Bible as her body grew numb and her stomach started to turn. Her head had ached for hours, but it was growing with strength and ferocity as cold sweat began leaking out of her pores.

"If we confess our sins, he is faithful and just to forgive us our sins, and to cleanse us from all unrighteousness." She re-read 1 John 1:9 many times over, hoping she could apply it to her own life and forgive herself, since it was clear her Heavenly Father had already done so.

Her tears grew in strength as she remembered dancing with her father and standing on his feet as they swayed across the parlor of their home. She remembered the beauty of her mother and her soft voice and sweet smile, that of an angel, sitting in her corner, sewing a hem on a dress that Annabelle had torn while playing outside. The sunlight through the trees outside her window and the housemaid and the cook all played through her mind.

She paused her sobs long enough to hear her mother singing in the foyer with the birds outside every morning. Her mother would sway back and forth and eventually her father would come downstairs and grab her waist to dance with her as Annabelle sat by and watched the love flow between her parents. She heard her mother's voice telling her she loved her, and she heard her father's voice saying she was his world.

This was not what they wanted for their baby.

This realization sent Annabelle spinning and she grew increasingly delirious. She couldn't stomach the thought of disappointing her parents. Not after everything she had already done to them in her life. While her parents promised her a long life of freedom and travel, exploring all the worlds she learned about as a child, she only took away their chance to make promises to each other.

She did not have a home anymore, for no place without her parents could ever measure up. Her heart had always wished to fly with the birds and run away from this life and its memories, but she sat in the pew, anchored to her guilt, drowning in her tears.

The sweat increased on her brow as her stress grew monumentally. Only able to open her eyes for a moment, she saw the minister walking towards her in a rush. He must have heard the doors of the church burst open with her and the storm brewing beyond its walls. Her vision became blurred and suddenly, he multiplied as she fell to the bench and lay motionless. Darkness consumed her. The very darkness she thought she had been running from for years.

****

"Is she going to be okay?" the little girl pondered.

"Child, you must wait until the completion of the story," she replied.

"She has to be okay, Grandmother," the girl continued. "God saved her, didn't he? He saves his children."

"My dear, God can do whatever he pleases," she replied. "Annabelle made a choice to go out into the violent storm and the consequences of her actions are her own. God will not force us to do things. Everything we do is our own choice, and God will always use the consequences of our actions for good, even if we do not immediately see it, but with every decision, there are consequences, nonetheless."

"Grandmother?"

"Yes, dear."

"I am sorry for interrupting. Can you please continue the story?"

"Yes, my dear," she answered with a slight chuckle to her voice.

****

And just like that, she was back in her own personal version of Hell. The screams, the blood, the metallic scent floating through the air. She ran as twigs bit at her feet and leaves latched to her hair similar to a leech. She had been told to run, and she had done so ever since, holding the world at arm's length, where it could not hurt her like this night did.

She couldn't breathe and the only light to be found was the luminescence cast down to Earth from the moon. She ran and ran until her legs gave out. Cascading to the forest floor, her body lay there a moment before crawling through the dirt to a burrow where she hid until daylight. Things were not so scary in the light of day.

The scene behind her eyes played over and over in a rushed sequence forged to break her heart and crush her soul. The guilt crashed through her as her mother's screams and father's pleas filled her ears. Eventually the scene slowed enough to be decipherable and as it began once more.

She was in her country home. Her father was a Duke but wished to live a humble life and chose to forego the family Estate for much of the year and grew his family in the summer home. It was big enough to be considered wealthy, but small enough to be considered home. It was here, in the English countryside where Annabelle grew. With few staff that became family as the years drew on, a quaint life was lived by Annabelle and her parents. Annabelle was free here. She roamed the gardens as she pleased and ran through the fields daily, the wildflowers nipping at her hem. She would skip through the woods and climb the tallest trees, and every morning, she would wake up to the sweet sound of birds and her mother's hums. It was a life some would dream of, and it was all hers.

One summer day, a horrendous storm rolled through the country as night fell upon the home. Annabelle, a mere child at the time, loved the storms that graced her summers. She would watch the rain trickle down her window and the lightning flash and dance across the clouds, black as night. Nothing could hurt her while she was wrapped in the safety of her family home. This night was just like any other. Her parents had tucked her away underneath her blankets and bid her goodnight with kisses to her head. A single candle burned slowly and quietly on the table next to her bed.

She had stayed up past what was reasonable for a child, but she did not take note of the fact for she was far too mesmerized by the storm. Her eyes glittered with every flash of light and her smile grew brighter as she felt the rumbles of thunder echo through her bones. The outside world was beautiful and blurred through the raindrops on the glass that separated her face from it. Fortunately for Annabelle, her love of storms just might have saved her life.

****

"Grandmother," the young girl began, tentatively, "what happened that night?"

"My dear," the aging woman responded quietly, "we have not yet delved into that part of the story. Patience child, we will get there." She continued with a chuckle.

The young girl only pouted and waited for her grandmother to begin speaking again.

****

It had been three days that Annabelle had slept and three days since Mr. Worthington had moved from the chair beside her bed, except to bathe and change his attire. Detective Cuttle had left the morning after he arrived, determined to find all the pieces to Annabelle's puzzle and hopefully assist in uniting the two.

The days had drug on with no noticeable changes in Annabelle's condition, causing the entire household copious amounts of emotional stress. The doctor sat by her bedside while draping a wet cloth along her brow to aid her persistent fever. It was at this moment that Annabelle began to whimper from the nightmare she relived repeatedly. The fire cast the only light across the room as she slowly and weakly stirred in the bed that did not belong to her, the room she was unfamiliar with.

Slightly delirious from her dream, Annabelle did not take much note of her surroundings, but when her eyes fell upon the man cast in shadows, with the same greens eyes that still looked like fiery dragons when the embers reflected in them, she let out a soft and tired sigh. Her emotions were a mess and her head was still spinning. Before falling back into her darkness, she let few words pass her lips.

"What have you done to me?" She asks, barely able to speak.

"I suppose the same thing you have done to me," he replied as she fell, once again, into unconsciousness.

The dream was no longer a dream, but in fact, memory. Young Annabelle was gazing out on the storm when she heard a loud and violent crash ring through the house, followed by quick footsteps. She assumed a branch must have caused damage to the house and heard her father as he went downstairs to check. It was not until she heard more crashes and bangs, and finally, her mother's shouts, that she grew increasingly anxious and agitated. Something deep within her told her that something was not right, and her small legs jumped from the bed to search for comfort, a comfort only her parents could bring.

She trailed slowly down the candlelit hallway and treaded carefully while descending the creaking stairs into the foyer of the home. Lifting her eyes once she reached the last step, Annabelle saw the wooden door cracked and twisted, hardly holding onto its hinges. Taking in a quick breath, she felt her heart start to pump harder and faster until she could hardly hear because of the blood flowing through her. It was as if she no longer had control over her body as her feet took tentative steps towards the parlor at the front of the house where she heard most of the commotion.

The candlelight from the foyer began to dwindle and Annabelle became cloaked in darkness as she neared her destination. She lifted her delicate fingertips and drew them along the wall that was decorated in velvet floral designs; another sign of her family's wealth. With each rumble of thunder, Annabelle felt her bones rattle and heart skip and with every bolt of lightning her anxiety grew higher and higher.

She could not hear the words being shouted but could tell they were getting louder as she neared the parlor, only confirming the fact that she was venturing in the correct direction. Tears began to pool in her eyes as dread and fear clenched around her heart much like a snake would do to asphyxiate its prey. Still she fought her emotions and ventured on. Her father was her hero, there was nothing he could not overcome, and if there was, Annabelle, as his baby, would do anything to help her parents stay happy.

The door to the parlor was cracked open and light poured out of the sliver and into the hallway. Stopping in front of the wooden door, the small girl held her eye to the opening and had to bite back a gasp at the scene in front of her.

Her parents. Her beloved and fearless parents sat in the corner of the room, dimly lit with few candles, with distinct fear in their eyes. In front of them was a man whom Annabelle could not recognize from the back. She willed herself to take deep breaths to silence the pounding in her head as the rest of her body stood frozen. She felt tingles erupt over her skin and knew her hands were becoming clammy. Suddenly cold, the young girl began to shiver, watching her parents cower in fear.

No matter how many silent prayers Annabelle sent up in those last few moments, she was not enough to save her parents. The man pulled out a large piece of metal that Annabelle now knew to be a revolver and shot at her father, silencing his desperate words attempting to coax the man to cease his action. Her hero let out a strangled cry as he crumbled to the floor as her mother fell into a fit of tears next to him. Her daddy was hurt, and Annabelle could not will her body to move to help him, all she could do was muster up a heartbreaking sob behind the door, an action she quickly realized was a grave mistake.

The man's back tensed and Annabelle witnessed her mother's eyes widen as her head whipped towards the door, where she met the frightened eyes of Annabelle.

"Baby, please," her mother began to whisper. "Run." She put on her best smile for her daughter in hopes she would follow her orders.

It was in this moment that the man chose to turn around, searching for the source of the cries. His eyes landed on Annabelle, and immediately glistened with recognition.

"Well, what do we have here?" He taunted, edging closer to Annabelle, as her mother began breathing frantically, still clutching onto her now lifeless husband.

"Mi-Mister Gunter?" Annabelle inquired through a whimper. She remembered the stout man who used to tend the family gardens. Her father had recently released him once he found him attempting to steal her mother's jewels. She could not understand why he was here or why he had hurt her father, but even a child could see he was not well. Covered in dirt and wafting a putrid sent off himself with every movement, Annabelle grew more nervous with each step he took in her direction.

"Well if it is not pretty little Annabelle," He continued, edging closer to the cowering young girl. "I am so terribly sorry you had to see me do that to your daddy," he exclaimed, although Annabelle doubted the sincerity in his words after seeing the smile on his face, yellow teeth on full display.

Annabelle opened and closed her mouth multiple times and the man began to reach for her, suddenly losing all the words of her vast vocabulary. She twisted at the last moment and tried to run, only to be pulled back by the deranged man and thrown onto the ground. The young girl landed in a pile of glass from one of her mother's favorite vases that had toppled over. All she could do was stare at the hand painted pieces scattered on the floor, not registering the large piece that had cut deep into her back. It was not until she heard an inhumanly growl come from Mister Gunter that she remembered herself and her situation.

The last thing she saw before she shut her eyes as tight as possible were his hands flying towards her face. It was in this moment that Mr. Gunter was pulled back violently by two thin arms, his grunts of discomfort causing Annabelle to whip her eyes open.

Watching her mother's curls fly through the air as she flailed around the man, attempting to grasp the gun, Annabelle felt a chill wash over her once again. Looking towards her father, all she saw was his motionless body and she knew the life in him was gone. The red that pooled underneath him on the floor told her as much. It was then that the tears that had been plaguing her eyes final decided to fall.

"Annabelle, run!" Her mother's shrill scream pulled her from her shock as she gazed up at her mother, fighting a losing battle, if only to give her baby a chance at life.

"Mommy!" She cried in return as she took a step towards her mother who continued to struggle with the man.

"No baby," her mother responded, scolding her for coming towards her. "I am going to be with Daddy, so he will not be alone, but first, I need you to run."

Her words were broken up by large breaths and grunts of pain, but Annabelle heard every single word.

"Who will be with me, mommy?" the little girl cried, not wanting her parents to leave without her. She knew she should run but could not bring herself to leave her mother alone with such a scary man.

"You will come back to us," she replied in a breathy voice, signaling her strength was fading. Annabelle's father tried to reason with the man and save his family, but without him here, her mother had to fight, and she was slowly losing. "You will come to us after you have lived a long and beautiful life." Tears began to fall out of Annabelle's mother's eyes as the fight was slowly lost. She would fight until her daughter was safe, then she would follow her husband home.

"Now, baby, RUN!" her mother shouted in strangled voice. "Run darling, run!"

"Run and live a beautiful and happy life baby!"

"Okay Mommy," Annabelle said through her tears and heartbreak as she turned and ran as fast as her small legs would take her out of the house. As she headed down the hallway she heard a cry of pain from her mother and a distant scream which sounded close to "I love you baby!"

She ran as fast as she could out of the house and into the woods as she heard more shots ring through the halls of her once beloved house. The only place she had ever known love and happiness. She ran straight into the night, through the rain that bit at her skin, cold as ice, and under the watchful eyes of the moon. She ran until she could not run anymore, only to drift into a dreamless and restless slumber on the forest floor until she was found, a crazed mess, the next morning, caked in mud, sweat, blood, and tears. None of her words could be understood as she screamed and shouted and cried in grief and confusion. She kept trying to run back to her house, but the family that found her on their morning walk had to restrain her until the constable arrived. It was not until Annabelle dragged them back to her house, having the location of her home being the only intelligible words she spoke, did the gruesome scene from the night before becoming visible in the light of day.

Annabelle cried and was forced to tell the officers as much as she could. All she wanted was to go inside and see her parents. Run to them and have them embrace her and tell her the night before had only been a monstrous dream, but such a thing would never happen. Annabelle was guided back into the house only to pack as many belongings as would fit in her small trunk and after having her wound cleaned and patched, she was shipped off to the closest family she had.

Her parents' home and the entire estate was given to her Uncle Monty, the last living relative on her father's side who had fallen out with her father years earlier. He could not find any compassion in his heart to care for Annabelle, beyond shipping her to Auburn Academy and paying for her entire education and an occasional new dress. Over the years, he stopped even doing that much and disappeared from the girl's life completely, not that she minded. She understood very quickly that she could never rely on him or any family she may have scattered around the globe. She could not even remember where in the world her beloved childhood home had been, not that she would ever go back now. The memory was tainted with evil, darkness, and sorrow; three things she had far too much experience with and would distance herself from wherever possible.

The scene continued to play behind her eyelids like a play on a stage, repeatedly while her mind attempted to escape this prison it found itself in. She had no idea what was occurring in front of her closed eyelids and was not sure whether she was safer in the confines of her nightmares or opening her eyes to the possibility of another one in real life.

****

"Grandmother," the small child inquired of her elder.
"Yes, Dear?"

"Did they ever catch the bad man? They had to have found him, correct?" Tears were filling the young girl's eyes as she looked up at her grandmother with fierce hope.

"I am not sure, Darling," she began to answer her granddaughter with a comforting smile. "No one told her anything of what happened after she walked out of her house with her trunk that day throughout her childhood. She did not hear another word about the horrible event after her parents were laid to rest."

"Yes, grandmother, but what about the bad man?" The young girl wanted her question answered. It was as if an answer would appear out of thin air if she asked the same question continuously.

"At the time, no one told her what happened to Mr. Gunter. She did not know if he was withering away in a jail, dead, free and living his life, or searching for her looking for revenge. The thought of him finding her one day washed through her nightmares as well. She was a mess. Always had been, and she perceived herself always being one. Her demons were simply too great to fight, and she was drowning in the sorrow she felt."

"But she was safe at Arrington, was she not?"

"The illusion of safety is all in our minds, child," her wise words filled the small child's ears. "You are as safe or as threatened as you let yourself believe, and when you wage war with your fears every single day, safety is not something that exists in your mind."

"So, Annabelle was not safe?" The little girl twisted her head to the side to show her confusion. She had only felt fear when her candles went out at night during storms, but even then, she simply went to her parents' room and fell asleep in her father's arms. How could Annabelle not be safe with Mr. Worthington around?

"Annabelle thought the promise of safety through Mr. Worthington was not deserved by her. She was fearful of what happiness could look like and mean for her, child. She did not think she was enough to keep the man happy, and she was afraid of once again being shackled somewhere with no way out. She did not want to be trapped again, as she was at Auburn. She had wished for freedom for so long, but she did not realize that the freedom she was wishing for was not freedom to leave, but a freedom to stay. Her fears paralyzed her into believing she had to run away from her problems, like Mr. Kennelworth, or Mr. Worthington's love. She thought that by making her own choices in life, she would be able to find happiness. By taking back the power of her future, she could find it. Unfortunately, the only way she would find happiness would be to fight her fears, not run away from them. That is what was hidden from her. She did not know how to fight her fears, thus causing her to run from those that embodied them the most. She feared hurting another person she loved, so she ran. By running, though, she hurt him more than she could have ever done had she stayed."

"Grandmother, I still do not understand." The young girl's face scrunched with frustration and confusion. She liked Annabelle and wished she could understand why she ran so much. She loved her home, why could Annabelle not want one? She did not know that Annabelle did not understand all her reasons either. She only ran from such strong emotions in hopes of saving both of their hearts.

"Let me finish the story, dear, then I will answer all your inquiries." The young girl only responded with a quick nod and a small smile, signaling her grandmother to continue.

****

"Thank you, doctor," Mr. Worthington stated the next day while shaking the man's hand. No more could be done for Annabelle medically, and now they only needed to wait for her to awake from the hellish sleep. Her fever was almost gone and her body, while weak, was growing stronger.

"While this is not a pleasurable moment, sir, I am more than happy to do my job successfully," the stout man replied in a gruff voice. "I am just pleased that I was able to help the young lady before the fever took her. She surely is much too young to die."

Mr. Worthington averted his gaze to Annabelle's form laying on the bed as he responded to the aging man's sentiment. "Yes, yes she is."

He did not bid the doctor goodbye and did not watch him leave. His eyes were glued to pale and sweat riddled face of the governess. Releasing a sigh and sinking deep into the chair next to the bed, Mr. Worthington read through the documents on his lap once more. He would be foolish to think he could hide from his business, even while tending to the maiden. It was not so bad, he thought. He could distract himself from the curiosity and pain he felt every time he glanced at the young governess lost in slumber only feet away from him.

He was lost in his own thoughts, staring at the pieces of parchment between his fingers when Annabelle shuffled on the bed, causing his eyes to shoot up and his anxiety to rise significantly.

As she opened her eyes, her whimpers from the fearsome dream finally ceased. She was no longer reliving her worst night. The light from the windows felt as if it were attempting to blind her. Mr. Worthington took notice and promptly closed the drapes, casting the room in the orange glow from the fire.

Finally, able to take notice of her surroundings as her weak arms attempted to force herself higher up the bed, Annabelle realized she was once again in the estate she had run from. Scared of his reaction and ashamed of her actions, Annabelle cast her eyes to her fingers which lay in her lap, refusing to look up at the face of the man she so deeply cared for.

"Why did you leave?" He questioned her.

"Why did you wish me to stay?" She threw back shortly. "Do I have not a right to make decisions on my own? I was not happy here, and so planned to move on."

"You were not happy?" He questioned, his voice taking on a vulnerable tone with a hint of weariness. "How can one be so unhappy at home?"

"This is not my home," she replied tersely, feeling the tears growing in her eyes. "I do not have a home, sir. All I wish for is freedom to venture off to find new employment."

"You have not been dismissed, Miss Faraday," he spoke to her in a lighter, softer tone. "You are not given leave to move on."

"What are you saying, sir?" She questioned desperately as she wrapped her arms around herself and rubbed the jagged scar that had been ripped into her skin. A constant reminder of the night she had spent life trying to forget.

"You will return as governess," Mr. Worthington stated as he placed his folded hands on the side of her bed, moving his body to the edge of his chair.

"You would put me in a cage?" She replied in anguish.

"I do not possess the strength to set you free."

His head hung low as he rose from his seated position and moved to the door. His footsteps paused once he reached the doorway to say in a whisper, "I haven't the will, either."

He then exited the room as Annabelle listened to his boots tap down the hall and fade away down the stairs. She turned her face from the door to the window. Even with the drapes closed she could imagine the birds dancing through the skies with no borders or walls holding them in. A tear fell from her eye as she believed her freedom had been stripped from her and her last chance to escape was stripped with it. She could not run from her nightmares any longer, for they had found her, and she had nowhere to go.

****

"Why did she not want a home?"

"I do not think it was that she did not want one, my dear," the grandmother replied. "I do not think she understood what a real home was. I do not think she believed herself to be worthy of such a place either."

"Grandmother, where is your home?" the little girl inquired.

"Come child, I will show you," she responded, slowly rising from her seat, stretching her aching joints, and beginning to move towards the door.

"But Grandmother," the child began with a pout on her face. "Is your home not here? What about the story?"

The elderly woman held out her hand to the young girl and beckoned her forth. "No, child. This is not my home. Do not fret little one, we shall continue the story on the way."

With a bright smile, the young girl jumped from her seated position and skipped towards the door to follow her grandmother on another adventure.

CHAPTER 13

Mr. Worthington did not visit Annabelle again that day. She laid, confined to the unfamiliar bed she awoke in for the remainder of the day, cloaked in darkness. The doctor came by only once more to assess her symptoms and a maid came through to offer her more blankets, deliver a doctor approved meal, and start a fire. She had been informed by the doctor that she had slept for three days and had been visited by most of the staff throughout that time.

The comfort she felt at hearing that those who called Arrington home still cared enough to check-in on her condition faded quickly as she was left alone after she awoke. Not one soul had knocked on her door, and very few footsteps were heard travelling down the hall, none ever stopping by her door. She knew in her heart she had hurt those who had cared for her so freely, and she had no idea how to repair such damage.

The unfamiliar room grew dark as the embers began to suffocate, much as Annabelle had been doing cooped away in a corner of the estate. She did not know where in the grand home she had been placed, but such luxurious rooms were only given to the grandest of guests, so it was clear she was not in the staff quarters. Her meal, a warm chicken soup, had been forced down her throat. She felt no hunger, but with a fear of Mrs. Nettles spoon, Annabelle ate as much as her stomach would allot. She did not wish to cause this household any more distress and being difficult would not be welcomed kindly.

Two more days of solitude passed with Annabelle's only interaction being that of the doctor and the maid that would help her bathe and deliver her meals. Her body still protested every movement and her sneezes and painful coughs were the only sounds that would crack through the silence that surrounded her. It took nearly all of her energy just to travel across the room to pull open the curtains that hid the windows light from her eyes. The mornings brought the birds to the sky, but the glass from the sealed windows shut out their song, forcing Annabelle to bask in their beauty, but not their music. After days surrounded by only her thoughts and regrets, she desperately needed to be bathed in light, for the darkness was clouding her mind more than ever, and she could not let it take hold of her body. The locks on the windows had been stuck. Annabelle could not force them open and those who could had yet to visit her.

Her solitude was thankfully shattered on her fourth day confined to the bed after she awoke. Light knocking sounded, drawing her gaze from the window to the door to see Miss Bowden creeping through the doorway, a cautious expression masking her face. Annabelle could already see the woman was nervous of this interaction, even though she had no reason to be. Annabelle owed so much to this head of the house. She had taken her in, taught her all she needed to know, allowed her to leave when she wished, and cared for the children when she could not. Love filled Annabelle's heart at the mere thought of the woman and seeing her in person only cause such love to grow. She would forever be grateful to the lovely Miss Bowden.

"Hello Dearie," the aging woman began. It was clear the number of stairs she had to climb to reach the room had taken its toll, but the woman persisted on until she settled on the edge of the bed Annabelle laid in. "And how are we feeling?"

Annabelle smiled as the back of Miss Bowden's hand pressed against her forehead, checking for a fever.

It was a maternal act, and a display of the care she had for the governess.

"I am well, Miss Bowden," Annabelle replied in a hoarse voice, having not used her vocal chords much in the past days. "My head aches still, but the pain is faint. I am told I should be allowed to walk on my own tomorrow so long as my joints no longer throb."

"I am so glad to hear that, my dear," wiping a tear from her tired eyes, Miss Bowden let a small smile lift her wrinkling face. "We all have been terribly worried for you, but Mr. Worthington would sooner fire us all before allowing us in your room while you are awake. He wishes for nothing to impede your recovery. Not even him."

"Do the children know?" Annabelle was still in shock of the realization of why she had spent so many days alone but needed to know the answer to her question. Miss Bowden needed no clarification before she gave an answer.

"Yes, my dear," she replied sorrowfully. "They are bright ones, those two. When they saw you being carried in by Mr. Worthington and up to this room, they hid down the hall and heard everything as he spoke to the doctor. It was not until I found them that they were removed from their spot."

"How are they taking it?" Annabelle was unsure if she wished for an answer, but knew she needed to know before confronting the children.

"Lucas is very upset," Miss Bowden responded, casting her gaze to the quilt that covered the surface of the bed. "Isabelle refuses to speak about it, but they are aware that you ran away. They are very confused, Annabelle. All of us are. We thought you had found happiness here."

Guilt immediately crept up Annabelle's spine as she listened to the words leave Miss Bowden's lips. If there were people she never wished to hurt, Lucas and Isabelle were at the top of her list. They had been hurt and abandoned by so many, and they did not cross her mind when she selfishly fled, but now she would have to seek atonement for her indiscretions towards the children.

Annabelle had opened her mouth to respond to Miss Bowden when the woman simply placed her hand atop hers on the bed.

"I do not know what haunts you so, child," the head of the house spoke in a comforting tone, as a parent would speak to a child. "But should you ever need to talk, I do hope you know I am here. I presume you will not be leaving again, at least for some time, and I make a lovely cup of tea, should you ever need one."

With tears brimming in her eyes, Annabelle flashed Miss Bowden a misty smile as the woman rose and strode to the door after kissing the young governess on her forehead with a promise to visit again soon. She could not be sure when that would be, as the children fell to her lot, but she would return.

As the door shut behind the woman, Annabelle once again found herself alone and a prisoner to her thoughts. Her heart ached at the thought of the pain she must have caused the children. She scolded herself relentlessly for such selfish acts. She had been so lost in her guilt and heartache that she did not think of the pain she would inflict on those who cared for her. She left in a panic, leaving a storm of hurt in her wake, only to return to the mess she left behind with no idea on how to rectify it.

After dinner, Annabelle fell into slumber with such thoughts still plaguing her mind. She realized her actions were wrong, and had only wished she had known so sooner, before she every stepped foot outside into the unforgiving storm. She would have saved those she cared for so much stress had she thought of others first.

It was on the fifth day in her confinement that Annabelle could move around the room with ease and little reluctance from her lungs. She feared leaving her room for the thought of running into anyone who had considered her family was far too daunting, but she did enjoy being able to move freely, no longer confined to a bed for the majority of the day. The maid had even been kind enough to deliver a few books from the estate's library to Annabelle to help her pass the time.

It was around midday when Annabelle found herself lost in the words of the Bible. Philippians 2:3 was haunting her thoughts.

"Let nothing be done through strife or vainglory; but in lowliness of mind let each esteem other better than themselves."

Confusion encapsulated her as she thought about the situation she had found herself in. In the morning her breakfast had been delivered by Miss Bowden who did not stay long, but only spoke well wishes to her. Lunch brought Mr. Longfellow to her door delivering her favorite soup from Mrs. Nettles as the man of few words swallowed emotion as he spoke of how pleased he was to hear her health was recovering. He brought with him a bouquet of bright flowers from the garden from Mr. O'Connor and smiled for the first time Annabelle had ever seen before he left.

This estate full of people were forgiving her for her actions so quickly. She had wronged them in the worst way and left without a word of goodbye, but no anger lingered in their eyes and no harshness covered their words. They simply wished her well, and she could not fathom why. She could not forgive herself for the pain she caused them, so why could they.

It was almost time for supper when she opened her eyes to the fact that these people understood the Bible much better than she ever did, whether they read the book or not. They had put aside their emotions and had put those around them before themselves. They would not throw cruel words at Annabelle, for they still cared for her, and would love her when she was not capable of loving herself. And while she could not fathom why they cared so much for her after knowing so little about her, she felt her heart warm at the compassion they showed her with their actions. They only wished for her to be in good health and return to their family, nothing more. This, Annabelle realized, was the unconditional love she craved.

Once again, though, she was broken out of her thoughts by a knock at the door. The last person she expected, though, was behind it. She had not expected black boots to cross her threshold, or a tired man to regard her cautiously. He stood at the foot of the bed where she lay. His posture was stiff, and his hands were clasped behind his back as he looked down towards her. She noted his unkempt appearance or wrinkled clothes and disheveled hair, and the mud stains on his knees.

"What have you been up to today, Mr. Worthington?" Annabelle questioned after a moment of silence. If he would not start a conversation, she would, making sure her curiosity is sated.

"I have been in the fields with the staff, Miss Faraday," he responded, not meeting her eyes. "It is in the fields where I do my best thinking."

Surprised did not come close to what Annabelle felt in this moment. She had seen the man fishing and hunting through the seasons and had even seen him assist the staff in clearing the fields when the gardens were being expanded, but she did not think he enjoyed such work. It seemed like a tiring task that a business man would look down on. Her uncle Monty would often berate her father for such things when Annabelle was young. She would listen in on their conversation when she should have been sleeping, but curiosity always seemed to get the better of her.

"Is that right, Mr. Worthington?" She replied. "And you do not see such work as menial or below you? I was told as a young child that no business man belongs in a field."

"And who, prey tell, told you that, Annabelle?" He shot back, clearly sensing the governess' desire to bicker. "It does not sound like such a thing your parents would say."

"And how would you know what my parents would say, sir?" She questioned shortly. "You knew nothing of them."

"Maybe so," he spoke, levelling his tone. "But I do know of you, Miss Faraday, and you were raised by them. I have seen you sit with the grace and poise of a queen and climb a tree better than a schoolboy in trousers. If your parents were so against a man of business in a field, surely they would not let their daughter go frolicking in the trees."

Annabelle found herself stumped as to what to say next. She did not mean for the conversation to turn into a heated discussion, but such things always happened when Mr. Worthington was around. Her emotions were heightened and were clouding her mind, and the haggard man in front had gotten the brunt of her frustrations. She felt sorry but could not find it in her to say such a thing at the moment.

"Regardless, Miss Faraday," Mr. Worthington spoke, effectively changing the subject. "That is not what I ventured here in hopes of discussing."

"What can I do for you, sir?" Her voice was shallow, nothing more than a whisper as defeat washed over her. She did not know where these fiery emotions were emerging from, but this was not her. This woman she had become was not the kind girl her parents had raised, and Annabelle was losing sight of how to return to that girl.

"Your future, Miss Faraday," he began. "That is what I wish to discuss."

It was in this moment that Annabelle rose her gaze to meet his. Her grey eyes were dull and lacked the spark Mr. Worthington had come to crave and his no longer looked like dragons spitting fire but burned bright like emeralds in the light of the sun that cast through the window. A starved man is what he resembled. Desperate for something Annabelle was sure she could not grant him.

"You look at me as though I hold the key to your sanity in my hands," she uttered, entranced by his piercing gaze. "With such awe and desperation."

"Oh, but you do. My very fate is dependent on your choices and your choices alone."

He had not moved his body, other than clenching his jaw when the conversation became tense. No other movements passed through his body as his limbs stood stock still.

"I am sorry to disappoint," she murmured from the bed she had been imprisoned in since she awoke.

"I guess it is well that I am a forgiving man then, Miss Faraday."

"Is that all, Mr. Worthington?" Annabelle questioned. "Have you only come here to remind me of your feelings towards me? Feelings I cannot reciprocate."

"Do no speak such untruths, Miss Faraday," he lightly chastised. "To answer your question, however, no. I am here to inform you that as you can now move on your own, you are expected to return to your role as governess in the morning. Miss Bowden is far too old to care for Arrington and the children."

"Very well, sir," she spoke. "I will see you in the morn."

A nod of his head was the only reaction she had gotten out of the man as her words had clearly signified that the conversation was over. Even still, Annabelle felt a sharp twist in her heart when he left without another word to her. She wished he would stay, and just sit beside her, but could not find the words on her tongue.

He walked out of her room not wishing to cause himself any more pain by watching her wither away under her heartache. He could only hope the letter had received from Detective Cuttle would bring good news. He had not opened the documents yet, nervous for the words that could be written on the paper, but knew it was necessary, and took the stairs to his study quickly praying for answers.

In the room she had been housed in, Annabelle prepared for bed. She was now able to move around much easier and was set to return to caring for the children in the morn, much to Miss Bowden's relief, but Annabelle's anxiety. She was not sure what a day with the children she had selfishly left behind would bring, but she could only hope she had not hurt their hearts as much as she thought she did. There were few choices she regretted more than the one to leave just days earlier, and she had spent the days since she had awoken working on ways to repair the damage her choice had left in its wake.

****

Anxiety rose in Annabelle the next morn as she prepared for her day. No longer confined to her bed or her room, Annabelle would be returning to her normal routine of caring for the children. This began with breakfast in the kitchen and ended with a day spent alone with the children in the study.

Taking her time readying herself, it became very clear that Annabelle was stalling the beginning of her day. She almost fooled herself into thinking this was just like any other day spent at Arrington, but even she could not trick herself that much. The birds that sang outside her window were not the same birds she had come to know, and no tree stood proud and tall on the other side of the glass. The bed where she laid was pressed against a different wall and the luxurious linens that lined the bed told Annabelle that such a fantasy could not be true. Everything had changed, and she had never been a fan of such a thing.

Dressed in her navy gown with white lace accents on the collar and the cuffs, Annabelle descended the stairs. She had only pinned the front of her hair back, allowing the length of it to cascade down her back as she nervously pulled on the lace details. She had not worn the dress in ages and felt as if the garment would give her the confidence she was lacking to survive the day. It was the best looking and most expensive dress she owned, other than the one for the ball that had been gifted by Mr. Worthington. If the dress could not do its job, Annabelle hoped the necklace she draped around her neck would. Her mother's jewelry that she had not donned in what felt like months. She could not remember the last time this necklace decorated her skin, but in a desperate attempt to feel close to what she had lost, she secured the chain and let her fingertips graze the jewel.

Not sure what the reaction would be to her appearance, Annabelle took the stairs slowly as she descended into the kitchen. The sound of pots and bowls and the cackles of the kitchen staff all came to an abrupt halt as soon as Annabelle crossed the threshold. All eyes were fixated on her as she stood in the doorway, her cheeks slowly turning pink. She was never a fan of such attentions and having not seen most of these workers since she ran left her uneasy. It was not until Mrs. Nettles dropped her spoon and ran to the governess that Annabelle knew she would be alright. Wrapped in the cook's warm embrace, Annabelle felt as if this was somewhere she belonged.

"Do not ever do that to me again," Mrs. Nettles spoke earnestly through the tear that were wetting Annabelle's shoulder. "I shall use my spoon so hard on you should you ever give me such stress again, do you hear me?"

The aging woman pulled away from Annabelle to look in the eyes as she spoke the last words, intent on showing her seriousness of them.

"Yes ma'am," a misty-eyed Annabelle responded softly.

"Very well," Mrs. Nettles replied before turning and walking away from her and pointing to a stool that sat at the counter. "Now, sit your little run away behind down in this seat and eat your breakfast that I made you."

A small smile graced Annabelle's lips as she followed the orders, feeling as if it were possible to make amends to those she had hurt.

The day continued to be uneventful after breakfast until Annabelle was left alone with the children in the study for their day's lesson after Miss Bowden had readied them. Annabelle did not expect the warmest of welcomes, but what she had received had not even been a possibility in her mind. She had spent so long working with these children to help them grow into intelligent and confident humans and she saw how one foolish decision reversed all of their hard work.

"Please speak to me," Annabelle desperate pleaded. The day had drug on like an eternity and the quick glances and silent stares were becoming too much for her to take. Isabelle would not acknowledge her existence and sat curled up on a chaise lounge near the fireplace, not speaking a word even to her brother. And her dear Lucas would pin her down with the harshest of glares and do the exact opposite of whatever she asked. She would ask him to sit and he would walk to the other end of the room. She would ask him to put away a book and he would pull another off the shelf and drop it at her feet. She could not even be disgruntled at their behavior for she had caused it. Lucas was angry, and Isabelle was broken, and it was all her fault.

"Annie, you promised," mumbled Lucas with a pout strong enough to break glass upon. His eyes were distrustful of the governess and his heart hurt at her betrayal. "Why did you not stay with us?"

"Did we do something wrong?" A very soft Isabelle spoke out, her eyes cast to the floor refusing to meet Annabelle's gaze.

Tears welled painfully in her eyes as Annabelle responded to the children who had stolen her heart and kept her anchored for the duration she spent at Arrington.

"No, my lovely children," Annabelle tearfully replied. At the sound of her sobs both children lifted their own misty gazes to her as she spoke. "You must believe me. You are the reason I stayed. My heart has hurt for so long and most days your smiles were the only cure. I love you both so and I made a mistake. I should not have broken my promise and I am so very sorry."

Weary gazes regarded her as she attempted to reign in her tears.

"I never wished to hurt you or damage your trust," she continued as she wiped at her wet cheeks. "I do not know how to make amends but do know that you both hold so much space in my heart. It was a lapse in judgement made in a time of heartache."

"I do not understand, Annabelle," Isabelle softly replied. "How can your heart hurt so much you run away from home? From those you love. My heart hurts when I stay away from those I care for. I always miss you when we leave on trips."

With her quiet and sweet words moisture filled Annabelle's eyes once again.

"I forgot that sometimes running away hurts more than staying, sweet Isabelle. It is hard for me to explain and I can only hope you never know such turmoil. Just please know that I regret it very much."

"So, you will not leave again?" Questioned a cautiously curious Lucas. "You will stay with us?"

Even though she had pretended not to notice, Annabelle heard boots echo in the hall outside the children's study and come to a stop right outside the door. She did not need to guess for she already knew the wearer of the shoes as she responded to Lucas' inquiry.

"Yes, dear Lucas," she replied with a shaky smile, acknowledging that she was now sealing her fate. "I will stay with you."

Cautious smile rose on both children's faces as they took slow steps towards her only to be engulfed in a tight embrace. Annabelle had missed their warm and the light that followed them. She did not wish for the darkness of their parents to weigh them down like the darkness of her past had, and so she would stay. If for nothing else, then to give these children a chance at a life filled with joy.

She was so lost in the embrace she did not hear the boots click back down the hall from whence they came.

****

As the grandmother continued her story, the pair walked through the home past many grand portraits and expensive tapestries, all of which were collecting dust. Down too many stairs for the grandmother's knees to handle and hallways that were much too long. Nevertheless, their journey lead them out the front door. It was in a field with deer grazing along the grass that they stopped for a short break, so the grandmother could catch her breath. She was running out of story and needed to reach their destination by the end for the child to truly understand everything. But for now, they stopped and breathed, looking down at the expanse of land that stretched on for miles, bathed in the light of the sun and God's beautiful nature. The grandmother could not deny that she adored it here.

"Has your mother told you many stories about her childhood?" The grandmother inquired while they stood together.

"Yes," The young girl responded. "Not very often, but Mother does tell me when she was my age, she and Uncle Alexander used to play cricket on this field."

The little girl spoke clearly as she held her grandmother's hand, upset that she did not spend more time here where her mother grew, and that she did not know as much about her childhood as she would have liked.

"Uncle Alex said that he once killed a fish when he hit a ball into the lake, but he could not have possibly known if it was his ball that killed the fish, right Grandmother?"

The aging woman simply let out a chuckle at the memory of her children's antics. Alexander, the eldest, had taken over the family business many years earlier, but had settled down at thirty-four with his dear wife with whom he had two young children, and her dear Sophronia had been married many years as well, gifting the aging woman her granddaughter, whom she walked with now.

"Yes, my Dear," the grandmother responded, pulling herself from her memories. "Your mother and uncle knew how to keep me on my toes. They never dared cross your grandfather, but testing my patience was another story altogether."

"Did grandfather travel often?"

"No child," she responded with a fond smile. "He rooted himself at home a year after your uncle was born. He hated leaving before then, but once he was given a reason to stay home, he never dared leave the walls unless I was by his side."

"Grandmother?"

"Yes?"

"Can you please continue?"

"As you wish," and they carefully began walking through the fields, slowly, as the story continued.

****

The sun had set when Mr. Worthington's mind had returned to the present. Annabelle thought the world had forgotten about her, but in storage in a run-down file office, her story was housed, and with enough monetary incentive, Mr. Worthington had paid to track it down. Detective Cuttle had dropped the file off on his doorstep in the early hours of the morning. With a hard pat on the back and a wish for good luck, the man was on his way back to London, as his leave from Scotland Yard was up and he was expected to return to work.

Holding the file hand delivered to him by Detective Cuttle, he read about the hellish night she had to endure once again. Her own statement, in her own words as a child. Her story. And with every line of ink on the page, Mr. Worthington's heart cracked once more.

How she had survived such an ordeal amazed him, and how she had such a kind spirit still baffled him. She finally made sense. More sense than she had ever made to the man. Every time she cast her brow to the floor, and each time she apologized for things that were never her fault. Guilt destroyed her, and she was forever looking for someone to grant her the forgiveness she could not find for herself. She wanted happiness but did not believe she deserved it. She craved love but settled for giving hers away. How could this young woman have lived any form of a life after that night?

The thought plagued his mind for the remainder of the day until he could not take it any longer and felt a desperate need to speak to the woman. She would not have to conquer this guilt alone. He would stand by her and support her, if only she would let him. And so, he set out to find her, knowing she would be putting the children to bed at this time. It was in the hall around the corner from the children's quarters that he found her, walking slowly, almost lost in a daze.

"Annabelle," the governess stopped in her tracks listening to the click of boots that she had run from many times before.

"Mr. Worthington," she turned to face the man. "How may I help you?"

He did not know any other way to tell her that he had read of her nightmare. She need not utter the words to him, which he knew would be far too painful for her to do, for he had found the answer for himself. All he could think to do was to pass the file into her small hands and wait. Her brows furrowed at the file now sitting between her fingers and her inquisitive stare to Mr. Worthington went unanswered for a moment as the man looked to be under a great deal of stress, refusing to meet her eyes. She continued to stare until he motioned to the documents in her hands and utter a quick "look inside." His rushed voice and panicked eyes caused anxiety to rise in Annabelle's chest as she flipped open the file.

Understanding quickly washed over her as she read the words that had passed her lips eleven years earlier. She was not angry at the man, for such an action was not a surprise to her. On the contrary, relief flooded her system at the knowledge that these words would not have to pass her lips a second time. He already knew. He had read her words. Pushing the file into his left hand, which he quickly clasped around the documents, the only part of this encounter she did not understand is why he still stood here in front of her with compassion in his eyes.

"Now you know my secrets, sir," she spoke in a desperately broken voice. "My deepest form of hell rooted and rotting in my heart. Do you now think less of me?"

"No, my dear Annabelle," Mr. Worthington responded fiercely, stepping closer to her. "Now I know I was right to think the world of you."

"I need to leave," she rushed as she attempted to once again turn away from this man and everything a life with him offered her, only stopped by his gentle hand on her arm and his words.

"You are free to stay."

"I cannot," looking in his eyes she pleaded with him to understand why she was the way she was. He knew her story, understood her guilt. Surely, he could not think she was deserving of happiness.

"It was not your fault," the certainty in his voice made her resolve break, as she desperately wished such a thing to be true.

"You were not there, sir," she explained, his hand still on her arm and her eyes still piercing his. "You cannot possibly know the grief I carry and the guilt that drowns my soul. They were my blood and I ran away."

"Do you hold guilt for a child listening to the last wishes upon the final breaths of a mother, or do you hold sorrow for not leaving with them as they walked into eternity hand in hand," he reasoned, only hoping she could understand that and eight-year-old child could not be to blame for such a tragedy.

"They left me here," she cracked, letting the tears rain from her eyes and her emotions cloud her heart. "My mother wished to be with my father, and they both left me here alone. I was but a mere child. If I could have saved them I would not be here alone, and they would not have had to endure such a treacherous death."

"Annabelle, there was no hope for your father," Mr. Worthington pressed. "He was gone before you ran away. Did your mother not have a right to give her life for the child your father perished to save. I believe you were left in your room that night for a reason. They wished for you to sleep through the night and go undetected. She was fulfilling the wishes of the man she loved, and then she was gifted the opportunity to be reunited with him once again, knowing you were safely away from the evil that stole them from you. But depriving yourself of love, are you truly honoring their wishes?"

"You did not know my parents."

"No, but they seem to have been wonderful to you, as mine have been to me, and my parents would have wished for my happiness," he could not reason with her any longer today and hoped leaving her with her thoughts and his words would allow her to let go of some of her guilt. This war would have to be won by her and her alone, but those that loved her would gladly pick her up when she fell and sharpen her sword when it grew dull. Tonight, though, there was nothing else he could do except keep her safe.

With that, he turned and walked the same way he came down the hall, bathing Annabelle in the dim candlelight of the corridor and moonlight leaking through the window, as only the stars heard her cries.

CHAPTER 14

Annabelle had returned to the quarters she woke up in days ago after she recovered from her moment with Mr. Worthington in the hall. The old room she spent her time in housed far too many dreadful memories that she wished not to relive. This new room brought with it a clean slate and a freshness her old one had not carried. Caring for the children, however, she was no longer confined to the room for the day's duration.

Annabelle had readied herself for the day, rubbing the pendant that once hung around her mother's neck, but now graced hers, for comfort as she descended the stairs and walked towards the kitchen. She had expected a normal day spent caring for the children, but what awaited her was far better than anything she could have imagined.

Crossing the threshold into the room expecting to eat her breakfast, Annabelle was met with the sight of her dear friend Emma laughing atop a stool as Mrs. Nettles told a vivid story as the kitchen staff watched her performance. She paused and looked on at the sight in front of her for a moment, not believing it to be true, until Emma's warm eyes met hers from across the room. The ember haired girl was out of her chair quicker than a cannon ball fires and barreled towards the governess.

"Anna!" her squeals were not met with delight by Annabelle's ears as a wince overtook her features, but warmth covered her heart like a blanket at having her friend in her arms. The embrace was tight and reassuring. Everything Annabelle needed in the chaos that continued to surround her.

"Emma," Annabelle took her friend's hand securely in hers after they separated, still disbelieving of the reality of this situation.

"I am so very glad to see you, but how are you here? I did not receive a letter informing you of your plans to visit." Confusion masked Annabelle's features as she wracked her brain attempting to remember an instance where Emma had chosen this date for her impending visit but coming up empty. Annabelle would have never agreed to such a thing after the week she had just endured but was thrilled to see her friend nonetheless.

"Your employer summoned me, Annabelle," Emma spoke with caution. She studied Annabelle's shock ridden face closely as she delivered the news. "A carriage arrived this morning with a message for my employer and instructions to deliver me here to Arrington to spend the day with you. I return home tomorrow."

"I am so sorry, Emma," Annabelle began, apologizing for disrupting her life. "If I had known he was planning this I would have told him to rid his mind of such thoughts. Is Peter angered by this? I would never wish you to rearrange your schedule for me –"

"Annabelle, stop!" Emma berated. "Once I heard you were ill there was no question in me making the journey and my dear Peter would not have it any other way. He will miss me, but I will return in the morn, so he does not worry. Do you not wish me to be here?"

Annabelle wrapped her arms around Emma in a suffocating hug in response to the thought. "I will always wish you here, Emma. I only wish to make sure you did not feel obligated to make the journey. It is very long, and you have a husband waiting for you." Pulling away to look Emma in the eyes, Annabelle continue with tears pooling, "but I am so very glad you are here."

Misty smiles were shared between the pair as they continued their hold, only to be interrupted by Mrs.

Nettles.

"My dears, I am so glad you have been reunited, but seeing as you only have this day together, should we begin with a breakfast?"

Annabelle sent a grateful nod to the cook as she began preparing plates for the ladies. They took their seats at a table in the corner, choosing to spend their morning with the staff and away from the extravagant dining hall. After the meal, Annabelle took Emma by the hand and led her around the estate, introducing her to the staff. Annabelle used the opportunity to show her friend where she had spent her days for the past year, but also to have reason to speak with the staff members once again. The level of comfortability she felt with them after her run away gone awry had lowered significantly, and she used the conversations she had while introducing Emma as a way to begin rebuilding the bridges she damaged. To her surprise, she was welcomed warmly by every staff member they encountered throughout her tour, further warming her heart.

It was after lunch that Annabelle had decided to show Emma the place that was so dear to her heart. Hand together, the pair ventured through the fields of Arrington, past the weeping willows at the forest's edges, into the meadow covered in rose bushes and bees. Emma gasped, and tears filled her eyes as she looked upon the stone slab that bared her friend's name.

"It is beautiful, Anna," Emma spoke while attempting to reign in her emotions.

"Yes, yes, it is," Annabelle responded, not making eye contact with her friend, only looking upon the resting place of her dear Catherine.

"He did this for her?"

"He says he did this for me, but I am glad it was done, never mind the reason," Annabelle replied, brushing off the gesture to Emma even though it was one of the loveliest things that had ever been done for her.

"Anna, let us sit," Emma spoke, finally looking at her friend.

Annabelle responded by walking closer to Catherine's grave and sitting down upon the grass where Emma joined her a moment later.

"What is on your mind, Emma," caution masked her tone as Annabelle expected what was to come.

"What happened?" Emma pressed, having been given very cryptic information by Mr. Worthington in a letter, demanding her presence and stating Annabelle needed her friend now more than ever.

"You would not believe me if I uttered the words."

"I will always believe you, Anna," Emma comforted in hopes Annabelle would choose to open up. "You need only trust me."

Weary eyes met Emma's as Annabelle weighed her options. This was her first friend at Auburn. A sister, not by blood, by circumstance, but loved just the same. If anyone would believe her, it was Emma. With no more rational thoughts convincing enough to stop her, Annabelle dove into her story head first, speaking every ill thing that had happened to her that night, just as she had so many years earlier. Emma finally knew of her past. She knew Annabelle was too beautiful, too graceful, and too intelligent to have been abandoned on Auburn's doorstep without reason, but no peace came to her heart by finally knowing her past. Instead, her heart violently broke at the thought of what she had been put through.

"Anna, why did you never tell me?" Emma was taken aback by what she had learned about her friend. In all the years she had known her, she never expected such a story to be hiding in her past.

"This was my sin to carry, Emma," Annabelle replied with a hoarse voice, refusing to meet her friend's eyes. She stared intently at the hands that lay in her lap, not wishing to see the judgement she was sure would mar Emma's features.

Clasping her hands around the ones Annabelle was so intent on gazing upon, Emma could not find an ounce of anger or judgement in her body for what her friend had been through and was determined to prove such things to her.

"But God forgives, Anna."

"What if I cannot forgive myself," holding back sobs, Annabelle finally locked her grey eyes upon Emma's comforting mocha ones, as if searching for the answer to every heartache that had been rained upon her life.

"I do not know the words to comfort you, sweet friend," Emma could only clutch Annabelle's hands tighter as she found herself at a loss for words.

"I do not believe words are capable of such comfort, Emma, so I do not blame you for being at a loss."

"My dear Anna," Emma began. "How could you have lived with such a thing weighing down your soul for so long? You must know this is not your fault. You could have not stopped a man so large. You were a mere child."

It was then that the tears rained free.

"My dear, Anna," Emma spoke slowly as she rubbed the back of her friend. "You have spent far too many nights sleeping on a wet pillow, and you know how I hate such things."

At her friend's gentle beratement Annabelle let out a soft giggle. Emma always knew how to remove Annabelle from her deepest and darkest thoughts, just as she did now. With a tight hug, both ladies rose from the grass and began the long journey back to the estate, bidding goodbye to Catherine for the day.

Once they had returned to Arrington, the pair had taken up residency in the children's study for the day's remainder. Emma had met and gushed over Isabelle and Lucas before lunch, squeezing their cheeks and squealing at their appearance, as they were dressed in their best garments for a day at the market with their mother and their uncle. Mr. Worthington had made sure his presence would not be lurking around the estate this day, as Annabelle deserved an uninterrupted time spent with her friend. Annabelle and Emma made themselves comfortable on the couches by the fireplace as they enjoyed an afternoon tea together after visiting in with Mrs. Nettles to make plans for the days next meal.

Emma had started the conversation, telling Annabelle of her work and her husband. She had purchased new drapes for her little home and had spent much time with her husband tending their gardens, planting as many flowers as would fit in the beds. The thought of the bright colors brought a smile to Annabelle's face. Her friend's happiness could always cause her own to grow. After spending a sufficient amount of time informing Annabelle of her life, and drinking two cups of tea, Emma saw an opportune time to change the subject.

"Your Mr. Worthington is quite the man Annabelle," Emma spoke in a tentative tone, knowing that her misconceptions about the man had led Annabelle's heart astray. Her bold nature caused her to avoid Annabelle's piercing glare and harsh intake of breath warning her to drop the subject. "I am so very sorry for the words I spoke on our last visit. It would seem that I was incredibly wrong to believe such things. Please forgive me, Anna."

"Of course, you are forgiven, Emma," Annabelle responded bluntly. She would always forgive her friend for such infractions. Her words were spoken out of true concern and love and Annabelle found no reason to hold her at fault for their inaccuracy. "Is that even a question? I knew you meant no harm, but please do not refer to him as my Mr. Worthington. The man is not mine."

"Only because you will not let him be," Emma began with the intent on forcing her friend to see reason.

"Emma—" Annabelle cut her off exasperatedly.

"Okay, I will stop," Emma interrupted. "But Annabelle, can I ask you something?"

Wiping her remaining tears that trickled from her eyes, Annabelle gave her friend a shaky nod.

"How can you forgive me so easily for my transgressions, but cannot find enough love within you to forgive yourself?" Emma knew her words would challenge Annabelle and what she believed, but that is exactly what the governess needed to find her happiness. "This evil inside of you will demolish you if you let it."

"I am afraid it already has, my dear Emma."

"No, Anna," Emma berated as she let go of Annabelle's hands and shot up from her seat only to pace the room in front of her, flailing her hands in the air as she spoke. "For if it had you would not find love in this world, but you look at those children with more love than their mother. You cry over our dear friend Catherine, and your heart breaks for a man you have deemed yourself unworthy of. You are not yet completely shattered. You simply need to reattach the pieces of your heart that have broken away."

"I do not have them all, Emma," Annabelle pleaded in a stern voice with her friend to see things from her view. "My parents took so many pieces with them when they perished."

"No one has a whole heart, Anna," Emma responded with a heavy sigh, stepping toward her friend in hopes of explaining such things to her. "We all are a little broken, some more than others, but that is why we find love. Entwining our hearts with someone else to fill each other's holes. Please allow yourself to be loved. I did not know your parents, but I know it is what they would have wanted."

Spending the rest of the night crying on her friend's shoulder telling her of every moment she had shared with the man of the house, Annabelle could not help but let her friend's words echo through her mind all through the night, haunting her, and maybe healing her. She was finally coming to terms with the knowledge that an eight-year-old could not have stopped the man who stole her parents. She had spent so long locking the memories away when the only way to be free was to speak them out loud. Thinking herself foolish, she only wished she could go back so many years and share her story then. She did not know with who, but even to speak her words to the stars would have been better than the darkness she locked beneath her skin and deep in her soul.

Emma bid Annabelle a sorrowful goodbye in the early morning after breakfast and left in a carriage to return home to her husband. Annabelle knew she would hear from her friend soon in letters and visits to the market, so the goodbye was not as bittersweet as ones she had before. No longer being distracted by Emma's presence caused Annabelle's anxiety to grow as she knew that her mind would wander back to the man of the house and everything that had occurred over the last week. With these thoughts lingering in her mind, it was no surprise that she readied herself as quickly as her hands could and walked to the children's quarters to ready them for the day. They had behaved the day before according to Miss Bowden and Annabelle was elated to hear the stories of their day that awaited her.

"Annie, Uncle Sheridan bought me a boat yesterday," Lucas gleefully told his governess holding up the wooden toy as they walked to the kitchen for breakfast, thrilled at the attention his uncle had been giving him over the past weeks. "He promised me that once he returns from business we will take it out onto the lake and see if it floats."

Annabelle's ears perked up at the word "business." She was not aware Mr. Worthington was leaving for business anytime soon and could not ignore the uncomfortable feeling that overtook her heart at the news. He was known to be gone for months at a time, and she was not sure she could take being away from him that long, especially with such conflicting feelings marring her heart.

"That is truly lovely, Lucas," Annabelle absentmindedly spoke as her mind wandered. Luckily for her, the boy did not notice her perceived disinterest and continued to wave the object around as they walked, much to his sister's annoyance.

"Lucas, please," Isabelle whined. "Put that thing down before you break something. Uncle Sheridan will be furious should you damage anything in his home."

At the thought of disapproval from his uncle, Lucas immediately ceased his movements and walked calmly next to the females as they ventured to the study. The children spoke of memories from the day before, which had been lovely in their words, while Annabelle continued to stress about the man of the estate leaving on business. The anxiety that coated her emotions at such information surprised her more than anything. It was clear her heart did not wish him to go.

Floors below the group, Mr. Worthington was deeply immersed in the work that would peel him away from Arrington when he was disrupted by an unexpected visitor.

It was still early morning when a knock rang out along the halls of Arrington shortly after Emma left. Annabelle was taken with the children in the study while Mr. Longfellow pulled open the large doors to the estate to reveal a messenger holding a parcel addressed to Mr. Worthington. The short man briskly handed over the parcel before racing away from the steps and mounting his horse to continue to his delivery. Accepting it gratefully, Mr.

Longfellow moved on to Mr. Worthington's office to deposit the large envelope.

As the door to his study was opened following a short knock, Mr. Worthington lifted his gaze to see the butler depositing the envelope on a table by the door before bowing and leaving the man to his work. He knew he should have finished the documents that lay spread out in front of him before looking into the object that lay feet from him, but his curiosity was piqued, and he could not help himself. Ripping open the envelope, the first thing Mr. Worthington encounter was a handwritten note drawn out in a messy scrawl of handwriting the man knew all too well.

Sheridan —

I did some digging for you, boy, and I thought this information may give your girl some piece of mind. No one should be forced to live in fear of such things their entire life.

Yours truly,

The best detective Scotland Yard has seen, Louise Cuttle

P.S. – treat her right, son. I believe this girl is a keeper

Opening the file that came attached to the note, Mr. Worthington could not help but breathe out a deep sigh of relief, for one of the questions that had plagued his mind had finally been answered. He would have to make sure to have the Cuttle's up for a meal the next time his parents were in town and send the man the best bottle of wine his money could afford. He owed the detective more than anyone knew.

Rereading the information multiple times, it took the man until after lunch was completed to decide how to approach the unwitting governess with this new information. He ate quickly in the confines of his study, having not left the room since the morn and only ventured out to find Annabelle after he was sure her teaching for the day was over. She would now be entertaining the children until dinner and all that was left for him to do was find her.

The group was not where he expected them to be. They were not in the study or confined to the walls of Arrington, forsaking the confines of indoors for the fresh air and warmth that awaited them in the gardens. Walking out a side door leading to the west gardens that sat just beyond the windows of the dining hall, Mr. Worthington was met with a pleasant sight. Annabelle stood looking over the children at the edge of the gardens as Isabelle skipped along the pathways pulling flowers from their bushes and stems. One could only hope Mr. O'Connor's son did not see the act, for he took great pride in his flowers and even fought Mrs. Nettles when she wished to pick some.

Lucas, on the other hand, stood firmly on one end of the path with a hard look of concentration coating his face. Mr. Worthington was not sure what was wrong with the child and was about to approach when the boy suddenly bent his knees and hurled himself forward. With a smile tugging at his lips, Mr.

Worthington thought back to when he was a child and would partake in a similar act to see just how far his legs could throw him, often forcing the staff to measure his jumps, hoping with each new leap he had landed farther than the last.

Drawing his attention away from the children, Mr. Worthington looked back to the governess standing in the same location. The only difference was her shoulders were now shaking slightly, most likely from giggles at the children's actions. Oxygen filled deep into

KIMBERLY MARIE

his lungs as he struck up the courage to begin the unpredictable conversation. God had brought Annabelle back to him, and with this in mind, he sent a quick prayer skyward wishing that this conversation would be had smoothly.

Annabelle found herself lost in the world of the children, giggling at their antics so intently that she was not aware of anything occurring around her. Her heart jumped when a voice cut through the peace she had accrued for herself today.

"Miss Faraday," a voice from behind called to hear. "May I please have a word?"

Mr. O'Connor was quick to call Lucas and Isabelle over to him in response to the situation. Both children willingly ran to man under the promise that he would teach them how to place a bridle on a horse in the stables around the corner. It was clear that they were not needed in the area of the upcoming conversation, and Annabelle, in such shock at the voice that had called her name, had not resisted the children's departure, choosing to only watch them skip away into the care of another.

"Of course, sir," she spoke in as firm a voice as she could muster, searching within herself for the courage to turn around and face the man. She did not have to spend long on her hunt though, for his boots clacked against the pathway as he came towards her, rounding her body until he stood only feet away, now facing her.

"It is customary for those participating in conversation to face each other, is it not, Miss Faraday?" Having not spoken to the governess in days, Mr. Worthington wished to ease into dialogue with the gentle ribbings he had come to look forward to so fondly. He could only hope she saw his efforts and reciprocated his actions, for this conversation would be difficult enough, and he did not wish her to be uncomfortable for the beginning of it.

A smile tugged at her lips as she rose her eyes to his. "Yes, sir, but you only asked for a word. I believe a conversation consists of more words than just one."

He could not stop the small smile that took over his features at her reciprocation. Her eyes held a familiar light that he had not seen in months and the color had returned to her face in a healthy manner.

"Forgive me, madam," he spoke to her eloquently through his smile. "May I please have multiple words then?"

With a light laugh she replied, "you may." The conversation was not tense like she thought. Talking to this man was easy, as infuriating as he was, but enjoyable nonetheless. She would miss him while he was away, she decided. The thought alone of his departure stripped the smile from her face and caused a solemn tone to coat her voice.

"You are leaving on business," her voice coated most of her emotions, but he was able to detect a hint of anxiety in her tone.

"Yes, Miss Faraday, I am," he replied stoically. He was not sure how she would respond to the information he was about to tell her and forced a serious tone to his voice in hopes of hiding the discomfort that surrounded him.

"For how long," her whisper was desperate as she gazed at the cobblestones they stood upon. The kind of words that made him wish to reach out to her, but he knew he could not. Not while she was still unsure of his feelings and not while he had such important information to relay to her. He would not further confuse her emotions and torture himself. She needed to make her decision about her life, and he only hoped this information could give her a little more piece of mind and speed up the decision-making process.

"A week, Miss Faraday," he spoke carefully, not able to read her reaction. "I leave in the morn, and that is why I felt this conversation was very pertinent. I did not wish to leave without sharing with you some new information that has come to my attention."

"Okay," the only word Annabelle could muster at this moment. A week was not as long as some of his other trips, but she was still not thrilled. Even when she was not speaking to him, knowing he was there brought a little slice of peace into her world and she was not sure how she would react with him gone.

"Miss Faraday —"

"Annabelle," she cut him off swiftly as her formal name passed his lips. At his confused glance she continued. "You may call me Annabelle."

The significance of her invitation was not lost on him, but he could not focus on this at the moment, as he knew this conversation needed to be had and could not allow himself to become distracted.

"Very well, Annabelle," he spoke her name after clearing his throat. "Shall we sit down for this conversation?" His arm motioned to the bench that sat underneath the limb of a tree a few yards away.

"If you deem it necessary, sir," she replied, staring at the bench that stood in the shade overlooking one of the many fields that stretched along the land of Arrington. She began walking to the bench as he met her strides. It was only when both parties were comfortably situated, and Annabelle looked up at him with expectant eyes, did he continue.

"This morning a messenger arrived delivering a parcel from London," he spoke in an even tone, looking upon her face for any sign of duress. "It was being delivered from Detective Cuttle, the man who informed me of your past."

He paused for an uncomfortable moment waiting for a response from the lady sitting next to him, but no reaction came. Her eyes stayed fixed on his and her gaze grew expectant, waiting for the rest of the information.

"In the parcel that was delivered was information that he gathered after returning to London that he felt I should be made aware of. It was document concerning a robber who was arrested nine years ago in Oxfordshire."

"I am very sorry, sir," Annabelle spoke, breaking his train of thought. "But what does this information have to do with me? Why should I be worried about a man who was arrested in a place so far from here?"

"Annabelle, your childhood home was located in Oxfordshire," he cautiously continued. "The man's name who was arrested for such crimes was Elmore Gunter."

At his words Annabelle's eyes grew wide. She knew now why Mr. Worthington felt the need to share this information with her. Her Mister Gunter, the man who lived on in her nightmares and haunted her every move, had been arrested nine years ago.

"Where is he now?" Annabelle asked in a shaky voice with tears brimming her eyes.

Feeling bold and needing to offer some form of comfort, Mr. Worthington took both of Annabelle's hands in his and held tightly.

"He was arrested for his crimes, having been caught in the act of robbing another home, not far from yours. He was foolish to stay in the area after he committed the crime against your family, but I cannot help but be pleased that he was a fool."

"Is he still in jail?" She could not help but tighten her hands in his as she awaited the answer.

"No, Annabelle," he spoke carefully. "He is not."

As tears slipped from her eyes, Mr. Worthington quickly realized his error and let go of her hands only to raise his thumbs to her cheeks to dry her tears. He could have just given her his handkerchief, but he could not help but wish for an intimate moment with the governess as he spoke his next words.

"Annabelle, he is no longer in jail because he is no longer living," the air escaped her lungs as her desperate eyes searched his face for the truth as she listened to his words. "He was murdered while in serving time for his crimes and now resides in a cemetery close to the prison he was sent to. He cannot hurt you any longer for he is no longer a part of this world."

Uncontrollably she sobbed, throwing herself at the man and clinging to him as if her own life depended on it. Her nightmare was over. He could not find her again and could not finish what he started. Hope flooded over her. Maybe now the nightmares could stop and maybe now she could forgive herself as the fear of her past finding her present existed no longer. She felt as if she should feel remorse for the man or send up a prayer but could not find such compassion in her. She simply allowed herself to be comforted by this man who had put so much effort in easing her troubles.

"I do not know what to make of you," she spoke her frustrations aloud as she moved out of his arms and rose. "Or the feeling that coats my heart's surface and have been absorbed within."

"You can make of me anything you wish, Annabelle," cautiously Mr. Worthington took a step towards the maiden. "So long as I am yours to make something of. Make me a fool, make me gentleman. You could call me back to Arrington on any trip and I would return if for nothing else than the promise that you would still be here when I arrived. I am yours. I have given my heart away a long time ago to a stubborn governess who did not think she was capable of such love that I feel for her, but Annabelle, I am yours, and I will gladly spend the rest of my life proving it to you."

"And what if I make you a liar, sir," her words held a faint glimmer of sarcasm. "For nothing else than to insure you would never prove me wrong, for I do enjoy being right."

"That is the one thing I will not allow you to make me," he spoke fighting a grin at her resilient spirit. "For when I speak my feelings to you, it will be clear that each of my words always holds the purest form of truth."

Taking two steps closer to her, he invaded her space in the best way possible, lowering his head until his lips almost met her ears. Society would see the gesture as scandalous and call the man a louse, but Annabelle had not been a respected member of society for years and Mr. Worthington simply did not care.

"So, when I tell you I love you," he spoke, his lips brushing gently against her ear with each word. "You will never doubt me. When I speak the world of you, you will not question my authenticity, and when I speak to you my dreams and tell you that you are the center of each one, my seriousness will be clear."

A sharp exhale pushed every ounce of oxygen from her lungs as her heart beat wildly and furiously beneath her chest. Her body vibrated as the world came back to her, bringing her senses with it. Warmth flooded her face as a satisfied expression overtook Mr. Worthington's as he noticed her reaction.

"If I did not have to leave you this week," he spoke once he took a step back and gave Annabelle a moment to collect herself. "I promise you I would not, but as fate would have it, my father has called me to London for business, but I shall return in seven days."

A shaky nod was all Annabelle could muster as her large grey eyes slowly got lost in his green. They were like a hedge maze that she did not know the answer to, forever making turns and only venturing deeper into the shrubs. He had opened his soul to her through his eyes to portray his truth, and the authenticity of it all had her mind muddled and her heart disordered. She felt so much for this man that she did not understand and could not put into words.

Lifting his hand to brush against her cheek, Mr. Worthington spoke his goodbye.

"I will see you in a week, Annabelle, but now I must go. Atlas is ready and waiting to deliver me to town."

At the mention of the black steed Mr. Worthington owned, Annabelle's mind was drawn back to their initial encounter, when she saw him as intimidating and dark as the horse he rode upon. How wrong she was.

"I will see you in a week," she murmured as he began to slowly step away, giving her the space, she needed to sort through her mind and emotions. Her heart ached once he walked away toward the stables from her.

The week that followed was one of the worst Annabelle had ever experienced. When she was not distracted with the children or the harsh demands that Mrs. Kennelworth made upon her about their education, she was thinking of a stubborn man who claimed to love her. It was clear Mrs. Kennelworth would not be leaving Arrington any time soon and if she did it would not be back to London, but to France to live with the safety of her parents. Each time she wished ill upon the woman, Annabelle always brought her mind back to the children and would say a quick prayer for their mother, wishing for her future to be kinder than her past.

"Dearie," Mrs. Nettles spoke as she readied breakfast for Annabelle on the morn of the fourth day Mr. Worthington had been away. "What is clouding your mind?"

"I am sorry, Mrs. Nettles," Annabelle politely responded. "But I am afraid I do not know what you mean."

"It is as clear as the clouds in the sky, Annabelle," Mrs. Nettles fired back with a fierce tone. "I will not be lied to. Something is ailing you and I wish to know what it is."

"I assure you it is nothing food can fix," Annabelle replied in a glum tone. She sat hunched in her chair, perfect posture forgotten, as she thought about her life, her heart, and the man that could not disappear from her thoughts, not matter how hard she tried to block him out.

"You miss Sheri, don't you," Mrs. Nettles assumed placing her spoon down to collect Annabelle's hands in hers. "It is alright to miss the man you care for, dear."

Wide grey eyes looked up at the woman as Mrs. Nettles realized Annabelle thought she had kept her emotions a secret.

"I have known long before either of you stubborn humans were willing to admit your feelings," she spoke to a confused governess. "You may have turned a blind eye to your emotions, but I always pay very close attention."

"What shall I do?" Annabelle did not see any point in arguing with the woman for it was clear she knew better than both her and Mr. Worthington.

"Do not do anything until you are sure of your feelings," the older woman spoke. She cared for both individuals far too much to knowingly cause either of them more pain. "Sheri does not return home for three more days. Take this time to analyze your heart and listen to what it wishes for. Only if you are certain of your emotions should you tell him so. Not a second sooner."

Nodding her head, Annabelle ventured out to do just that. She spent the next days counting down until his return and wrestling between her mind and he heart. Both organs disagreed with each other and could not come to terms. She cared deeply for this man and missed him dearly while he was away, but she had not had a proper home in so long that she did not know what awaited her should she accept one. She still had childhood dreams she wished to accomplish and deep seeded fears she needed to overcome. She could not reverse this decision once it was made, and that scared her more than anything.

The sun hung brightly in the sky on the day Mr. Worthington returned to Arrington, and it continued to shine brightly as Annabelle rushed through the estate with the sole purpose of hiding from him.

Hiding from this man had become her specialty. Whenever she was not ready to face him, angry with him, or locking her emotions away from him, she hid, and he rarely found her. The second she heard he arrived back to Arrington, she could not decide if she wished to disappear from sight, or run into his arms, but after sneaking down the grand staircase that connected the wing she had been staying in since her return to the foyer, she decided on the former. It took one look at his silhouette and one click of his boots to cause a stir of butterflies to erupt in her heart and sweat to coat her palms. Her nerves could not take an encounter with the man she had missed so dearly, and so she hid.

It was this expedition that led her outside past the gardens and into a familiar field on the grand estate. Having just come from the stables, Annabelle could only hope Mr. Worthington would not look for her here, rather spend his time inside going over the stack of papers that had been accumulating outside his study doors during his leave of absence. Seeing the familiar tree, now covered in lush leaves and home to many animals, Annabelle could not help but put her climbing skills to work, mounting the lowest branch and raising herself up from there until she sat on a sturdy branch about half way up the trunk, able to look over the grounds of Arrington from her vantage point. The wind whistled through the leaves as the birds sang songs. Such peace had to be appreciated so Annabelle could not help but to lean her head back and close her eyes absorbing the serenity that surrounded her here.

It was only when the birds became louder that she opened her eyes, noting that one of them had landed not far from where she sat, nursing its nest before flying off once again.

She always wanted to be a bird. Her father promised her she would fly and accomplish life's greatest accomplishments. She had a life of promise, travel, and adventure awaiting her at her parents' side and in one night everything she had been looking forward to had been stripped from her. It took her far too long to realize that happiness was the absolute greatest success.

With these thoughts clouding her mind, she pulled and prodded at the bark of the same tree Lucas and Isabelle had sprinkled seeds on for the first time so many months ago. Her eyes lifted to the nest where eggs laid waiting for their mother to return home and keep them warm. In this moment Annabelle's eyes were finally opened.

She could be a bird and fly as far and as wide as she wished, but even the birds have a place they call home and a family to care for. She had to leave her nest earlier than most, but that fact should not have stopped her from creating a nest of her own, with a man who was willing to build it with her. Her confusion was still present, but with a large exhale of her breath life had made a little more sense.

"Maybe a home is not so bad," she pondered, still holding her gaze to the nest on the branch above. "A tree cannot reach the tips of the sky without equally deep roots. Just like a bird will not venture out into the wind without a nest to return to."

****

"Grandmother, did Annabelle stay?"

"Why yes, my dear," the grandmother replied with a smile on her face, moving her wrinkles and gracing her laugh lines. She was remembering her life. Her stubbornness. The man who said and did all the wrong things, but still stole her heart. She spoke with a renewed spirit as she remembered that tree, that still stood on the estate. "But she did not decide until she spent hours sitting in that cursed tree staring at the birds as if they would up and speak to her and tell her what to do. She realized she loved her stubborn and rueful man who said all the wrong things and had always loved him. The hearts choices are not be ignored or regretted and so Annabelle accepted the love she felt towards him. This realization had impacted her so much so, that she flew down from the tree and through the house much to the confusion and amusement of the staff she rushed past in her mission. Her manners were forgotten completely as she pulled open his study doors violently without any notice. The poor chap barely had time to stand from his chair and was not allowed words before she jumped on him, almost knocking him over, I have you."

The grandmother paused from her story to let out a breathy chuckle as tears welled in her eyes. Recounting her life was difficult, but she was so pleased with where she ended up, she would thank God for it every day and tell her story as many times as He wished her to, just to give back a small fragment of what He had blessed her with.

"It was then that they kissed," she continued. "It was a kiss she would remember during the long nights when he was away on business or the cool mornings after a row. After that kiss they broke apart only long enough for her to tell the man she loved him, causing him to initiate yet another kiss, not letting her out of his arms for the remainder of the day. A marriage followed shortly after. I am sure he was convinced Annabelle would change her mind and run off once again. Little did he know that he did not have to worry about that occurring ever again. She was happy with him, and such bliss could not be found anywhere but in his presence."

She took yet another pause, as they neared their destination, walking through tall grasses to the border of the trees. She looked down at her granddaughter, who looked up at her desperately, wishing for the end of the story to be just as glorious as she hoped it would be.

"They did not live a happily ever after," the grandmother said softly. Quickly noticing the look of sorrow pass the little girl's face, she continued. "Life is not easy, and we are not always happy, but they were as happy as they could be, as often as they could be it. Remember little one, love can solve many problems that logic cannot. The heart is much smarter than the head."

The little girl smiled brightly at her grandmother. "Grandmother are we almost to your home?"

"Yes, child," she replied with a sad smile. "My home is just beyond those trees."

The anxious young girl began skipping with her steps, excited to see the place her grandmother had told her about. They passed by the ripe branches of the weeping willows and descended into one of the prettiest meadows filled with rose bushes and trees that housed many birds. She could not believe how beautiful her grandmother's home was. The sunlight peeking through the trees glimmered off the rose petals as the pair walked hand in hand towards the open grass.

Two headstones stand here now, separated by about 20 feet between them. Next to one of the stones stands an old wooden cross, small in comparison, but made with the purest forms of love, many years ago. Tucked away in the corner of the meadow was Catherine's home, and in the center of the meadow, where an empty patch of grass lay next to the second stone, was hers.

Standing above his gravestone, listening to the birds sing to her, a single tear rippled down her wrinkled face as she grasped her granddaughter's hand tighter. Without allowing her eyes to stray from the wording on the stone and the portrait carved into it, the woman simply spoke, "Here, Child. This is home. He is my home, and here my body shall lay when my spirit returns to him."

Sheridan Worthington
Beloved Husband, Devoted Father

"That is Grandpa, Grandmother," recognizing the face of her grandfather embedded into the stone, the little girl raised her eyes to look at her, noticing her tears. "Do you wish to be home with him?"

"It has been a long three years, my dear," was all she could say in return in a tired voice, the tears growing more ferocious as she remembered her love.

"Now dear, your mother waits for us at Arrington and your father shall be here soon to collect you," Annabelle began after taking a moment to compose herself, glancing down one of the many products of her love with Sheridan Worthington. "We need to get back before the meal is ready."

With more questions than answers at the end of her grandmother's lovely story, the girl simple silently nodded and turned around, never letting go of her grandmother's hand as they strode back towards Arrington.

****

THE END

ACKNOWLEDGEMENTS

To all the people who never questioned this crazy journey. Your love and support are the only reason I am where I am today.

Thank you.

Barbara Hanna
Larry Hanna
Lois Hanna
Kayla Cosner Amos
Joan Wright
Donna Stefanick
Everyone who told me to keep going

The Sun At Down
First Edition
Copyright © Kimberly Marie 2019

ISBN 9781916070646

CPSIA information can be obtained
at www.ICGtesting.com
Printed in the USA
BVHW071318210419
546103BV00001B/185/P